SMARTgirl

Also by Rachel Hollis

Party Girl
Sweet Girl

SMARTgirl

Rachel Hollis

This is a work of fiction. Names, characters, organizations, places, events, and incidents are either products of the author's imagination or are used fictitiously.

Text copyright © 2016 by Rachel Hollis
All rights reserved.

Published by Lake Union Publishing, Seattle

www.apub.com

Amazon, the Amazon logo, and Lake Union Publishing are trademarks of Amazon.com, Inc., or its affiliates.

ISBN-13: 9781503953260
ISBN-10: 1503953262

Cover design by Cortnee Brown
Cover layout by Paul Barrett

Printed in the United States of America

For my big sister Christina Wilber, who gave me *Twilight* and demanded I read it immediately. The rest is history.

Chapter ONE

A happy little sigh escapes me as I grab my iced caramel macchiato off the table in front of me.

"Do you believe in love at first sight?"

Max glances up from across the cluttered surface of her desk, a scowl already in place. Her look quickly morphs into confusion instead. Falling in love has softened a lot of her edges, but being agro is a conditioned response, and she has to work hard not to bark or growl like she used to. My mom has a rescue dog that's exactly the same way.

"Who, me?"

I look around the bakery's small office for dramatic effect. She owns the place, and I'm here to help her design an upcoming event. We're clearly the only people in the room.

"Yes, you."

She shakes her head slowly.

"No." She runs a hand through her choppy pixie cut. "I genuinely hated Taylor when I first met him."

The memory of their first meeting makes me smile. She was combative and beautiful; he was antagonizing and gorgeous. They were like a sexy, combustive yin-yang symbol, and even if she didn't realize it at the time, there was always something special between them. The first angry diatribe she hurled his way was laced with it.

"And now you're in love with him." My voice comes out a bit wistful.

"Yes." She nods slowly. "And now we're in love." She looks bemused, as if every time she remembers this fact is a new and lovely surprise.

I grab my oversize shoulder bag off the ground and dig around in it for some Swedish Fish. I toss one into my mouth before I pull out the other snack bag I brought for her.

"You need some protein?" I shake the baggie. "I have almonds. You like the dry roasted, not the raw, right?"

She smiles at the bag and snatches it from my hand with a thank-you. A year—even six months—ago, she would have been annoyed with me for offering. But six months ago she was still trying to hide how sick she can get if her blood sugar gets too low. Six months ago she was still battling anyone who tried to be her friend, let alone tried to care for her in any way. She's doing so much better at not having to be so flipping self-reliant all the time. A handful of nuts go into her mouth as she considers me.

"Are you still coming to dinner this weekend?"

I nod and pop another Fish.

"It's Sunday Supper. Of course I'm coming to dinner."

Sunday Supper is something that Max's mom came up with a couple of months ago. Now that mother and daughter are getting along better, and Landon, Max's roommate, is in full happily-ever-after love with Brody, Max's big brother, it's a chance for Viv to see "her kids" once a week. My best friend Landon and I were jumped into the "her kids" gang awhile ago, and I look forward to these dinners all week because (a) Max's folks, Charlie and Viv, have a stellar personal chef, and (b) if Max's other brother, Liam, isn't out of town on business, he'll be there too.

"Miko, are you asking about love at first sight rhetorically," Max queries, "or is there some specific reason you want to know?"

I didn't realize she is still studying me. There's a question in her dark-brown eyes that I can't answer. The small heater pumping warmth into her tiny office is necessary since neither of us dressed appropriately for the chilly LA day, but it suddenly feels stifling. Max is wearing jeans and a tank top of all things—but that's mostly because she spends a lot of her day baking around hot ovens. I've got on an oversize T-shirt that keeps sliding down off my shoulder and tight-fitting sweatpants pushed up to just below my knee—but that's mostly because I'm a bum on weekends. It's cool, though; with my wild hairstyle and stylized sloppy clothes, I assume people think I'm headed to a hip-hop dance class instead of home to bury my head in a book. I reach back for my hair to busy my hands.

Months ago, when my hair finally grew out past my shoulders, I was so excited that I had the black ends tipped in cobalt blue to celebrate. But today the length and the style I worked it into feel smothering. I wind my locks round and make a bun to get my hair off my neck, using the delay to come up with a response. Max isn't an idiot, and that question has been in her eyes more and more lately. Sometimes I think I should rip off the Band-Aid and just blurt out the words, but I can never seem to find them. And even if I could, there's no way Max would handle the news of my crush well. She *barely* handles the fact that Landon is dating her older brother Brody. She definitely won't like the idea that I'm trying to do something similar with the only single male sibling she has left.

I mean, I get it—Max has only two brothers, and it'd be kind of weird if both her best friends ended up with them. But then it's not our fault their whole family is gorgeous now is it? It's like their entire clan came from one of the good districts where tributes are tall and muscular and look like Greek gods. The rest of us mortals are just struggling to stay alive in the Hunger Games and are nowhere near as pretty.

"No." I use one of the hair bands that is always on my wrist to tie up my topknot. "I was just curious."

She studies me a moment longer before looking back down at the spreadsheet on her computer. She's got to be so proud of what she finds there. Not that she's rolling like Gatsby, but she has turned a profit every single month since she opened the bakery she'd dreamed about having since she was a little girl. It'll take her years to repay the loans she needed to create this business in the first place, but at least she's proving herself, which is all Max ever really wanted.

Even with her success she doesn't take all of the credit. Since one of her new life skills is the ability to ask for and accept help, she incorporated us into the mix as well. She'd readily admit that part of the reason she's done so well is that Landon and I have encouraged our event clients to book some of their smaller private parties here. We've produced at least one event a month since she opened, which brings a sizable addition to her bottom line. Those events and subsequent profits have also given me something to talk about with Liam, who's a part owner of his sister's bakery. Which works out well for me, since looking for excuses to talk to Liam has pretty much become my part-time job.

The sound of my knuckles popping one after another fills the silence—it's a terrible habit I only partake in when I'm nervous. I watch her continue to look over her work, totally oblivious to the fact that my stomach just took a nosedive.

Man, she's seriously going to kill me when she finds out what I'm planning.

———

"Your hair looks so pretty—I love when you style it like that!" Landon calls to me across Max, who's in the passenger seat, through the rolled-down window. She's wearing a dress the color of raspberry sherbet and a hairdo usually found only on Barbie dolls—and she's totally pulling it off.

Max, who can't seem to help giving me crap, piles on.

"Yeah, it almost looks like you brushed it today."

I open the door of the beat-up SUV, toss my oversize vintage bag on the backseat, and then slide in after it. Max is totally rocking a sort of sexy tomboy thing with her ripped boyfriend jeans and a tight-fitting angora sweater right now, but only because Sunday Suppers are a dressier affair. Typically she can't even be bothered to wear matching socks.

"Brushed it *and* used a curling iron." I put an elbow on each of their seats and lean in conspiratorially. "It's like I'm a real live adult. Can you even believe it?"

Landon giggles and turns the volume back up on Pandora's Dolly Parton station (Dolly is her second-favorite human, right behind Brody), and I slide back to buckle up.

Their surprise is valid, since my mane is usually a wild, unruly mess. It takes forever to force it into a style, and since it's been like that my whole life, I usually just don't fight it. Having a Japanese father means that my hair, like a proper samurai, battles any power that attempts to conform it. Having a mother who can trace her wavy-haired Irish ancestors back multiple generations is the only thing that gives my curling iron a fighting chance.

Max glances at me over her shoulder.

"And where exactly does one find a shirt in that particular shade of neon?"

I run my fingers lovingly down the arm of my vibrant-green blouse. This top is fabulous; I don't care if she tries to insinuate otherwise.

"I'll have you know that this came from Nordstrom."

Max throws me a patronizing grin.

"Nordstrom Rack is *not* Nordstrom."

I make a show of admiring my manicure, a shimmery purple color called Waka Waka—apparently the Muppets have really great taste in lacquer—before responding.

"Careful, pet, your Beverly Hills is showing."

"I haven't lived in Beverly Hills in years, and you know it," she bites back.

"You can take the girl out of the—"

Landon doesn't let me finish.

"Children, *behave.*"

I stick my tongue out at Max.

When she pretends to scratch the back of her head with her middle finger, I fight a smile.

Gods, I love my friends.

I've always been really close to Tosh, which is more than most siblings can say. And I've always had friends—friends I could call to grab coffee, see a movie, or hit up a convention with. But I never had *best* friends until I met the girls in the front seat. Now I can't imagine what I'd do without them. If it weren't for Landon, I'd still be designing events for Selah Smith instead of running my own company. If it weren't for Max, I wouldn't have a constant sparring partner and unlimited access to baked goods. And Liam—if I hadn't met Max, I wouldn't have met Liam.

Because here's the thing: I fell in love with Liam Ashton on December 31 last year. Two weeks ago, after spending yet another Halloween without someone to create a thematic couple's costume with, I decided it was time to make him love me back. Admittedly, eleven months is kind of an eternity when you're in love, but I never was one to rush the ending, so that doesn't deter me. If anything, it'll make a fabulous story that we'll tell our grandkids. *Oh, Papa and I met at a bar on New Year's Eve. He was on a date with someone else, and I was on a date with a bottle of tequila!* We'll obviously be super cool grandparents who tell stories about bars and tequila. Gods, we'll make the cutest old people ever!

But first, I've got to get him to ask me out on a date. A date where we'll go to dinner or dancing or to the bookstore, or maybe it'll be something simple: a jog in the park (I'll have to learn to jog) or cooking together (I'll have to learn to cook). No matter what it is, though, I know it'll be romantic.

It will be romantic, because I am romantic. A hopeless romantic actually, and I've been waiting my entire life—all twenty-six years of it—to find my lobster, my French angelfish, my prairie vole. In case you aren't familiar, those are all animals that mate for life. And Liam? He's my one great love. I knew it from the very first time we spoke. And yes, I sort of thought my one great love would be more like me, but in retrospect that is pretty silly. I mean, hello, *opposites attract* is one of my favorite tropes!

And we couldn't be more opposite. In fact, in all the books I've devoured (and there must be thousands at this point), I've never once read about the blond Viking god falling for the zany Asian friend. Can you imagine that book cover? I can, and do. All. The. Time.

I smooth the edge of my Aztec-print pencil skirt and wonder what he'll think of this outfit. My clothes may be loud (all my favorite colors usually are), and true, most of them are from flea markets or secondhand vintage shops (it's not like I can afford anything else), but I don't wear anything that isn't inspired by current trends. I've been designing parties and rooms and graphics since long before I went to college for the degree. I'm constantly aware of which colors are trending, what fashion is on the way out, and how to pair mismatched prints together in an outfit so that it ends up looking perfectly cohesive. Max might make fun of me for shopping at outlet stores, but you'd never know my designer labels were marked-down clearance or miracle finds at the Goodwill unless I told you.

Because I'm a designer, I always see clothing as a way to style myself the same way I might style a room. Because I'm a book nerd, I tend to imagine design in terms of the words I want to convey instead of just colors or themes. When you design, it's aesthetically pleasing to group things in threes, so I always choose three words that I want to invoke with a given look. Today my outfit says *stylish, fun, noticeable.* Whenever I know I'm going to see Liam, the last word is always the same. I've tried outfits that say conservative or flirty, passionate or wild, but the last word is always, always *noticeable.* Because in the last year, his notice is the thing I've wanted most.

"Oh good, you've found the wine." Viv laughs as she gives me a side-hug.

I squeeze her in return and point out the open bottles on various surfaces of their expansive back patio.

"I believe your husband is giving us a lesson in viticulture by offering up a bottle from every winery on the Central Coast. It wasn't difficult to find the alcohol."

"It never is," Max adds sardonically before giving her mother a hug as well. "I think the directions to the nearest bottle of alcohol are written on the Ashton family coat of arms."

"We have a coat of arms?" a slightly gravelly voice asks from behind us.

Just like every other time I've heard his voice, chills race down my arms. Just like every other time, I have to give myself a moment before I can fully face him, and when I do, I still can't catch my breath.

Liam Ashton is kind of perfect looking. He's tall with dirty-blond hair that's gone so long without a cut that it's almost at his shoulders. It has the slightest wave to it, so it curls in on itself and sometimes gets caught underneath his collar. I don't blame it, though; I want to get caught under his collar too. What is it about a man with long hair? I used to think it was ridiculous, the kind of thing you'd find on romance-novel covers in the eighties. But then Liam grew his hair out, and I realized it was actually the hottest, most beautiful thing a man could do. Last time I saw him he'd just come from a workout, and he had his hair pulled up in a man bun. Honest to *dog*, I thought I was going to melt into the floor like a dying witch.

I'm pretty sure he spends most of his waking hours at Barker-Ash's multimillion-dollar offices, but whatever is left over must be spent at the gym. Because his body . . . Holy hell, his arm muscles are bigger than my leg muscles—or would be if I actually had any kind of musculature in my legs. And the things those arm muscles do to the dress shirt he's wearing should be illegal.

"Miko?"

I blink once. Twice. *Crap!* Was I ogling him again instead of following the conversation? Literally everyone is staring at me, waiting for some kind of response, only I have no idea what they've asked me. Max's eyes narrow, and I swallow an unladylike gulp of wine.

Oh well, I'll wing it.

"Yes," I announce confidently.

Both of Max's eyebrows rise.

"It wasn't a yes-or-no question," she tells me.

My eyes dart around the patio at the assembled group looking for an answer. Charlie and Viv are smiling encouragingly; Brody is playing with Landon's fingers, so he's no help; Taylor keeps rubbing small circles on Max's hip with his thumb while she stares me down; and lastly, there is a set of deep-blue eyes the exact color of San Francisco Bay during a storm. They're like a swirling vortex, and I fight the urge not to get sucked into them every time. So no help from any corner.

"Um, purple?" I try again to answer Max's question.

Those stormy eyes spark with humor.

"Are you just throwing out random answers now?" Liam asks congenially.

I fight the urge to pop my knuckles and shrug instead.

"I thought I'd give it a shot." I have another sip of wine to appear casual.

"Let's go in for dinner, and you can tell us all about it," Viv says, reaching out for Charlie's hand. I nod thoughtfully.

"About purple?"

It's an odd topic for them to choose, but I could probably write a thesis on the color if they needed me to.

Landon smiles kindly at me. "About all of the press coverage Max is receiving because of the bakery design you did for her."

"Oh, right." I grin at Viv and Charlie. "That *is* fun, isn't it?"

My wedge pumps carry me in the direction of the dining room, but Liam's voice pulls me up short.

"It's *fun*?"

"Sure." A golden piece of hair is losing the battle to stay tucked behind his ear. I look at it rather than his eyes. It's easier for me that way. "It's really neat that the Flour Shop is getting so much love."

I glance up from that strand of hair in time to see a look of incredulity flit across his features.

"It's neat? You think it's *neat*? Do you understand how hard it is to get press like that without even trying? *Dwell*, *LA* magazine, *Angeleno*, *Apartment Therapy*? Nobody just *falls* into coverage like this, and somehow a design you sketched out on the back of a napkin is garnering attention from everybody." His good humor is bordering on exasperation. He never really gets annoyed—he's far too charming for that—but I like to believe I'm the only one who gets him close. "Do you have any idea how much it would cost to have a PR firm try and snag that much press?"

Max steps back through the doorway in time to catch his last sentence. She frowns at her brother.

"Of course Miko knows. *Do you have any idea* who she is?"

I grin at her.

"Well, that sounded ominous. If this were a paranormal romance, that line would be the point in the book where I reveal some totally rad superpower."

Liam looks from his sister to me in confusion.

"I'd likely choose telekinesis." I tap the edge of my wine glass, considering. "Though a solid argument can be made for the advantages of elemental manipulation."

Both of them blink at me like tall, beautiful owls. I sigh internally.

Nobody got my PNR joke. What else is new?

Since I can't pop my knuckles, I take another drink instead. I think it's time to find my seat rather than just stand here awkwardly.

"No." His gravelly voice slides down my spine even though he's talking to his sister, not to me. "Who is she?"

Max's smile twists sideways before she answers.

"Google it."

———

I can tell by the look on his face during dinner that Liam did exactly what Max had told him to before sitting down at the table.

"Miko Jin. Full-ride scholarship and graduated with honors from the Rhode Island School of Design," he reads off his phone as he drops down next to me on the Matisse sofa. I've dubbed it thusly because it's sitting underneath a real-life, honest-to-gods Matisse. Charlie and Viv have an incredible collection of art, but this one with its burst of vibrant color is my favorite. Each Sunday after dinner everyone typically has a drink or a coffee or samples Max's latest dessert, but I've learned that if I park myself on this sofa, he'll wander over and sit with me. I wonder if he even realizes it's become a pattern. I do my best to look stoic while he keeps reading.

"Best known for having designed the Chelsea Club, the bar at Up Market, Mos Eisley's West Coast headquarters, and Jonathan Julian's flagship store." Blue-gray eyes look up from the screen. I don't tell him that every single one of those projects was a trade or something I did at an insane discount in exchange for the press exposure he's so impressed by now. That's how almost everyone gets press in a new field: they give their work away for free until they garner enough attention to charge exorbitant fees. I'll go ahead and let him believe I'm already at the exorbitant-fees stage; that seems way more legit. "There are more design awards here than I even knew existed, and more celebrity events than I have time to list. How old are you?"

Design awards are awesome; they also don't pay the bills. And the celebrity events? Until recently my former boss was the one growing rich off my work designing those. The age question is funny, though. I'm not sure what my age has to do with any of the things I've done. But I figured out awhile ago that Liam finds me interesting and that for some reason, finding me interesting tends to throw him off. Oh sure, it's fine to make jokes and share anecdotes, but he usually never really seeks out any real information from me. It's like if he doesn't really get to know me, he doesn't have to take me seriously. Finding out that I'm more accomplished than he imagined forces him to take a closer look. I wonder, not for the first time, if he's thrown off because he doesn't want to be intrigued by me and it bothers him that he is. I don't know whether to be flattered or annoyed.

I answer him on an exhale. "Twenty-six."

He stares at my face for a beat too long, and it actually feels like a physical caress on my skin. I wish I could wear his gaze around like my favorite vintage bolero.

"You've accomplished quite a bit for someone so young."

"So have you."

He tucks his phone back into his pocket.

"We're not talking about me."

My smile kicks up to one side.

"Aren't we?"

Liam leans back into the cushions of the couch and crosses his arms. He's the picture of casual innocence. I don't buy it for a second. I can see something working behind his eyes.

"Why would you say that?"

I cross my legs, meaning to come across as prim and all-knowing. His eyes follow the movement of one leg sliding against the other.

Score one for the pencil skirt!

"Because you're gathering actual information."

"And?"

"And we never share actual information. Not since that first conversation anyway." He looks away from me. Maybe it was wrong to bring that up here. I try to change the subject by answering his earlier question. "And because you're angling, and if you're doing it now, it must be because you want something from me."

With a silent laugh he falls back into the easier conversation like the moment before hadn't happened.

"Now that's a loaded statement."

His delivery is so perfect; it's sexy and playful and full of swagger—and I get it. I totally get why he is one of the most notorious players in Los Angeles, because in this moment, I'd play any game he wants.

"Don't flirt with me." It's the exact sort of thing a proper blue-stocking would say to an impertinent duke. But it comes out strangled, because my throat doesn't want to let the words escape my mouth.

He leans closer.

"Why can't I flirt with you?"

He's just trying to ruffle my feathers—but holy Moses Paltrow-Martin, is it working! My heart is bouncing around like that little blonde girl in the "Chandelier" video.

"Because you never follow through. You flirt and tease, and later you'll pretend it didn't happen."

I could say more—I *want* to say more—but I kind of can't believe I had the *cajones* to say even that much.

The real intensity between us dissipates like morning fog, replaced by a lazy grin that he pulls on like a well-worn jacket.

"I have a proposition for you."

My sigh comes out shaky. I hope he doesn't notice.

"What do you want, Liam?"

Gods, I like saying his name.

"I want to—"

In the split second before he finishes the sentence, my brain rapidly fills in several possible endings.

Take you on a date. Take you as my wife. Nibble your toes. Nibble your neck. Give you lots and lots of beautiful mixed-race babies.

Sadly, that's not how he finishes the sentence at all, and I'm so surprised I have to ask him to repeat himself.

"Hire you," he says again. "To design my new restaurant. What do you think?"

What do I think? Liam's family members are some of the most successful restaurateurs in America, and a project for Barker-Ash is the exact kind of thing that could propel my design career into the next stratosphere. This is the type of opportunity that makes it possible to triple your going rate—or, at the very least, to buy the designer clothes from the *actual* designer. This could be huge for me and my career. But honestly, my career doesn't even factor into this equation. What I think is that forced-proximity romance is one of my favorite literary tropes, that's what I think! I take a deep breath and try to sound casual and only barely interested.

What I say is "What do you have in mind?"

Chapter TWO

When I get home that night, Tosh is still exactly where he was when I left: sitting at the massive reclaimed-wood dining table he bought from Taylor a few months ago, working feverishly on a laptop that's worth more than my life. Based on the number of empty Snapple bottles surrounding him, I'm guessing he hasn't moved from that spot all day. He always gets like this when they release a new app.

I drop my bag on the table and start to gather up the bottles, but he still doesn't pay any attention to me.

"Kitoshi!" I snap my fingers in the space between him and the screen. He finally blinks up at me.

"Did I do it again?" He slides his beanie backwards off his head and runs a hand through his flattened hair.

"Yes." I gather up the rest of the bottles, walk them into the kitchen, and toss them in the recycling. "But your response time was less than a minute, so that's better than usual. Do you want me to make you something to eat?"

My brother unfolds himself from his chair, and by the time he's at the large center island in his state-of-the-art kitchen, his beanie is back in place. In polite society Tosh actually has a really cool fauxhawk, but he's down to the wire on his latest project, and even at thirty, that beanie is like his security blanket. He grins.

"Are you implying that you suddenly know how to cook?"

"I'm *implying* that I can make you a turkey sandwich or open a can of soup." I spy the recycling bin now filled with bottles. "Based on this trashcan, I'm guessing you've been living off Snapple Half 'n Halfs all day."

He rubs a hand down his face in exhaustion and sits on the nearest barstool.

"That would be superb. I'll eat two of anything you'd care to make."

I heave open the door to the massive Sub-Zero. The giant refrigerator holds mostly bottled and canned beverages with all of the labels facing out, because disorder drives Tosh insane. We are alike in all other aspects, but his OCD is such a counterbalance to my disorganization that I sometimes wonder how we came from the same parents. Beyond the soda cans and bottles lined up in straight formations like a Communist army, the fridge also holds the ingredients for a sandwich, a frozen burrito, and milk for the Cocoa Puffs. Other than that, it's just a really expensive box. But, like most of the things my brother owns, no expense was spared, even if he has no intention of utilizing it.

I pile each sandwich with enough turkey and provolone to choke a pony and then slide the plate across the counter to him. I've read *Chocolat* enough times to know that making food for someone is a great way to show your love. So even if I've only got rudimentary skills and a knowledge of cuisine that can best be described as "kid friendly," I still do what I can.

"Are you almost finished with work?"

He looks totally beat, like he hasn't slept in days. I'm almost positive that's the case.

"I'm really close. Just fine-tuning and checking for bugs. How was your dinner?"

I can't stop my happy little inhale.

"It was great. Liam asked me to design a new restaurant for him."

Tosh looks up from the half sandwich left in his hand. Seriously, how do guys eat so fast? It would take me most of an afternoon to work through that much tryptophan.

"You sure that's a good idea, Koko?"

I cock my head to one side to peer at him dubiously.

"Aren't you the übersuccessful businessman who's always telling me to take advantage of my design cred?"

The look he gives me is the same one he's been turning on me all my life. I'd bet that the day our parents brought me home from the hospital he had this *who you trying to kid?* stare down pat.

"And aren't you the one who's told me at least a hundred times that Liam Ashton is the love of your life and the future father of your unborn children?"

"So?"

He looks concerned.

"So, do you really want to start off this love affair of yours as his employee?"

I start to clear up the sandwich ingredients.

"Beggars can't be choosers."

A scowl crashes into his features.

"I hate any scenario where you describe yourself as the beggar."

He winces when I pop my knuckles. I hurry across the room and grab a bottle of water out of the fridge to cover up my tell.

Having devoured both sandwiches in no time flat, he comes around the island to put the plate in the dishwasher. When he's finished he throws an arm around my shoulders and drags me in for a quick kiss on my head.

"You know I support you in all things, yes?"

I nod because I do know this. Tosh is my first and longest-running best friend, and he very rarely goes "big brother" on me. He's the most accepting and supportive person in the world. There's nothing we don't talk about, no part of my life he doesn't know. The fact that we're so close is why I agreed to be his roommate. I knew he was worried about my ability to support myself while starting a company and wanted to keep an eye on me; he knew I wanted free cable. It works out for both of us.

"I will always be supportive of whatever you want to do, but it bothers me that you've been interested in him for so long and haven't even gone on a date. What's wrong with this guy that he's not equally obsessed with you? If you like a woman, you ask her out—it's that simple."

I pull out from under his arm with a scowl. "Yeah, so where's your girlfriend then?"

"I don't have a girlfriend; I have a company. I can only handle one kind of drama at a time." He turns and grabs a water of his own. "But we're not talking about me. I'd like to go on record as saying that I'm concerned."

I try to sound flippant. "Duly noted."

His lips purse as he considers me a moment longer. Finally, thankfully, his curiosity overrides his concern.

"So tell me about this project."

———

I agreed to meet Liam at the location of his new restaurant, a meeting that we set up via text. He was very professional and concise, not flirtatious in the least. But all I could think was *ShOMG! Liam and I text each other now!*

I am somehow able to find street parking right out front, which is a small miracle on a chilly afternoon in West Hollywood. I hop out of the car and make my way towards the front of the building.

The busy street is packed with the kind of people who can afford to shop at the PDC down the block and spend whole afternoons lunching at the upscale eateries that fill the neighborhood. Even though I'm ten minutes early, Liam is already waiting for me in front of a nondescript single-story brick building.

It's a weekday, and I'm guessing what he's wearing is just his everyday look, but I had no idea how I'd react to him in navy-blue slacks and a matching cashmere sweater with just the tiniest hint of his white T-shirt peeking out along the neckline. And the brown leather oxfords to match? I don't have words—I have heart palpitations, but no words for how handsome he is.

He's typing feverishly on his phone, but he stops to look up as I step onto the sidewalk. I watch his stormy blue eyes take in my outfit: a charcoal cardigan over a blousy white button-down half tucked into black leather ankle pants and my black wedge high-top sneakers to add some much-needed elevation. Today my words are *professional, stylish, noticeable.*

He looks past me to my car and smiles briefly before gesturing for me to head inside.

"Not what you expected I'd drive?" I ask as he tugs open the heavy door.

"Actually, where you're concerned, I've learned that things are never what I expect. However, upon discovery, they make absolute sense." He silences his ringing phone and drops it into his pocket. "A mint-condition vintage Mini Cooper, for instance? No, I never would have imagined *anybody* rolling up in that. But having seen it now, I can't imagine you driving anything else."

It makes me inordinately happy to hear the term *mint condition*, because my granddad and I worked my last three years of high school and part of my freshman year of college on that car. The paint job was something I was able to afford only after taking on a side gig designing the packaging for a dog food company. That cherry-red paint was purchased with the proceeds from my job with the Barkery. I had them add a small black paw print to the corner of the driver's side door for good luck. Even if Liam doesn't understand my style, I think he at least appreciates it.

"Thanks."

He shakes off the thank-you with a smirk.

"It wasn't a compliment per se."

"Sure it . . ."

The sound of my voice trailing off bounces off the walls and echoes back through the cavernous room. The space is massive— at first glance I'd guess seven or eight thousand square feet. The walls are stripped bare, the floor is dirty, cracked cement, and the entire place smells just slightly of mildew. But the ceiling . . . Gods, the ceiling is *incredible*.

It features vaulted white wood in a bowstring-truss style and skylights that let the afternoon sun spill in, lighting up the entire space. It's gorgeous; I'm enraptured. And just like every other time, a switch is flipped. It's like taking a filter and laying it over the top of a picture. The look of everything changes and comes into focus. In an instant, I don't see how it looks; I see how it *should* look.

Brick, tile, glass, pendant lights, greenery, raw wood grain, a bar that runs from one side of the room to the other. It's going to be gorgeous!

I blink and the bartender in my mind morphs into the man of my dreams. Liam's curiosity is evident in every line of his face.

"How long was I out of it?"

I fight the urge to pop my knuckles while he considers me. I can only imagine what I just looked like.

"Ten minutes, maybe more. It's cool, though. I took a phone call and answered a couple of emails."

My fingers itch with awkwardness, and I wiggle them for lack of anything better to do. I really need to figure out a sexier nervous tic. Heroines in books are always biting their lip; maybe I should try that too.

"Sorry, zoning out like that tends to happen on a new project. I think it's sort of a family trait."

His brow furrows.

"Why are you chewing on your lip like that?"

My top lip springs free from my teeth with an audible pop.

"Um, I'm looking for a new nervous tic? I'm considering lip biting."

The smallest smile plays across his face.

"Out of curiosity, what was the old nervous tic?"

My sigh is resigned. I hold up my hands like a magician and proceed to pop each knuckle in the same pattern I've done it in all my life. Index, middle, ring, and pinky knuckles and then a double thumbs-up, before bending my thumbs for one last pop. I started doing that last one after a year of clarinet in the seventh grade.

He winces.

"I *know*. That's why I was trying to find an alternative." I bite my lip again. "How does this look?"

His pained expression is almost comical.

"How does it feel?"

I try it again a few times.

"It feels like an English bulldog trying to gnaw off the top half of its face."

His bark of laughter is loud in the empty space.

"Yep, that's exactly how it looks. For the record, I'm pretty sure you're supposed to bite your bottom lip—and just on one side," he adds almost as an afterthought.

"Noted."

When I realize how ridiculous this conversation is, I grin. I love that I've encouraged him to participate in the ridiculous with me.

He clears his throat.

"So, what do you imagine for the space?"

I spin away from him to look at it again.

"You're still dead set on the vegan Latin fusion thing?" I wrinkle my brow. Even the *words* taste gross. I can't imagine what the food will be like.

"*Upscale* organic vegan Latin cuisine, yes."

I nod, my eyes stopping at the skylights again.

"OK. I'm thinking Spain. But, like, Spain as described by Gabriel García Márquez, and it has a baby with an Ian Schrager hotel."

I spin back around to face him.

"Do you see what I mean?"

His phone rings again. He doesn't even glance to see who it is before silencing it. For once he doesn't make a smart-aleck comment or tease me. He actually looks like he's genuinely trying to see what I see in the room. Finally he shakes his head.

"I know the definition of each of those words; I just don't have any idea what you mean when you use them together to describe a restaurant."

I push a mass of blue-tipped hair out of my face and walk over to stand next to him. My hair is basically a physical manifestation of my mood at any given time. When I'm designing, it tends to get just as excited as I am.

"OK, let's start from the bottom and work our way up." I point out the busted concrete below our feet. "For the floor I'd suggest—wait, what's the budget?"

"Extensive."

I grin.

"My favorite kind." I tap the floor with the tip of my toe. "I'd start with a reclaimed wood then. We'd stain with something really light, but the natural color of the individual planks would look like a rich tapestry, juxtaposed with the white ceiling. I'd set the bar to run along the entire wall there. Gods know people are going to need a cocktail when they realize they've wandered into a place that only serves vegan food. The bar façade could almost be a statement piece unto itself—Mexican tile or possibly Moroccan." I considered it for a moment. "But a bold pattern for sure. Black and white, maybe? I know Márquez was Colombian, by the way. When I mention him on Spanish vacation, I just mean the style and flair of Barcelona but brushed by the vintage elegance in one of his books. You with me?"

A quick glance up at him makes my heart stop. There's something that looks almost like pride on his face. It's incredibly sweet but also terrifyingly like the way you might look at your little sister—or your little sister's friend. The last way I want Liam to be feeling about me is fraternal. Ugh!

I hurry on to describe the rest of it in detail. The large metal pendant lights, the long communal dining tables, even the servers' uniforms: white button-downs rolled up at the sleeve, a different shade of the hipster aprons we sourced for Max's bakery. Throughout my description Liam nods politely and asks intelligent questions, but I get the impression that he still can't visualize most of what I'm describing.

"Would you like me to draw you a picture?"

He nods.

"That would be great. You can send over the information about your retainer, and then maybe you could get me a CAD to show the rest—"

I'm already digging a Sharpie out of my giant shoulder bag.

"Do you have any paper?" I ask him.

He blinks dramatically and holds his arms out to the sides to show that he isn't actually concealing a drawing pad on his person.

"Smart-ass," I grumble before dropping my bag onto the dusty floor and pulling a hair tie off my wrist. Once again the mass of blue and black goes into a topknot on my head. As I'm halfway to the ground, Liam realizes what I mean to do.

"You don't have to get down on the—" Just as my knees hit the ground, he finishes, "Floor. This really isn't necessary. You could just send me something later, and then you wouldn't be covered in plaster dust."

I'm already drawing out the perimeter of the room on the cement floor. I work quickly, and with each passing minute the design I see in my head comes to life on the ground below me. As I'm shading in the tile work, I get dust on my white blouse. My sleeve drags across the edge of the marker while I sketch the floral centerpiece by reception. When I push it up my forearm to keep it from further ruin, I notice that Liam's gaze isn't anywhere near my drawing. It's planted firmly on my butt.

With a gasp, I realize it's not even his fault either, because I'm on all fours, on the ground, in tight leather pants. I quickly sit back on my calves and cover my face, utterly mortified by how that must have looked. Gods, I've been moving around too!

"I wasn't trying to be provocative," I whisper through dusty fingers.

I really wasn't either. I was going for professional and inspired, like Jo in *Little Women*. Not hoochie and obvious, like the cougar with a side pony in *Dirty Dancing* who keeps trying to steal Johnny from Baby.

It takes him a second to respond, and when he does his voice is gruff.

"With you it doesn't seem to matter."

I let my hands fall into my lap. His outstretched fingers are already there to help me up.

"Miko." His voice is strained. "Please get off the floor."

I let him pull me to my feet, and then go about dusting myself off to try to gain some composure.

"It's incredible," he says.

I look up, startled. Is he still talking about my—oh, nope. He's talking about my drawing on the ground below us. I stare at it along with him. It's the size of a poster, and since I've drawn rooms like this thousands of times, the detail is crystal clear. It looks almost exactly like what I see in my head. Dirty floor or not, if I'd had colored markers, it would have been perfect.

His phone rings again, dissipating most of the emotions in the air around us. He glances at the screen, then back up at me.

"I have a four o'clock."

I don't know what I thought he was going to say, but dismissing me for a meeting wasn't it. How did we go from him checking me out to right back to business? It's always like this too. One second it's intense and I can feel the attraction between us like a third person in the room; the next second I worry that I've imagined everything. Maybe I have. Maybe I'm just like Peeta in *The Hunger Games*, and I'm going to have to start asking people if things are real or not real. Which sucks, honestly. Who wants to be Josh Hutcherson? At the very least, shouldn't you get to be the Liam Hemsworth of your own life?

Ugh! I'm sort of ashamed that I'm not better at this. Because surely if I were a practiced flirt, he wouldn't be able to switch gears so quickly regardless of whether or not he wants to, right? I glance up to find blue-gray eyes burning into mine. Before I even realize what he means to do, he touches my lower lip with his thumb and tugs it out from my teeth.

"That is *exactly* how you're supposed to bite your lip." He drops his hand to his side as if just realizing what he's done. He takes a step back from me, straightening the cuffs on his shirt like the simple act will help reorder his thoughts.

It happened so fast!

I didn't even have the time to take it in or pay attention to the nuance of having his hands on my face! Gods, if I had known, I would have closed my eyes to memorize the feeling. Or wait, no—I'd keep them open and take in everything. Is his sweater more navy than indigo? Are his hands well manicured? Does his skin smell like anything specific? I'd vote for lemongrass or pine if I got to choose, but I'd be totally fine with any scent if I only

knew what it was and could commit it to memory. But now that's
not going to happen, because I wasn't prepared and I didn't pay
enough attention. This is the worst! Worse than that time I finished all the books that had been published so far in a series a full
year before the final book came out. Worse than that time someone suggested that *The Bronze Horseman* was the next *Outlander*.
This is even worse than the time I met one of my favorite authors
at a signing and she was super rude and I went into an emotional
shank spiral for weeks!

Liam breaks into my swirling thoughts with a question. I don't
hear what he says, but I know I should answer him in some way. I
want to ask him to put his hands on my face again, but that doesn't
seem appropriate. Quick, Miko, say something!

"Have you ever had a Crunchwrap Supreme?" I don't know
why it comes out as some kind of angry demand.

He takes a step back after my nonsensical reaction.

"Uh—no, I can't say I have."

"Well"—I point at nothing in particular—"you should. You're
really missing out."

On that genius pronouncement, I give up and head towards
the front door of the building. Because really, bringing up the Taco
Bell menu is a new low in my repertoire, and even I know when to
run for cover and regroup.

"So I'll look for your email this week?" he calls after me.

"Yep!"

I make it all the way to my car before I admit it to myself: OK,
not my best work.

Seriously, how many times am I going to trip out and say something insane in front of him? I really need to come up with some
kind of plan so I don't keep finding myself in these situations!

I shake my head in annoyance and turn the key in the ignition.
Honestly, not *one* of my favorite book heroines would ever bring
up a flattened fried burrito as the follow-up to the hero touching

her lips. I mean, jeez, even Cinder acted more natural than that, and she was half cyborg!

Chapter THREE

"Hey, Casidee," I call to the open doorway.

"Yes ma'am," she answers before she's even all the way inside my office. Taylor's little sister is almost as tall as he is and certainly way too close to my age to be calling me *ma'am*. But she's also southern and apparently can't lose the manners no matter how many times I've asked her to. Landon, unsurprisingly, thinks she's the greatest thing ever.

When Tosh offered to let Landon and me have some office space in Mos Eisley's massive HQ, I jumped at the chance. Max might feel weird about getting help from her family, but my brother's company offices are state of the art and utterly gorgeous. There is a full-sized basketball court surrounded by vintage sports memorabilia and a kitchen that *Fast Company* described as "tech geek meets luxury chic" in an article last year. That same kitchen also always has at least ten kinds of cereal in the huge glass jars that line one wall. And each one of the six executive offices has a totally different feel, completely designed around the person who sits within it, but all of them feature the same color scheme—no easy feat. Plus, since I refused to let him pay me when I designed every single detail of the space, getting to use a couple of small offices now for a significant friends-and-family discount feels like a fair trade.

I gesture to the chair in front of my desk.

"Can you close the door? I need your help with a project." Outside the glass wall of my office, a programmer rides by on a skateboard long enough to hold a family of three. After two months of working here, neither of us pay him or his hipster transportation any attention. We've learned to live with the super nerd testosterone that constantly permeates the air and the forty or so computer guys who are ever starstruck by any sort of uterus among them. Casidee, with her kind of alien beauty, her adorkable glasses, and the fact that she understands a lot of their esoteric geek humor, has become a sort of deity here. It was because of that understanding of geek and nerd culture that she's sitting in front of me now.

I'm ready to move forward with the plan I've concocted for Liam, and since it's extensive, I need a partner in crime. After all, a proper heroine needs a sidekick, and neither Max nor Landon would approve of my idea. Max would have a heart attack for obvious reasons; Landon would worry that I was going about it the wrong way. Neither of them would appreciate the pageantry of the whole thing.

Cas sets a notepad in her lap and pulls a pen out of the knot in her hair. The whole mass of dark-brown locks falls down past her shoulders like a shampoo commercial.

Gods, why can't I ever pull off anything so graceful?

She looks across the desk at me expectantly as I hand over the Word doc I created. Her expression remains bland while she reads through it. At this point she's used to oddball event themes or weird directives from me, so there's no shock—yet.

I wait a minute longer, wondering if my hair looks as excited as I feel, because I'm seriously fighting the urge to fidget. My outfit today says *energized, focused, determined*, which translates to a neon-pink, way-too-big sweater, black cigarette pants, and some kicky boots. I slide on my oversize tortoiseshell reading glasses mostly for dramatic affect.

"Can you tell me what all of those have in common?" I ask.

She looks at the list again.

"They're all famous literary romances." Her Oklahoma twang makes the entire sentence more charming than it has a right to be. "The scenes you highlighted are"—she checks the list again—"something iconic the heroine did to garner the hero's affection."

I smile happily. I knew she'd be the perfect accomplice.

"Exactly."

"Are we recreating these for an upcoming event? The scene from *Gone with the Wind* might be difficult, but if we—" She waves the paper at me. "Can I write on this?"

When I nod, she starts making notes in the margin. I heart her enthusiasm.

"It might be hard to recreate the antebellum South but not impossible—"

I pop my knuckles. It's my office, after all, and nobody is allowed to stop me.

"It's not for an event."

She frowns in confusion.

"Is it just some inspiration for a mood then? That seems easy enough—"

"Not per se. It's for me."

Seeing that she is still confused, I lay it all out: from the first interaction with Liam to the list in her hands and how I plan to use it to get what I want.

"I've put a lot of time into this, Cas. The books are listed out in order of—I think—the most effective moments. Well, some of them got bumped to the top of the list, because I loved them regardless of how well they worked for the character in the book, but still. It'll be a sort of punch list for things to try. What do you think?"

She's slowly shaking her head in denial.

"I think this is a really, really bad idea, Miko."

I deny her denial by stuffing a piece of gum into my mouth.

"This is an excellent idea," I say around a bubble. "The best I've ever had."

"I don't think I can—"

"What did you say to me, Casidee Taylor? When you applied to be our part-time, sadly underpaid assistant and I told you I was concerned that you didn't have enough experience, what did you say?"

"But this is—"

"'I'll do anything,' you said. 'I'm a hard worker and I want to learn everything you have to teach me and I'll do anything.' Those were your exact words, I believe."

Her shoulders slump in resignation.

"I meant, like, cleaning icing out of a ballroom carpet or helping a bride hold her dress up while she uses the bathroom. I didn't think it would include something like this. It doesn't seem right."

I cross my arms. "Why not? It's not like it's underhanded or scheming—"

"It's a little scheming," she interrupts.

"But in a totally harmless way," I argue. "It's not like any of this will hurt him."

She can't be more than twenty-two, but the look she turns on me then is pure disbelieving matriarch, as if she's already seen way too much in less than a quarter century.

"He's not the one I'm worried about."

The statement is foreboding, but I refuse to hear it. I'm only allowing positive thoughts. I'm going to *Secret* this into being, just like Oprah and Rhonda Byrne say to. I point to the paper in her hands.

"Let's make another list. In *Sense and Sensibility*—"

"Oh Lord," she groans.

I ignore her.

"In *Sense and Sensibility*, Marianne Dashwood gets desperately sick after wandering the grounds in her melancholy over the loss of Willoughby. Then Colonel Brandon, dashing hero that he is, rushes off to rescue her. This in turn allows them the necessary alone time to realize they're in love with each other. What does that tell you?"

"That travel during the Regency era took four times as long as it should, and without modern medicine even the common cold could kill you."

I doff an imaginary cap at her well-placed sarcasm, then carry on in spite of it.

"No. It tells you that taking care of someone who's sick makes you feel nurturing and powerful."

My eyes must be alight with mad glee, because she knows to ask the follow-up question.

"And?"

I pop another bubble.

"*And* we need to Google what I can eat to make myself violently ill without inflicting permanent damage!"

Cas drops her head into both her hands.

I smile and add a second piece of gum to my mouth.

———

"Everything is set for Cora's bridal shower this weekend," Landon says around a sip of her hazelnut latte. "Cas is going to meet the rental company there in the morning so we can have a slightly shorter workday."

We've wandered down to our favorite coffee shop to go over the details of this weekend's celebrity event. Having an office is amazing, but if we didn't force ourselves to leave, we would spend whole weeks chained to our desks. I stir a bit more sugar into my cappuccino, which effectively destroys the leaf design the barista must have worked so hard on.

"So we'll work a fourteen-hour day instead of a fifteen-hour day?"

Landon aims a playful smirk my way.

"It's been six weeks without a Saturday off. I'll take whatever perks I can get."

I stab a forkful of lemon cake. We ordered it to share, but I'm basically bogarting the whole thing, since she's too preoccupied checking the timeline.

"Do you think it should alarm us at all that we're working, like, a hundred hours a week?"

She looks down at the plate between us with a frown, then swipes a bite with her fork before answering.

"I think that we've worked a hundred hours a week for a long time. At least now we're the ones actually making money off of it. And speaking of all the work, did you finish that CAD for Barker-Ash? I'm dying to see what you're imagining."

I actually have finished the design for Liam. In fact, we have a meeting later this afternoon to go over it. But even though Landon has agreed to help me manage this project (since keeping things organized and on time is not my strong suit), I still don't want her involved just yet. I want Liam to see the design first, and I want us to work alone as long as we can, because it feels more special that way. I look around the crowded café rather than meet her eyes. I'm a pretty terrible liar, and whatever is on my face usually gives me away.

"Not completely." It's sort of the truth. I haven't figured out the perfect oversize plant for the alcove by the women's restrooms.

"Mm-hmm." She sounds disbelieving. "And have you finished the outline for your insane scheme to win his love in a plotline straight out of a romantic comedy from the nineties?"

I didn't know cappuccino foam could actually travel backwards through the trachea until it shoots out my nose in evidence. I grab a napkin off the table in front of me and cough into it a thousand times before I can speak again. Landon looks . . . *concerned* is the most polite description I can give it.

"How did you find out?"

She sighs patiently and pulls a piece of paper out of her events binder.

"If you want to embark on some nefarious plan, it's probably best not to leave a copy on the printer-copier we share." She looks down at the list in her hand with a frown. "'Jo and Laurie—a reverse *Little Women*.' What does that even mean?"

I eyeball the doc in her hand, noting my list of possible scenarios along with Casidee's loopy cursive. That particular idea involved a shared hobby and possibly a sibling with some sort of wasting disease—neither of which Liam and I have, so I chose to ignore her question.

"*I* didn't leave it on the printer. I'm guessing that was the handiwork of our former assistant."

Landon waves away my comment.

"She's not a former anything, and I'm sure she's only trying to help."

I angle my head to study her better.

"So which is it—you found it on the printer or Casidee is trying to help?"

Landon suddenly becomes way too interested in the chalkboard with today's specials. I slam my hand on the table.

"Snitch!"

"She's not a snitch—"

I cut her sentence off with a look.

"OK, well, she is a snitch, but only because she's worried about you. Miko." She bites her lip nervously. "This plan is kind of crazy. More than kind of—it is really crazy. As in my aunt Judy dropped her basket and had to move into a special home for people who heard voices—that kind of crazy."

Ouch.

Hearing it from my assistant was easy enough to brush aside, but hearing it from my best friend definitely stings. My hair is clinging to my neck defensively, and I push it out of the way along with her worry.

"It isn't crazy. It's inventive and cute and just as good a means to garner attention as anything else."

She looks at the paper skeptically.

"You've included transmutation as a *viable option*. It's number three on the list!"

I pop my knuckles.

"It worked in the Guild Hunter series," I grumble.

"Because she was dying!" Oh man, she's exasperated now. "And she didn't even actively *choose* to become an angel; he did it to save her life and—" She cuts herself off and runs her fingers through her perfectly blown-out blonde hair to try to restore order. "My point is—if you like him, why not just go about it like a normal person? Why not ask him out the normal way? Why not invite him on a date or to coffee, or tell him how you feel?"

These are the same questions Casidee asked me the other day, only I don't feel as comfortable telling Landon the truth. But the reality is, I know exactly why I'm choosing this route, because I've thought about it a million times. In life I strive for honesty, most of all from myself. The honest truth is I know what makes me special, and I'm also glaringly aware of what makes me weird.

"Because I'm not a *normal* person. Because I'm not sure what the regular way would be. I've had two boyfriends in my whole life, and Liam is utterly different than either one of them. Because I've been trying to work up to something for almost a year, and I'm no closer than I was then. Because nobody understood my *Game of Thrones* costume *again* this year, because I didn't have anyone to dress up as Drogo and carry my dragon eggs! Because at least this feels like a real plan. And because this gives me something fun to focus on, instead of the way I feel when I imagine him never seeing me as an option at all."

She winces sympathetically. "And how is that?"

I toy with the button on my sweater.

"Invisible. And short on air." I look her in the eye. "Don't you get it? I'd rather try with everything I've got. I'd rather go down in a giant crap-ball of flames than strike out with something as generic as getting turned down for coffee. He's my lobster."

She's shaking her head slowly, equal parts horror and sympathy on her face.

"He can't be your lobster, Miko. You barely even know him."

This is where she's wrong.

"I know what I know."

She continues to stare at me while the din of the café carries on around us. I stir the remaining foam in my cup round and round until it dissolves into liquid as murky as my thoughts. Her resigned chuckle pulls my attention back up to her.

"Lord, Max is going to kill us when she finds out."

I push my hair out of my eyes and lean across the table towards her.

"Us?"

"Well, I can't very well let you try and pull this off alone, now can I? You might be the greatest designer ever, but your execution is terrible."

I can't believe she's going to help me, though I probably should have given her more credit; Landon has been my wingman since jump street. I don't know why I thought she'd let me down now, but I'm so grateful. I thought Casidee was going to be an asset in this whole scheme, but it seems as if she's so positive something bad is going to happen that she's making up excuses every time I want to walk through the next steps. I mean, I know the possibility of breaking and entering or securing a horse and carriage in modern-day Los Angeles wasn't exactly listed in Cas's job description, but you'd think she'd be excited about the possibility to do something besides make copies and answer the phone. Kids today.

I take an excited swig of tepid coffee.

"What do you think I should do first?"

"First"—she pulls a pen out and starts writing on the list—"you should start with a bit more subtlety—"

"I've had nearly a year of subtlety, Landon. It's time to go big or—"

"You are not kicking off this insane plan by making yourself sick, Miko!" Her little blonde eyebrows narrow as she reads my notes for the first plan. "Ipecac syrup is no joke, and if you puke all over him, I doubt even you can bounce back from that."

I cross my arms with a huff. She's right, which is super annoying.

"So what then?"

"How about number fourteen?"

I glance at the line she's pointing to.

"A bit subtle if you ask me," I grumble.

Her response is deadpan. "Your blouse is the color of a traffic cone. You could do with a little more subtlety."

––––

My mother would die a thousand times if she knew I'd read *Fifty Shades of Grey*. Even if I admitted I read it with my hand covering my mouth in shock, and occasionally I had to hide under my shirt like a turtle because I was totally embarrassed. But regardless of the questionable prose or the unironic use the term *inner goddess,* no one can deny its contribution to the romance book zeitgeist.

It's become an icon in the romance-book world by people much more experienced than I am, so it seemed like I should include it on the list. But really, there is very little I could use from the plot that didn't involve things way too inappropriate to even contemplate. So the scene that made the list was the interview from the beginning of the book. It really is the first time the hero takes notice of the heroine, if for no other reason than she doesn't cower and is dressed badly. I'm physically incapable of the latter, but the former I've got in spades. This whole scheme is made all the better by the fact that Liam asked me to meet him at his office. Given that the plan was coming together so nicely, I figured if I was going to take this on, I was going to do it right. I spent last night reading that scene over and over, trying to memorize all the questions and nuances. At the last minute I dropped my iPad with the e-book on it into my purse in case I needed it for reference.

I can't believe it was Landon who realized number fourteen on my list made a much better option than number one. Sometimes I get so caught up on the way something might look that I don't take the time to ask myself whether or not it's in any way realistic. It's one of my fatal flaws.

"Stella, are you kidding me?" I demand playfully as Liam's fifty-something assistant opens the door to his office for me. "You have to try coconut oil. It works for *everything.* It makes your hair shiny, your hands smooth. Sometimes I drink a spoonful just to counterbalance the quantity of gummy bears I eat in the course of a week."

She smiles sweetly.

"I absolutely will, Miss Jin. Thank you for the tip."

"Oh, and I hope Frank feels better soon. I've heard plantar fasciitis is super painful."

She thanks me again and closes the glass door behind her as she leaves.

If the confusion on his face is anything to go by, Liam has been watching the whole exchange from his desk.

"Do you two know each other?"

"Stella and me? No. I mean yes—we do now. We just met on the walk over from the lobby."

"You got all of that in a three-minute walk from reception?"

I'm fairly certain the answer is obvious, so I just shrug and take a seat in the chair in front of his desk. Today my outfit says *classy, sassy, noticeable*. He's wearing a tailored black suit and a crisp white shirt. The formality of his clothing is in direct opposition to that golden Viking hair that brushes against his collar every time he turns his head.

He nods at the skinny gray tie I added just before I walked out the door this morning—it's so Christian Grey of me.

"Business attire?"

I flash a grin.

"Something like that."

An exposed brick wall lines one side of the room, and the floor-to-ceiling windows behind his desk look out over Little Santa Monica in Beverly Hills. The wall that faces the hallway is made entirely of glass so you can see into the other executive offices along the corridor. The other wall was once white, but now its twelve-feet-high by however-many-feet-wide expanse is filled with graphics. Not framed images or posters, but actual drawings done right on the wall in bold black ink. I get up from my chair to look at it more closely. It's a collection of hundreds of small pictures, words, or graphics that share no commonality other than the style they're drawn in. It's a mismatch of imagery and feelings that is no less powerful for appearing to be cartoons at first glance. Apparently Charlie isn't the only member of the family who collects art.

"Is this Goodman?"

When he doesn't answer, I turn around to ask again. He's sitting on the front side of his desk, studying me, though I have no idea when he moved closer.

"I did it again?"

He nods. "Now that I know you're not having a stroke when you zone out like that, it's actually really interesting to observe." He gestures to the mural beside me. "I carried on for several minutes about his process and how long it took him to draw it out. When you started to trace the rain cloud with your fingers, I realized that you weren't actually listening. It is Timothy Goodman, though. Good on you for recognizing his work."

I tuck my hair behind one ear and walk back over to my seat.

"My creative crush on him knows no bounds. Have you seen his Instagram account?"

His brow furrows, and he shakes his head.

"Well, trust me—if you followed him, you'd understand."

He walks around to his chair and takes a seat himself.

"So do you have the design on your Mac, or do you need—"

"Actually, I was hoping I could ask you some questions before we begin."

I wonder if he means to look at me so intensely or if I'm imagining it. Now that I'm about to actually try this out, I feel nervous. I reach into my bag and grab my iPad; it's a digital security blanket.

He raises a questioning eyebrow. I open up my iPad and punch in my code. Immediately my Kindle app opens right to the page I need.

"To design your space, I need to get a better feel for, well, you."

This is a total fabrication. I've already designed the restaurant based on the space, but he doesn't need to know that.

He leans back in his chair and crosses his arms. The movement makes his biceps tense like they're ready to attack. I wish they would.

He clears his throat. I look down at the iPad and ask the first question.

"Right. Um, to what do you owe your success?"

"And this is . . . ?" He lets his words trail off in a question.

"Part of my creative process."

OK, it's not. But that doesn't mean it *couldn't* be part of my creative process going forward.

"My success?"

"Yes, to what do you owe it?"

"Who says I'm successful?"

I can't tell if he's trying to engage in some kind of a debate or being deliberately obtuse. I make a point of looking slowly around his stylish office inside his multimillion-dollar headquarters in Beverly Hills.

"Um, *Forbes*?"

He rubs the back of his neck. The gesture looks surprisingly uncomfortable.

"Shouldn't you ask, to whom do I owe my success?"

"What does that mean?"

"Oh, I don't know. I suppose it's easier to become successful if you have a father who's worth millions to begin with."

It might have come across as self-deprecating if it weren't for his tone. I'm a little thrown off. In the book, the question is answered with total unwavering confidence. I never expected any other kind of reply. I tilt my head to study him better. He's not serious about the secret to success, right? He can't possibly believe his father is the only reason he's made it this far. I scan the page of the book for another question that might be a follow-up, and when I don't find anything that makes sense, I just respond honestly.

"I know for a fact you've worked just as hard, if not harder, than anyone else to get where you are. I've never seen anyone so driven to succeed."

There goes that lazy grin.

"So you don't buy nepotism. How about charm? I've been told I'm just oozing with it. It makes for faster deals and easier partnerships."

When he doesn't continue, I glance at the page again, looking for something else to ask.

"Um, do you have any interests outside of your work?" I ask without thinking.

He looks at me in confusion. "Yes. I work out, I enjoy golf, I spend a good deal of time with my family." He frowns. "Not that you and I are exceptionally close or anything, but I thought you'd be familiar enough with me to know those things already. Surely you have enough of an understanding to mark that off the list of your client questionnaire."

Stupid. Of course I know those things already!

"Just doing my due diligence," I reply moronically. I scan quickly for another one before I can ask something else without thinking.

"Would your friends say you're an easy person to get to know?" It's word for word from the book, and it makes no sense in the context of our conversation. He stares at the iPad in my hands with a frown.

"Yes, I suppose they would, though I'm not really sure what this has to do with—"

The screen of my iPad starts to dim from disuse, and I jab my finger into it to wake it back up. In a hurry to move our conversation along, I recite the first sentence I see on the page with a question mark after it.

"Does the submissive agree to be—" Halfway through the line my brain catches up with what I'm reading, and I make a sort of strangled gagging sound, cutting off my words.

Dear sweet mother of dogs! My stupid e-book skipped to a later chapter, and I just read the word *submissive* in a place of work, during a business meeting! Hysterical laughter bubbles up inside me, but I tamp it down. A few more seconds and I would have asked him the rest of that question and then promptly committed seppuku with the Montblanc on his desk. I shut down the tablet and toss it into my bag like it's on fire.

"Did you just—"

"Nope," I cut him off. "Let's just move on."

He opens his mouth to answer. Closes it. Opens it again.

I am such an absolute idiot! Why, oh why did I choose something so risqué as my first choice? Even as I ask myself, I know the answer. I want Liam to see me as a woman, not as his little sister's friend. While that scene is mild, the book is sexy. I somehow thought some of that sexy might rub off on me. Which is ridiculous! Given my experience with awkwardness, I was absolutely asking for something embarrassing like this to happen! So now not only does he think I'm a weirdo, there's an excellent chance he thinks I have Tourette's or design red rooms for a whole different clientele on weekends!

I look out into the office beyond his and will myself to find the composure necessary to ask a relatively normal question.

"What is your role within the company?"

He looks utterly confused, which I suppose is the kindest reaction he could have when my weirdness hits level ten.

Liam looks out the wall of glass into the hallway, where Barker-Ash employees bustle around like a swarm of bees. "Let's put it this way: if Dad is the captain of the ship and Brody is the muscle, I'm the big-bosomed wench they send to shore to sweet-talk new sailors into joining up."

I shake my head in total disregard for his answer and grasp the new conversation topic with both hands.

"First of all, that's not even historically accurate. No ship captain kept a wench on staff to lure new sailors."

The grin breaks into a real smile.

"Are you sure?"

I cross my legs in a huff.

"Of course I'm sure. Do you know how many love stories I've read that take place on the high seas?"

He rests his chin in his hand with a bemused expression.

"Oh, hundreds, I imagine."

"Exactly. So I know what I'm talking about."

"I'm thrilled at least one of us does. Pirates, was it?"

I scowl.

"It was *your* allusion, and you know it was about sailors! But that's not the point."

"There was a point? How exciting."

"We were talking about your success."

"I believe we were talking about maritime wenches."

I can't help my smile.

"Incidentally, that would make an incredible band name."

He smiles back.

Our conversations always become this fast-paced banter. He's witty and funny, and that makes for the best partner to verbally spar with. He's also an expert at leading us away from any conversation in which we discuss something deeper than the weather. I came here with an interview in mind, because discussing work seemed at least a bit more substantial than trading pleasantries. I won't let him wave the discussion away.

An idea occurs to me. I grab my phone and pull up a page on *Wikipedia* before responding.

"Liam Ashton," I read off the screen with the same tone he used when reading my bio weeks ago. "Graduated from USC. Started in the mailroom at CAA. After being promoted to an assistant, he transferred to Barker-Ash as an account coordinator."

He shrugs. "So maybe I thought being an agent might be an excellent way to meet beautiful actresses. Or ultimately I was a slacker, and I found it easier to transfer to the family business, where I wouldn't really be held accountable. Much less demanding."

What is his deal? Why is he insisting on being so flippant?

"Right. I'm sure it had nothing to do with the fact that your father worked in that exact same mailroom right out of college. A terrible job that hundreds of people apply for but only a handful actually get." The fingers he's been drumming restlessly on the desk stop moving. "And starting as the lowest peon at one of the most cutthroat agencies in the world is the perfect job for a slacker. And that transfer wouldn't have anything to do with the fact that Barker-Ash doesn't hire for entry-level positions? Anyone who applies here has to have experience, even if your last name is written on the wall. And the eight venues you've launched and made profitable—that was all just a result of your charm? Dude. You work endlessly. You're professional and smart and great at your job—"

His eyes narrow. This is getting way too close to a real conversation.

"Did you learn all that on Google as well?"

I shake my head. "I don't need Google. I know you already."

We stare at each other, brown eyes clashing against blue gray. That feeling that's always there between us grows and intensifies until I think I might vibrate out of my skin. His mouth looks sharp and angry. I don't know when my eyes drifted there, but I imagine for the thousandth time what it would feel like to kiss that tension away. His harsh tone shatters the moment.

"This isn't going to happen."

My eyes fly back up to his. There's total conviction written onto every one of his features. I can't believe he said it. I can't believe he acknowledged there was anything *to happen*. I should take a minute to revel in the fact that he's admitting to anything, but I'm too focused on what he said, and all I can think about is why. Why can't this happen?

I don't realize that I've asked the question until he responds.

"You want the truth?"

My surprise at his sudden willingness to be honest doesn't make me hesitate long.

"Always."

He considers me, and whatever he sees in my face must be enough of a reassurance, because after nearly a year of dancing around it, the truth is exactly what he gives me.

"You're gorgeous, Miko." The little smile he delivers that line with is so sweet I feel like we're millimeters apart instead of sitting across a desk from each other. "Do you think I don't notice how gorgeous you are? You're also young and naive—five years and a lifetime away from where I am. You're a family friend and, as of a couple of weeks ago, a business associate. Do you think I don't see the way you look at me?" He leans across the desk and points at my tie. "Do you think I'm not imagining at least eight different ways I could use this tie on you? Do you think I don't know that forcing my imagination is why you wore it in the first place?"

There's no moisture in my mouth. Literally none. The entire thing is a dry desert choking off all words and giving heat stroke to any clever response.

"You've always been kind to me," he says meaningfully. "You're also beautiful and so wonderfully weird." He grins slowly. "And I'm curious to know what that combination is like in a more intimate setting. But I don't do relationships. It might sound cliché or trite, but that doesn't make it any less true. My professional life is difficult and demanding, so I keep my personal life easy and laid back. Anything with you would be far too complicated, and complicated doesn't interest me at all."

I think I blink at him—I can't be sure. As if summoned, Stella taps on the door and enters to remind him of his next meeting. He stands and I jump up too, suddenly unsure of where to put my hands or how to gracefully lift my bag up off the ground. I must knock it into three separate things on its short four-foot vertical climb from the floor to my shoulder.

"We'll have to review the layout another time," he tells me, sounding for all the world like we haven't discussed anything more interesting than an RFP.

"Yep," I tell him on my way out the door.

Once I make it down the hallway and into the relative safety of an empty elevator, I sigh despondently. Gods, I really have to get a better departing line.

The melancholy about my lack of witty comeback doesn't last long, though, because my head fills with everything he said. The whole way back to my office, I go over the monologue he just gave.

How did my interview questions take us so off track? And was it off track if we actually talked about what's going on between us? And what about his speech? It was kind of a prick move. I mean really, if you think about it, he basically just told me he was interested but not interested *enough*. He can date half the town, but *I'm* too complicated? And I'm naive and young and apparently transparent, since he *did* notice not only me but also all my less-than-stellar wiles.

I wipe my hair back out of my face. I should be pissed, or annoyed at the very least. My head bounces in agreement with my thoughts. Then, just as quickly, I'm shaking it at the notion, because who am I kidding? I'm the opposite of pissed. Someone else might be upset or put off, but my heart keeps latching onto all the other words he used: gorgeous, beautiful, kind, *wonderfully weird*. And now I know something I didn't before. It's not that Liam doesn't like me back; it's just that he's not convinced we'd be good together.

My hair falls in my eyes, likely pulled there by the wild energy I'm putting off. Yes, he is kind of a jerk, but *jerky hero falls in love with sweet heroine* is one of my favorite tropes!

Chapter FOUR

"It didn't work at all like I thought it would," I grunt as I push the small faux–French Regency sofa back at an angle. Moving furniture is a precarious mission when you're wearing a stylish cocktail dress, but event planners are supposed to blend in, which means we have to look similar to the party guests. We might do the work of teamsters, but we're dressed like the hostess of a high-end steak house. Stylish but conservative, with sensible flats and enough body spray to cover up the eighteen layers of sweat we've accumulated over the course of this day.

Landon shoves a club chair forward two feet to align it with the ornate vibrant-blue rug we just moved.

"How so?" she calls over the heavy bass beat wafting through the walls from the reception next door.

It's the fifth time we've changed the layout of the lounge area for this wedding's after-party. We have half an hour before the guests will wander into this ballroom from the one next door—it's the kind of event transition that's only possible if you're hosting a party at a five-star hotel. That segue from reception to after-party is the last and final stage of a wedding that cost more than half a million dollars. They'll come in here sweaty from dancing and looking to soak up the top-shelf liquor with the midnight snacks we brought in just for that purpose. The new lounge setup looks great, just like it did in the four iterations before this one. Changing things around is totally unnecessary, but we've already been on-site for fourteen hours, and we've found that the remaining time flies by much faster if you keep yourself occupied. I swap the throw pillows in one lounge area with those from another.

"Because not only did we not grow any closer, but I actually somehow managed to piss him off by asking totally innocuous questions."

"Are you sure your questions were innocuous?"

"Yes." I add one more side table to my arrangement and then plop myself down on the closest flat surface. "He doesn't like talking about his success, apparently. That question took us on a random and thoroughly agitated tangent."

I bounce on the cushions as she plops down beside me.

"Wait, isn't the success question the very first one in that scene?"

I gesture emphatically since this is my point exactly.

"So you managed to throw him off right out the gate?"

"Yes!" I pull a bag of Skittles out of my pocket and pour some into her hand before she can even ask. It's a known fact that calories don't count on event days, since we're so busy setting up that we basically consume only coffee and random snacks. Today my food pyramid is made up of a latte, some Corn Nuts, and the other half of this bag of rainbow-flavored candy. With all the furniture moving, I could eat an extra-value meal and still be in a calorie deficit for the day.

"Throwing him off would be fine if that was my intention, but I was honestly just trying to make conversation. How am I supposed to get to know him better if I have no idea what his reaction is going to be to anything I say?"

"Girl, that is every new relationship ever! I once got so mad at Brody I didn't speak to him for the whole afternoon."

I grasp my imaginary pearls in feigned shock.

"Not a whole afternoon!"

She bumps me with her shoulder and giggles.

"Shut up. I was really upset."

I roll my eyes.

"And what did he do to make you so mad?"

Her heavy sigh makes a blonde curl bounce around her face.

"He said that Britney wasn't a real singer."

Discretion is the better part of valor. I keep my mouth shut.

Landon, on the other hand, gets more upset with each word.

"He said she was a pop star who imploded under the pressure of fame and a lot of other rude things about her songs. Can you even believe that? He never once took into consideration how hard 2007 was on her or how terrible the grow-out on that buzz cut must have been. Also, the *Blackout* album was incredible—one of her best ever! Not a real singer? Please!"

I bite a lime-green Skittle in half to stall for time.

"And so you didn't talk to him . . . because of Britney Spears?"

She nods.

"It seems ridiculous to you too, I'm sure, but we all have stuff that sets us off that other people won't ever understand. Just because you don't understand it doesn't mean it won't sting when it's brought up. It's like how upset you get when an author turns what should be a trilogy into an unending series."

I swallow the candy in my mouth before it's completely chewed, so I'm choking when I try to explain my vehemence for this topic.

"Because she's toying with characters *we love* in order to sell more books! Just land the plane and give them their HEA," I cry in exasperation. "It's not fair to any of us to keep manipulating our emotions!"

Across the room Cas slips through the door and points at her wristwatch in a silent question. Landon holds up ten fingers, a sign that our brief respite has come to an end. We struggle to our feet to get ready for the crowd.

"See, this is my point. Very few people would understand getting so ticked off about an author's artistic choices—"

I snort. *Artistic choices* is a generous description, and she knows it.

"Just like very few people would understand why what you said got under his skin."

I nod slowly in agreement.

"So then what do you suggest I do next?"

She considers it for a moment.

"Well, a conversation didn't work. So maybe an option with less dialogue and more action?"

Landon reaches for her headset and radios our tech team to open the doors. Like some kind of magic, the air wall splits in two, creating an entrance for the guests. Almost immediately people start to trickle through wearing tuxedos and dresses rumpled from hours of dancing and the arduous job of lifting Cristal to their lips throughout the night. Regardless of their couture ensembles, they make a beeline for the stations of street food we have set up around the room. No matter how much money they have in the bank, people are helpless against greasy food when they're fighting a buzz. I'd kill for something from the Kogi truck right now, but we never eat in front of guests. Fingers crossed they'll have some left by the time we wrap up.

"Something with action, you think?" I ask as Casidee joins us.

"What has action?" Casidee is already scanning the crowd, looking for possible problems. Even event assistants learn early on the possible implications of a dance-floor brawl.

Landon quickly turns to face me.

"Not like Lara Croft kind of action. Just an activity of some kind."

"Oh man," Casidee groans when she realizes what we're talking about. "Please tell me you're not considering Lara Croft! Beyond the obvious reasoning, that makes zero sense as a means of starting a relationship."

I scowl at her. "What do you mean 'beyond the obvious'?"

Casidee's gaze goes to Landon and then back to me again, apparently urging her to deliver this news.

Landon grins. "Girl, you know your legs aren't long enough to pull off those shorts with combat boots."

Casidee nods in agreement, and I shoot them both disgruntled looks.

"A, you're both rude, and two, *Tomb Raider* is not on my list and you know it."

Landon shakes her head slowly as they both start to walk away to greet the guests.

"Yeah, well, I also know that you keep adding to that list every few days, and your definition of a love story is getting more and more nebulous," she says.

I swipe my hair out of my face.

"There is nothing nebulous about the Professor and Mary Ann. Theirs is an unending love!"

Their laughter is so loud that it actually manages to make its way back to me over the sound of the enthusiastic jazz band in the corner.

———

As far as the interview went, I had a great idea, but I didn't plan for what would happen once I was actually in his office beyond asking him questions and occasionally biting my lip. That *always* works in the books, so I have no idea why it doesn't yield any actual results in real life. I should have had a stronger plan in place. I should have known I was never going to get real results with something so simple.

Landon has now mentioned that I should try something with action. She's also told me to try a bit more subtlety. The latter isn't really in my wheelhouse. What's the point of trying any of the things on my list if I'm just going to tiptoe around him? Isn't that what I've been doing for the last year?

I nod at my own wisdom and drop a Sprite bottle into my shoulder bag. Liam asked me to meet him at the restaurant again to go over the plans that I didn't get to show him the other day. I will start off this interaction like I did the last one. I'll make conversation and see if I can get us away from our usual line of chatter. But worst-case scenario? I'm drinking what's in that bottle.

On the drive over to West Hollywood, I already feel nauseous. Just researching ipecac syrup is enough to make anyone retch, and my gag reflex is already pretty bad. First of all, they don't even sell it anymore—at least that's what the snooty pharmacist told me when I asked. So I did more research and found some homeopathic stuff you can buy over the counter. The Internet also had some recipes to create your own, but the thought of mixing egg yolks and boiled okra together made me want to puke just reading about it. No way I could actually get something like that in my mouth.

The whole thing is a little crazy—I know. But it has to be done. It worked in *Sense and Sensibility*, and who am I to argue with Jane Austen? In that book Marianne gets sick and Colonel Brandon has to take care of her. I am almost certain that if I were to get sick, Liam would step up in the same way and we'd have a prolonged period of time alone, which would have to lead somewhere, right? I figure I don't even need to be too bad off either. The recommended dosage (at least according to the Internet) is two tablespoons. If I have one small sip from the bottle in my purse—which is equal parts Sprite and syrup—it should be enough to make me believably ill without inflicting permanent damage.

I park my car and hurry up the tree-lined street to the restaurant, wearing my favorite white jeans with holes in each knee. My black booties match my black T-shirt and the black tuxedo jacket that always makes me feel pulled together in a way that says *professional, controlled, hip*. When I slip in through the propped-open door, Liam is already inside on a phone call wearing a charcoal-gray suit that probably costs more than opening your own Subway franchise. An empty folding table is next to him in the center of the room, which I assume is the location for me to lay out the plans. As I walk over, he smiles at me before turning away to finish his chat.

I pull the large printed plans from my shoulder bag and lay them out on top of the dusty tabletop. He must have pulled this table out of a back room or something; the whole thing is filthy. I use a tape measure I brought with me to hold down one corner and my makeup bag to hold down the other side. I try my cell phone on the third corner to keep it all from curling in on itself, but it isn't heavy enough. I should have thought to bring some kind of weight or something. As Liam ends his call, I pull the Sprite bottle out to hold down the last edge of the plans.

We look down at the large paper together.

"What do you think?" I ask expectantly.

"It's the cover page with your company logo."

What a spoilsport.

"I know, but it's still pretty," I grumble. I move all my little weights back to turn the page and then lay them all out again.

This page is a perfect color rendering of the image I see in my head. The bowstring-truss ceiling with whitewashed wood, the exposed brick walls, the bar I love so much. It looks totally perfect.

"This looks fantastic."

His smile is like sunshine.

It takes me a minute to realize his mouth is still moving and I'm missing the words.

"I'm sorry?"

"The elevations, can I see them?"

I jump to move the weights back again and turn to the page we need. A large plume of dust flies up with the massive pages and then settles again. Liam feigns annoyance.

"I'm sorry, my liege, but you're the one with the decrepit table. I'm just trying to do your bidding."

He ignores my tone and looks down to inspect the plans. His eyes scan them and then look out across the room.

"You're imagining the shelving goes up that high?" His brow furrows. "That seems a little extreme."

"Not at all." I move around the table and walk to the far wall to point it out. "If the bar is as high up as I'm thinking, then this shelving makes sense. You need the—"

"Yech! What is this stuff?"

I whirl around in surprise at Liam's screech and then race across the room in a blind panic. He's staring at my Sprite bottle in disgust, and I'm not sure how to react or why he has it or why the cap is off. I do the only thing I can think of: I slap it out of his hand like it's on fire. He jumps backwards, away from the flying bottle and the subsequent puddle at our feet.

"Why did you do that?" we both yell at the same time.

He's looking at me like I'm insane, and for once I can't even blame him.

"I got dust in my throat. I didn't think you'd mind if I had a drink of your soda. What was in that?" he says.

Oh Zeus, Athena, and all the other gods! How much did he drink?

"How much did you drink?" I demand.

"I don't know—a few gulps, why?"

His panic is starting to catch up with mine.

Crap! Think, Miko!

"Uh, it's just been in my bag for, like, two or three weeks. I'm worried it might make you sick."

Oh crappity crap, is it going to make him sick?

"Is that all?" His shoulders relax, and he chuckles a little. "You scared me. I thought it was something really bad."

Really bad, as in medicine to make you puke that I got from some website called Moon Goddess Homeopathics? My laugh comes out a little maniacal. He throws me a curious glance before heading back over to the plans.

Should I tell him? Should I warn him in some way? The bottle said it wouldn't take long to kick in, so I was going to ask him for a ride back to the office and "get sick" on the way there. But now . . .

"So are you thinking that we'll get this marble façade from a local artisan?"

He sounds totally fine; he looks like a Nautica ad. Maybe I'm overreacting. Maybe the Moon Goddess's potions don't work on someone the size of a linebacker. I walk over to stand next to him, eyeballing him for any signs of distress.

"Actually, there's an artist down in Mexico I'd love to use," I tell him carefully.

"Of course there is." He rolls his eyes playfully.

You probably can't roll your eyes if you're on the verge of total stomach failure, right? I let myself relax a little.

"And this here." I point out the seating areas. "I'm imagining it will be a sort of mix and match of Old and New World."

The smallest wrinkle appears between his brows. He rubs the frown away with his fingertips. Maybe he doesn't like the idea of mix and match?

"I mean, we could do it as one or the other, but I just thought—"

He rubs a hand across his stomach.

I curse internally in two languages and some elfish I learned last summer at the Renaissance faire.

"Are you . . . ?"

My voice trails off as the look on his face grows sort of panicked.

"I am so sorry," he says abruptly. "I think I have to go."

He hurries off towards the door, and I hurry after him. Oh man, what if he gets sick while he's driving and wrecks his car? Should I tell him what happened? Should I call poison control? Oh gods, this was so stupid!

"Liam, maybe I should give you a ride."

He whirls around, clutching his stomach with both hands. His eyes are wild, and his face is covered with sweat. If only the beautiful unisex bathroom with its antique fountain turned hand-washing station and the toilet stalls I fashioned after a confessional booth in an old church were already installed. But they've only plumbed the water main, and the fancy toilets are still in crates lining the back wall.

"I think your Sprite was bad," he groans. "I think I'm going to be sick!"

OK, I need to take control of this situation before it gets worse.

"Stay right there!" I yell and sprint back to grab my bag. I don't even get the plans or any of the items off the table. I just grab my purse and my car keys and race to him. He's leaning against the wall by the door, and his face is nearly green. He's covered in sweat, and he keeps swallowing.

I am going to burn in Hades for this.

I grab his elbow and tow the sick giant to my teeny tiny British car. He doesn't even protest when I tuck him into the passenger seat, which really shows just how far gone he is. Once I get him inside and myself in the driver's seat, I pull out into traffic like a bat out of hell. It's only then that I realize I don't actually know where he lives.

"Where do you want me to—?"

My sentence is covered up by the sound of him gagging. I fight the bile in my own throat.

"Oh God," he moans into the hand covering his mouth. "I am so sorry. I just can't stop—"

He gags again, louder this time. I drive faster.

He groans painfully. "Maybe it was the Indian food I had for lunch."

Sweet merciful baby angels, not Indian food!

"Oh God." His eyes go wide in panic. "You have to pull over!"

I look around wildly. "I can't pull over, Liam. We're in the middle of rush-hour traffic!"

Crazy eyes stare into mine. "You have to!"

I reach for my neon-green shoulder bag with one hand and dump the contents into the backseat. I shove it into his lap. To his credit, he does manage to look even more disgusted by the suggestion.

"It's your purse," he groans.

"It's from Target!" I yell back hysterically.

Apparently that was all the convincing he needed. Between one blink and the next, Liam buries his head in the oversize tote and starts puking up his guts. At the first sound of his retching, my gag reflex kicks in like Pavlov's dog.

I will not puke! I'm the one who made this mess, and at the very least I can try to get him somewhere where he can throw up into a toilet like a human being. I roll down my window as fast as the vintage crank will allow to get air into the car, which now smells like the worst parts of—no! I will not think about what it smells like in here!

I look over at him in concern. Sadly his hair, which I love so much, keeps sliding forward into the bag along with his head. Two seconds later we're at a stop sign, and I pull the hair tie off my wrist and gather his now sweaty locks into an awkward bun at the back of his head. For a year, all I've wanted to do was touch his hair. I never thought the first time would be to hold it back so he could projectile vomit into my favorite bag.

I rub his back in small circles like my mom used to do for me when I was sick. "I'm so sorry."

"I'm so sorry," he moans back to me.

"We're almost to your parents' house, OK?"

I'm not sure where he lives, and Charlie and Viv are closest. At the very least the housekeeper will be there to open the door for us.

He nods slowly, still clutching the sides of the purse around his face like a protective shield. When I think about the fact that his head is trapped in the same synthetic leather as his puke, I gag again, only this time it's not just a gag. This time I throw up along with him.

By the time we make it to Charlie and Vivian's house, I've ruined my favorite white jeans and he's ruined my purse. I'm not even sure I can ever air my car out long enough to get rid of the smell. When Maria opens the front door, she's so flustered by the sight of us that she starts speaking rapidly in Spanish. Liam stumbles to the closest bathroom, and the sound of him in there almost sets me off again. Honestly, I can't even believe he has anything left to throw up. I sneak up to Max's old bedroom and commandeer a T-shirt and some old sweatpants that fit me once I roll them at the waist a hundred times. The dirty clothes go into a trash bag Maria so helpfully provided. My purse goes into the garbage. Rest in peace, old friend.

When I walk into the hallway, I can hear the sound of the shower next to the boys' old bedrooms. Liam must have found his way up here.

I sneak over and knock on the door.

"Liam? Can I get you anything?"

"Miko," he groans over the sound of the shower. "If you have an ounce of pity in your soul, you will leave here right now. I promise I will call you tomorrow, I'll have your car detailed—I'll give you a hundred million dollars. Just please, *for the love of God*, don't make me embarrass myself any more in front of you today."

I wince and move away from the door when I hear him dry heave.

Like I said, I am going to burn for this one for sure.

———

When I tell Landon about everything that happened on the phone that night, she is laughing so hard that she almost hyperventilates. When she calms down enough to ask if Liam is OK, and I assure her that I received a text from him verifying that my rotten Sprite hadn't killed him no matter how hard it tried, she starts laughing again.

"You're really not helping me here." My exasperation must be evident, because she finally stops laughing.

"I know, girl. I'm sorry." She chokes again, takes a deep cleansing breath, and starts throwing out words rapid-fire. "Hairless cats, mom jeans, growing out bangs, paying back my student loans, forgetting to shave one armpit—"

And people act like I'm the weirdo in this friendship.

"What are you doing?" My demand makes her pause.

"I'm thinking of things that make me sad," she tells me seriously. "You told me to stop laughing, and it's the only thing that works."

"Oh—well, you're right. Hairless cats are really upsetting."

"So are hairless dogs," she adds. "Like when they shave off all of a dog's fur just because it's summer. It seems so rude. How do they know he wouldn't prefer to have hair even if it makes him hot?"

I nod, even though she can't see me. "Some allowances must be made in the name of looking good."

"Exactly!" She pauses long enough to take a sip of whatever she's drinking. "I do like it when they shave Pomeranians to look like a lion, though. Now *that* is adorable!"

And just like that we're off on the topic of dog haircuts and her aunt's cousin who once got bit by a Doberman and lost a finger but still plays a beautiful dulcimer even with the nine-finger limitation. And I'm laughing and considering dulcimer lessons, and even though we never get around to figuring out what my next—hopefully much more subtle—plan is with Liam, I feel so much better than I did before I called her. Which was her exact hope all along, I'm sure.

Chapter FIVE

In *Twilight* there are so many great options to choose from that it was difficult to narrow it down to one for the list. So I didn't. I added several different choices and figured that when the opportunity presented itself, I'd know which one to choose. When Landon suggested something with an activity involved, I remembered that scene where Bella almost gets jumped by some street thugs and Edward rescues her. Sure, the rescue is heroic and he's battling the urge to go vampire on everyone, but my favorite part is their drive back home. Being locked in a car together for a lengthy period of time has a way of drawing out conversation. I'm just hoping a conversation goes better this time than it did the last.

As for our last interaction, I will be the first to admit that mistakes were made. Nearly poisoning Liam to death and ruining my favorite purse are definitely cause for concern. I recognize now that I made a bad choice with the whole syrup idea. I mean, in the book Marianne Dashwood clearly had a respiratory problem, and I decided to go rogue with something gastrointestinal. I consider the fact that my car still reeks of chicken tikka masala as a justified penance for a badly thought-out plan.

This time I've got a great plan. This time I've got a whole slew of ideas, and whether he likes it or not, my brother, Tosh, is at the center of most of them.

I throw him a side eye, but he's too distracted by whatever is on his phone to notice it.

"You have to put that away when we get inside," I say as we walk slowly towards the Ashtons' ornately carved front door.

His fingers are a blur as he types out instructions for whichever of his poor underlings are being forced to work on a Sunday.

"I know, Koko. You've said it at least twelve times."

"Because it's rude to openly flaunt your obsession with your iPhone in front of new people. If they were old acquaintances or your lifetime best friends—"

"Or an annoying younger sibling."

I point at him emphatically. "Yes! Exactly. But otherwise it's just—"

"Rude. I get it." He puts the phone in the pocket of his jeans and then crosses his arms to stare me down. "You know, some people might concede that it's also rude, or at least slightly selfish, to insist a person accompany you to an event when said person is horrendously busy at work. To go so far as to beg and plead and send a hundred text messages demanding they come along—"

I shake my hair out in agitation. "Well, I—"

"And *then*, when said person finally relents, to spend forty-five minutes instructing them on what to wear." He raises an eyebrow in annoyance, and I tuck my hair back behind my ears demurely.

He has me there. I did possibly spend a little too much time figuring out my outfit tonight, and when I finalized what it would be, I had nowhere to turn my frenetic energy except to what he should wear. For Sunday Supper this week I chose an empire-waist baby-doll dress, which would feel like summer were it not for my Kelly-green old-man cardigan and my tan Frye boots. The dress and cardigan say *casual* and *innocent*, and the *noticeable* is all in my hair. It's a gorgeous blowout with plenty of shine and body. My dress might not be trying too hard, but my hair came to play.

"It's just that they've never met you, and I wanted you to look right." I ring the doorbell, a distraction tactic that doesn't work.

"And what is the *right* way to look, exactly?"

I give his outfit a once-over: good jeans, form-fitting dress shirt with a button-down collar, casual blazer, and Converse. He also styled his hair into an awesome fauxhawk, but only after I threatened to burn his beloved beanie if he didn't. It's not that he doesn't have great style—he does. But given his workload and his annoyance at my forcing him into this, chances are he would have opted for something super casual. Because he works in tech, people who don't know him sometimes don't take him seriously, and when he's dressed like a Seattle teenager circa 1992, it doesn't exactly help his cause. The truth is that Tosh is one of smartest and most accomplished businessmen I know. I'd be willing to wager he's got as much money in his bank account as the Ashtons do, if not more. I just don't want anyone judging him unfairly.

But I can't say any of that without embarrassing him, so I change the subject rather than answer.

"Did I tell you they bought this house from Tom Selleck? Apparently he's still totally loaded from all that TV in the eighties."

He looks over the grounds as if noticing how palatial everything is for the first time. "Do you remember the time Dad dressed up like Magnum, P.I., for Halloween and Mom was Higgins?"

A college professor and a copy editor, our parents could not be nerdier if they tried. But they're also two of the happiest people you'll ever meet and thoroughly comfortable in their overall weirdness. I get that from them. Their themed Halloween costumes are the stuff of legends. I get that from them too.

I smile at the memory. "Gods, he loved wearing those short shorts. It was so inappropriate."

"And his fake mustache kept falling half off his face, but Mom thought it was so funny, she wouldn't tell him to fix it."

The memory has us both laughing so hard we're nearly in tears, which is how Liam finds us when he opens the door. He looks radiant once again; all signs of his bout with forced bulimia are nowhere to be seen.

Tosh has hung out with both Brody and Taylor before, so he must realize who this is. His laugh dies instantly.

Liam extends his hand before I can introduce the two of them. "Kitoshi, right? It's nice to finally meet you."

They shake hands like they're going to be graded on it later. As we walk through the house, Tosh makes polite conversation but doesn't engage with Liam the way he normally would when meeting one of my friends. He's usually personable and friendly. With Liam he's all one-word answers and indifference. Man, these two are going to laugh about this meeting someday years from now when we're all on a family vacation together.

I follow them back to the kitchen, and I'm surprised to find Viv and Charlie busy at work and the smell of fajitas filling the space. I've never seen them cook before; I actually didn't even think they knew how. Maybe their chef got mono or something.

"Oh, you're here!" Viv calls, already wiping her hands on a kitchen towel and hurrying over. "You prefer Tosh, is that right?"

Tosh reaches out to shake her hand, but I could have told him Viv would have none of that—she's a hugger.

"We're so excited to finally meet you," Viv says cheerfully. Charlie has to wait for her to unclench before he can shake Tosh's hand.

"Thank you so much for having me over," my brother tells them politely.

I drop my purse on a chair and go around to each person, giving hugs and kissing cheeks, with Tosh following behind. I don't bother to get anywhere near Liam since technically we should have hugged hello when he opened the door, but he didn't offer and I'm not going to throw myself at him—at least not without some alcohol in my system.

"Can I help with something?" I ask.

"No." Viv waves me away with a perfectly manicured hand. "We're almost done with the tacos. Grab yourself a drink, and have some of that queso Landon brought. It's got to be five hundred calories a bite, but it's worth every one."

I follow the direction of the knife she's using to point down the counter. Brody and Landon are drinking beers near an elaborate spread of chips and salsa and a giant bowl of melted cheese that Landon considers one of her specialties. Liam walks around them and goes to work next to Viv chopping vegetables.

Oh gods, please don't let him be good at cooking too! I can't make a meal to save my life, and if this man has some culinary prowess on top of everything else, I might actually just have to kidnap him. A Stockholm syndrome kind of love is still love, right?

I force myself to look away and find something else to focus on. As usual, Max is whipping up some kind of cocktail, and Taylor is . . . I'm not really sure.

"Taylor, what are you doing down there?"

His voice comes out muffled from where he's half bent under the kitchen table.

"This table wobbles a little," he calls back. For good measure he shakes it to prove his point.

"It drives him insane," Max tells us as she lines glasses with salt. "You want one of these?"

Both Tosh and I nod in unison.

"It doesn't drive me insane," Taylor says.

"It does. He's been fretting over that table for weeks, but he doesn't want to offend Mom and Dad, so he hasn't offered to fix it," Max says with a smile.

Taylor unfolds himself from beneath the table, his height and muscles and tattoos in direct opposition to the sweet smile he gives Max and the lazy drawl of his accent.

"Jennings, you know I've never *fretted* about anything in all my life."

"Even when we did events?" Landon asks. "I seem to remember you rewiring an alarm once during a blizzard at Sundance."

"Ugh!" Max scowls at her. "Don't bring up Selah—it's bad juju."

Both Landon and I yell mostly incoherent things at the mention of our horrible former boss, and Brody throws a handful of tortilla chips at his sister.

"Dude, you know you're not supposed to use her name. She's like Voldemort!"

I take a sip of the margarita she just handed me with a scowl on my face. Fresh citrus hits my tongue, covering the fire from the tequila almost completely and wiping out some of my annoyance at the mention of my former boss.

"It doesn't matter now." Max hands Taylor his drink and accepts his kiss on the cheek. "Taylor no longer works there as of Friday."

Landon gasps and I squeal. It's loud enough that everyone stops what they're doing to look at us.

"This is so great!" Landon says, standing up on tiptoes to give him a hug.

I follow suit while Taylor chuckles self-consciously.

"Yeah, well, all the cool kids are starting their own businesses, so I thought I'd follow suit."

"You're not just starting." Max fits herself against his side. "You've been successfully designing furniture for years; now you're just doing it full time."

"That's awesome, man." My brother taps glasses with Taylor. "Let me know if there's anything I can do to help."

Taylor grins.

"Beyond the order you just placed for forty-three desks for your office, you mean?"

Now it's Tosh's turn to look embarrassed.

"That's entirely on Koko. You know she's the arbiter of style. I just do whatever she tells me to."

I sigh dramatically. "If only every man was so easy to tame."

I'd meant it as a joke, but if I'd thought about it for even a second, I wouldn't have said the words at all. There are way too many people in this room who know way too many things for me to make a joke like that. Unfortunately Viv isn't one of those, so she doesn't resist an opportunity to tease.

"Oh really? And is there a particular man you've set your cap for, darling?"

Charlie turns off the burner on the stove and comes to stand behind her. Everyone in the room is looking at me with varying degrees of interest, but I feel Liam's gaze the most.

"Of course." I try to sound breezy. "And as soon as Prince Harry will condescend to answer one of my love letters, I'm sure we'll be very happy together. You know I've always wanted to be a princess."

The sound of everyone's laughter is punctuated by the front door slamming.

"We're here!" Malin yells from the front room.

The baby of the Ashton family apparently has little regard for the craftsmanship of the front door, because she slams it with a crash. Malin is blonde and carefree in a way only gorgeous girls in their early twenties can be. She comes waltzing into the kitchen with Casidee Taylor in tow. In quick succession she's kissed both her parents and purloined a drink from Max.

"Is it time to eat yet?" she asks between sips. "We're starving!"

"It is." Viv jumps into motion. "I'm just lining it all up here on the butcher block, and you can make your plates buffet-style. We'll sit in the dining room."

Malin is first in line to make her plate, a whirling dervish in blue cashmere. At first glance she'd be easy to dislike—that much beauty and energy usually is. But once you get to know her, you can't help but find all that enthusiasm charming.

"How did the apartment hunt go?" Charlie asks his youngest.

"I hated most of them," Malin says, adding some rice to her plate.

"Why am I not surprised?" Brody teases.

"Cas hated one of them too," she hurries to add.

Casidee pushes her glasses up on her nose.

"There was a half-naked man sitting out front," Cas says by way of explanation.

Malin bumps her with her shoulder. "Come on. He was kind of cute."

"He was dirty and covered in faux fur."

"I know," Malin says, popping a chip in her mouth. "It was, like, sexy John the Baptist."

Charlie chokes on a swallow of beer while Viv throws Malin a chiding look.

"That comment seems inappropriate," Viv tells her.

"No, I totally get it." Landon grabs a plate from the stack and starts to assemble a taco. "The first time I saw Brody, my brain sort of short-circuited and I kept thinking he was like Jesus in human form."

Brody's laughter comes out as a bark. "What?"

Landon looks up from her plate and bites her lip nervously, apparently only just realizing how odd the statement sounded. Then she shrugs happily and keeps piling on the cilantro.

"I can't help it. You're the most beautiful person I've ever seen."

Brody's response comes out quietly on an exhale. "Ditto."

It's only one word, but it's filled with emotion loud enough to melt every heart in the room. There is a single beat of silence, but it's broken when a kitchen towel flies across my field of vision and hits Brody in the head. Everyone else piles on with boos and gag-ging sounds, and it's only made worse when Brody comes around the bar and gives Landon a kiss not in any way appropriate for a family dinner. They're both laughing when they come up for air.

"But did you find a place?" Charlie attempts to steer the con-versation back to more suitable topics.

Malin smiles happily. "We sure did. You're looking at future residents of Culver City. Try to control your jealousy."

"Culver City is great," I tell them both.

"And it's safe," Taylor adds.

"Yes, whatever you do, don't consider anything so distasteful as Hollywood," Max adds with fake disgust.

Her parents still haven't gotten over her living east of La Brea.

"Wait, you two are moving in together?" Liam asks.

So far he's been sipping a beer and only observing, a rarity for him since he's usually carrying the conversation.

Malin and Casidee share a confused look.

"We are," Malin tells him.

"So Landon lives with Max. Landon dates Brody, Max's brother. Then Max dates Taylor, Landon's friend. Now our little sister and Taylor's little sister are becoming roommates. Have I got that right?"

The girls nod and grin.

Liam lifts a finger from his beer bottle and uses it to point at everyone in the room. "This whole group is getting a little incestu-ous, if you ask me." His eyes find mine for a single second before he continues. "I'm just going to tell you right now, Tosh, I am in no way interested in being your life partner, no matter how much you look like Jesus in human form."

Everyone laughs, but I have to force the sound from my lips. At the mention of his name, Malin realizes she hasn't met Tosh yet and greets him with the same hug she greets everyone else with. She must get that from her mom. When it's my turn I go through the motions of filling my plate up, but the implication in Liam's look makes me uncomfortable. He played it off as humor, but I feel like the declaration was for me.

"What *don't* you have on that taco?"

I've been moving so slowly down the buffet line that Liam and I are the only ones left in the kitchen. I look down at my plate along with him. The tortilla is barely visible around the heap of toppings. I've never met a taco ingredient I didn't like.

"Was that little announcement for me?" I ask the pile on my plate.

His sigh brings my gaze up to his stormy blue eyes.

"You're not very good at this, you know. You're not supposed to ask me things like that. It just confirms why I need to make that comment in the first place."

I look away from him.

"Was it a warning?"

"Just a statement of fact. I can see what you're hoping for every time you look at me. I worry that everyone else can see it too."

I shrug helplessly.

"So what if they do?"

His sigh is louder this time. I can actually see him trying to think of something to put me off. "I'm dating someone."

I'm mostly sure my flinch isn't as pronounced as it feels. It's like when Kate Daniels finally lets herself love the Beast Lord, Curran, and she makes him dinner, but he never shows up, even though he promised he would. She's devastated, because she doesn't know that he was actually being attacked by shape-shifters, but when she sees him again, she pretends to be totally unfazed.

Yeah, just like that.

I force myself to face him and to sound as indifferent as possible.

"You're always dating someone, usually multiple women at once. This isn't news."

His eyes narrow. "Don't pretend to be indifferent to my lifestyle, Miko. I know you're not the kind of woman who dates casually."

I'm fairly certain it will always come back to this with him. He's selling any relationship short by not even giving it a chance. More than that, he's selling himself short. How does he know he wouldn't like a relationship if he's never actually had one? And even if I hate that he's using it to create another barrier between us, he's right about the way I feel. I hate his lifestyle. Over the last year I've seen him with too many women to count. It wouldn't be as terrible if I thought he was looking for forever. But what he has in mind is fleeting, the absolute opposite of what I believe in.

I believe in love and monogamy. I believe in the way Brody plays with Landon's fingers when he thinks no one is watching or the way Taylor can't seem to stop kissing that same spot behind Max's ear. I believe in a lifetime of love like that of my parents, who I still find slow-dancing in the kitchen to Nat King Cole when I visit home. I believe in all of that, and I want it from Liam so badly that it makes me feel frantic. But I also believe he's convinced himself not to want any of those things. For whatever reason, he's blindly averse to the idea of a committed relationship, and I don't stand a chance with him if he thinks that's what I'm looking for.

"You don't know anything at all about the kind of woman I am." I let the lie fall right out of my mouth. Because of course it's a lie. He does know what I want; he can see it in my eyes.

He opens his mouth to respond, but Max interrupts.

"What are you guys doing?"

My gaze flies to hers across the room and then back down to our full plates. How long have we been in here? I screw up some courage and actually sound pretty convincing when I smile and head towards her.

"Oh, Liam was just regaling me with stories of his latest conquests."

She looks surprised. "No wonder you've been in here all this time." She smiles. "That's a long list."

"Yep," I agree. "And growing longer by the second."

I throw a wink over my shoulder and don't wait around to see his reaction.

See, all I have to do is keep up the pretense that I'm totally chill about this whole thing. All I have to do is act mature and worldly so he takes a chance on us. If he'd just take a chance, then I know he'd eventually fall for me. It took Bella ages to convince Edward to let down his guard. Why should my own love story be any different?

———

"I'm not falling for this," Liam says a couple of hours later as he swings the passenger-side door to his Mercedes open for me to get inside. I stumble but catch myself in time—mature and worldly, remember? I stop short of getting into his car and turn to flash him a smile.

"Fall for what?" I ask innocently.

He shakes his head in exasperation even as a small smile plays across his lips.

"You're a terrible actress."

I acknowledge that this is probably true by sinking down into the leather seat. He gets into the driver's side and pulls his obnoxiously expensive car out onto the road. I stretch my legs out into the line of heat wafting out from the vent and wiggle my toes in my boots.

"Do you mind if I put my feet on your seat? I'll keep my socks on."

He looks startled, as if I'd asked if I could take off my clothes instead of my shoes. I'm guessing worldly and mature women don't ask to sit crisscross applesauce on men's butter-soft Italian leather seats. I must remember this.

"No, go ahead," he says warily.

I slip out of my boots and wiggle my toes in freedom.

He eyes my brightly colored Avengers socks. "You have a thing for superheroes?" he asks.

"I have a thing for Stan Lee."

I cross my legs in the seat and cover them nearly to the knees with the billowy skirt of my dress. It's a twenty-minute drive to Santa Monica. I figure I should at least be comfortable.

"It's actually kind of incredible."

His arm muscles move and stretch underneath the sleeve of his shirt as he shifts the car into one gear after another.

"What's incredible?" I murmur.

"The way your brother got mysteriously called into work and couldn't give you a ride home."

"Oh, there's nothing mysterious about that. Tosh has a new app coming out. He works almost nonstop."

"And everyone else?"

"What about them?"

"Everyone else couldn't give you a ride either?"

I give him a huge smile.

"You know you're the only one who lives on the Westside too, Liam."

I like saying his name so much that the single word comes out a whisper. I worry about using it all of the time, so rather than sound like a deranged parrot, I save it up and use it sparingly like rations on a desert island. The only problem with this is that my emotions usually spill out with it.

"And what if I had plans?"

The demand in his question pulls me back into the moment. I look out my window at Beverly Hills sparkling just outside of the glass.

"You don't have plans," I answer confidently.

We come to a stop at a red light, and I can almost feel him pulling on his arrogant persona.

"Don't assume that just because it's late on a Sunday that I don't have any plans to meet up with a date—"

"You meet your mother every Monday morning for breakfast." He freezes, utterly still. "You told me, remember? How you have to get up early to drive to Santa Barbara and how she looks forward to it all week long, because you're the only one who—"

"Don't." His tone has a hard edge. "You don't know what you're talking about."

I look right at him now, absolutely refusing to be denied this one truth.

"Sure I do." I touch the scar on the back of his hand gently with my index finger. "You just wish I didn't."

He pushes into first gear, effectively dislodging my hand. I've managed to piss him off again, just like the last time. So it's on to plan B, which is to back off. Being alone in the car with him for the next half an hour feels intimate enough. I look out the window, remembering the night he got that scar.

———

Liam and the leggy redhead he brought to New Year's had been arguing for most of the night. I doubted anybody else noticed, since they weren't sitting at our table, but I was fascinated by it. I knew he was Brody and Max's brother, and I knew he was a big deal at Barker-Ash, because our company did so much work with them at the time. I knew his handshake was solid from our one brief introduction. I also knew that he was beautiful. That was the end of my knowledge about him, and I was intrigued enough that I couldn't stop staring.

It was New Year's Eve, the DJ was awesome, the club was alive with energy, and everyone around us was having fun. Everyone except for Liam and the Amazon woman. He kept having to take calls on his cell phone, and I watched her grow more and more frustrated as the night went on.

    It was nearing midnight, and he'd just sat down with her again, only to have his phone ring for the millionth time. I saw him apologize to her and watched her snap enough to chew him out. Having never had any kind of public tiff, I was kind of mesmerized watching it go down, even if I couldn't hear what they were saying. Her red hair was flying this way and that, and just when it seemed like she was really narrowing in on her central thesis, he looked down at his phone. I'm guessing it was buzzing again. She tossed out a line, something that made his eyes narrow. But just as quickly, his face cleared of all emotion and he shrugged. On his way out of the room he had his phone to his ear, but he stopped long enough to say something to the general manager, who had shown us to our seats. Jessica Rabbit got up in a huff and grabbed her bag, and when she passed him, the GM followed her out—I assumed to get her a cab.

    Before I could think better of it, I was following Liam as he retreated down a long dark hallway, past the kitchen and towards the office. Because we'd done events here in the past, I knew where he was headed, and I followed him right to the door. He didn't close it entirely. I stood outside in the shadows, straining to hear his voice over the bass that shook the walls even all the way back here.

    "No, it's OK. I wasn't busy." He moved back and forth like he was pacing. "Did you really? That's wonderful," he said patiently. For a moment he disappeared from view. He resumed his pacing with a full bottle of whiskey in his hand. He'd already had multiple cocktails tonight, and I wondered how he could remain standing. At some point he leaned against the wall near the door; in the dark, empty hallway I did the same. The conversation continued with him answering softly and gently, almost as if he were speaking to a child. I didn't hear him hang up, but I did hear the crash when the mirror broke into a million pieces. I rushed into the room without stopping

to consider what I was doing. Liam spun around wildly when he heard the door slam behind me, his bloody hand dripping onto shards of the broken whiskey bottle beneath his shoes.

I nodded at his hand.

"Is there a first aid kit in here?"

If he found it odd at all that I mysteriously appeared in the room, he didn't say it. He took one step and then another before his back hit the wall. He slowly slid down it to the floor.

"In the closet," he said as his head fell back against the wall behind him.

I grabbed the first-aid kit and sat down beside him. I was infinitely grateful I had decided to wear a romper that night instead of a cocktail dress, or that position would have been a whole lot more scandalous. When I reached out to inspect his bleeding hand, he pulled it back quickly.

"You'll ruin your outfit," he mumbled.

He seemed totally drained, like all the energy in him had fallen to the floor along with the whiskey bottle. I'd only ever seen him full of life, and this side of him made me sad. I lifted his hand again, careful to keep it away from the electric-blue material of my outfit, and slowly cleaned him up. It was not one cut but several, and they were deep enough to scar. He watched my hands work on his, neither of us saying anything.

"Ex-girlfriend?" I asked just to fill the silence.

"No." He shook his head sadly.

I wrapped the gauze end over end to create a bandage and tied it off carefully.

"Who, then?"

His eyes narrowed. "It's none of your business."

I grinned. "Tell me anyway."

He looked at me for a full minute before responding. "It was my mother."

I wadded up the used gauze in my lap and got up to deposit it in the trashcan.

"Oh, that's not nearly as seedy as I was hoping for."

"Will you grab me the other bottle while you're up?" He gestured at the collection of decanters in the corner.

I rolled my eyes at the request. "I think you should probably have some water instead." I started across the room to grab him a bottle of Evian, but his voice stopped me short.

"I said it was my mother, not my stepmother. Not Viv. My biological mother, Elizabeth. She's struggling to adjust to a new medication they've started her on. The nurses in her assisted-living facility have already had to sedate her twice in the last month. She's calmer if she can speak to me, so I keep answering even though she's manic and only repeating the same story over and over. She doesn't even realize we've talked twenty times today already." He sighed heavily. "She doesn't realize a lot of things."

I must have stared at him for a full minute with my mouth hanging open. I was totally unprepared for that. I glanced at the bottles of liquor in the corner and headed in that direction.

"Did you say you wanted the bourbon or the gin?"

When I turned around holding one in each hand, he smiled sadly.

"Both?" he asked.

I nodded and sat down beside him, handing him the bourbon and taking a swig of the gin myself. It was fairly dark in his office with only the lamplight, and the moment felt safe, perfect for secret telling.

"Why is she calling only you?" I asked him.

He took a long pull.

"Because I'm the only one who takes her calls."

"How is that possible?"

He looked away from me, telling his secrets to the dark office.

"My parents' divorce was messy." He swallowed. *"She cheated on him . . . more than once. Brody never forgave her. Dad either. We were teenagers then, and she was always off on one adventure after another. She was—is—flaky. They didn't really have a reason to talk after the papers were signed."* He took another drink.

"As a little kid I thought it was magical how much energy she had or how excited she'd get about something. She'd flit from thing to thing like a butterfly, and I just thought it was her personality. She was always a little bit manic, but she didn't really experience the deep depression until after they were apart. It was like each year after the divorce, she got progressively worse. At first it was little things: spending all her money on a new business she wanted to start and then deciding she hated it a month later. I realize now that Dad was her straight man, and without him there to keep her in check, she started to implode.

"I tried—I tried so hard to help her, but it was early in college, and I was too focused on my own life to pay much attention. A few years ago it got . . . bad. I've had her in care ever since." He looked at me suddenly. *"It's a state-of-the-art facility, not an asylum or anything. It's like a five-star hotel . . . only with orderlies and psychiatric care."* He tried to smile then, but it didn't get anywhere near his eyes. He took another drink.

"Why didn't you tell Brody about this? She's his mother too."

For a single moment his eyes flooded with tears, and I could feel his pain like my own.

"She wasn't always like this. She used to be so . . . special. And when she started to get really bad, she begged me not to tell anyone. Brody hasn't spoken to her since the divorce, and neither has my dad. I don't blame them for that, just like they don't blame me for still choosing to have a relationship with her. She didn't want them coming around out of pity." He looked out over the dark room. *"I didn't tell anyone, because she asked me not to."*

The words broke my heart. I wanted to hug him so badly my fingers tingled with the need to do it. Instead I let my head fall on his shoulder, as if we were old friends instead of people having their first-ever conversation.

"So why tell me?" I asked.

My head rose and fell with his sigh.

"Because you're not real."

I chuckled softly.

"Why do you say that?"

"Because you took care of me," he said conversationally. "Nobody ever takes care of me, so you can't be real. I've had too much to drink, and so I imagined a fairy with big brown eyes and wild hair so I had something beautiful to think about it."

I almost choked on my words, trying my hardest not to break the spell of this moment by getting emotional. I tried to keep my tone light.

"You believe in fairies?"

His lips brushed the top of my head before he whispered into my hair.

"I do now."

I fell in love with Liam Ashton at that exact moment.

———

Liam doesn't say much when he drops me off in front of Tosh's house, except to point out that my brother's car is in the driveway and he is clearly at home. I just thank Liam for the ride and walk slowly up the steps to the front door.

I wanted to press him into talking more, but I worry that, given all the emotions I unleashed in him today, I won't like the results of that particular conversation. I hadn't meant to bring up that night, especially since we've never acknowledged that it happened at all. We sat on the floor for the longest time as he told me all about his mother. I guessed he'd never told the truth to anyone, and because he was locked in the unreality of the night and the moment, it felt safe to tell me. But as the time ticked by, he seemed to come back to himself, and just like in *Cinderella*, the magic was lost.

When I saw him at Max's birthday party months later, he didn't even acknowledge me, though I caught him staring again and again. When we finally spoke at a dodgeball game, he pretended like it was the first time we'd met. I kept staring at him that day, trying to figure out what his game was or if he'd been so drunk that he genuinely didn't remember our conversation. But then we went to breakfast as a group, and he was all smiles, congenial and telling jokes. Nobody but me noticed how often he touched that scar on his hand.

Chapter SIX

"Why are we doing this?" I demand as I clomp along beside Max.

She's running down the street in workout gear, looking like a gazelle. Beside her, Landon looks like jogging Barbie. I feel like a disjointed mule. Running is not my love language.

"Because you said you wanted to get in shape," Landon calls across Max to me.

"No," I grunt, barely able to speak over my lungs threatening to implode in my chest. This is what Hazel from *The Fault in Our Stars* must have felt like. Where's an oxygen tank when you need one? "I said I needed to work out to counteract all of the licorice I've been eating lately. I never said anything about getting in shape, and I certainly wouldn't willingly ask to run."

"It's just three miles." Max grins at me, masochist that she is. "And we're almost back to the car."

Only three miles. I grumble it in my head since I just used up all of my air supply on that last diatribe. I hate running, but I also just want this ungodly exercise to end, so I refuse to stop and walk, because then it's going to take even longer to get back to the car. When we finally make it back around, Max suggests we stretch out our legs. I take this as an excuse to crumple to the ground in a heap and then do some random stretches I remember from eighth-grade PE.

"I'm going to miss you guys next week," Landon tells Max. "I had so much fun with y'all last year."

"We'll see you, like, two days later. It's not like you're going off to war."

Landon smiles.

"Well, I don't know about that. I've never brought a man home to meet my parents, so I'm not totally sure how Daddy is going to react."

"I'm more interested in how Brody is going to react." I wink at her. "I've met your family, and that's a whole lot of Texas coming at a person at once. I can't wait to hear how he reacts to them."

"Speaking of parents, I'm super disappointed I won't get to meet yours." Landon smiles at me.

My parents are coming to visit for Thanksgiving, and my mom is making a big lunch for us at Tosh's place before we head to the Ashtons' for dessert. Viv was nearly apoplectic when she heard they were coming into town and wouldn't be coming to her holiday feast. She insisted on us joining them in some capacity. We agreed to come over for dessert. No one in my family is very good at baking, and everyone has heard about Max's culinary creations, so it was an easy sell.

"Well, it should be a hoot to watch. My parents are absolutely nothing like yours," I tell Max.

"Thank God for that!" Max grins. "Who could handle that much micromanaging in one holiday?"

"Speaking of holiday managing"—I wink at Landon again—"does Brody know you'll be sleeping in separate bedrooms at your parents' house?"

"Of course he knows." Landon laughs at the frown Max is shooting my way. "Just like you know that we don't—"

"I thought we talked about my disinterest in this particular conversation," Max gripes.

"Yes, let's change the subject, please." Landon adjusts her ponytail. "Let's talk about Brody and my parents, because Miko's right—there is a whole lot of southern coming at him at one time."

"Oh, Brody has always done well with parents. The Barkers absolutely adored him."

Max says it while folded over in a butterfly stretch, so she doesn't see Landon's face morph instantly into confusion. She must realize what she's said, though, because she sits upright quickly.

"I'm sorry, Landon. I didn't mean to bring her up so flippantly."

I look back and forth between Max and Landon, having no idea what they're talking about. Landon bites her lip.

"What are you talking about?" she asks.

Yikes! I guess I'm not the only one.

Gruff or grouchy or pissed or teasing—I have seen Max a lot of different ways. But at a loss for words? Never.

She gapes at Landon like a fish.

"It's nothing," she says finally, finding enough composure to attempt to sound casual.

Landon frowns. "If it's nothing, then why not just tell me what you're talking about? Who are the Barkers?"

"Barkers as in Barker-Ash?" I add.

Max glares at me.

"Don't look at me in that tone of voice." I glare right back. "You're only making her more nervous by being secretive about it."

Max stands up and dusts off the seat of her pants. We stand up too.

"You should ask Brody about it," Max tells her.

"I will." Landon bites her lip again and nods. "It's not that I haven't known something happened in the past. I knew—I just didn't know how to ask what it was. But it's not your place to tell me. I get that. I'll speak with him about it."

Max walks the few short steps to the car while awkwardness comes off her in waves. Landon's voice halts our progress.

"What's her name?"

Max pauses in between one motion and the next and then sighs in defeat. She looks down at her shoes and shakes her head slowly, clearly battling with herself on who she should be loyal to. It's too late now, though. She's stirred things up, and any woman can understand wanting to know at least the name of the ex with whom the relationship ended so badly nobody wants to talk about it. Particularly when that relationship apparently went down with the daughter of his father's business partner.

"Sloan," Max says quietly. "Her name is Sloan."

———

Brody and Landon are flying to Texas tomorrow, so we all agreed to meet for drinks on Tuesday night. I've asked her several times whether or not she's talked to him about whoever this Sloan creature is, and she's told me repeatedly that she doesn't feel like discussing it. She says she's come to the decision that his past doesn't affect their current relationship, and she seems genuinely sincere in the statement.

"He's had enough crazy ex-girlfriends hounding him about details of past relationships," she tells me as we walk down the street to the bar. "I told him a long time ago that I couldn't be upset about something that happened before I even met him, and I meant it. If he needs to talk to me about it, he will. Until then I'm not going to stir up a bad memory that isn't currently affecting my life in any way."

We slip inside the lounge out of the cold.

"Dude, you're way more mature than I am," I tell her as I pull off my jacket.

She fluffs her perfect golden hair a few times and then throws me a wink. "Tell me something I don't know."

I fuss with my own hair and try to think of something truly shocking.

"Um, I didn't finish the third book in the All Souls trilogy."

Landon actually gasps and looks at me like I've grown a second head. She grasps my hand like I might be sick or something. "But you love those books!"

"I love the first two. The truth is I think I love them too much. When the third one started to go off the rails, I couldn't handle it, so I just stopped reading."

Landon shakes her head slowly back and forth. "What would Deborah Harkness say?"

I return her look sincerely. "I hope I never have to find out."

She laughs so loudly that people turn in our direction to stare. I spot our group in the back corner.

"Come on." I nudge her ahead of me. "Let's get some wine. This conversation about Matthew and Diana has upset me."

I follow her through the crowd to a long communal bar table where the usual suspects have gathered. Brody envelops her in a hug and then gives me a perfunctory kiss on the cheek. I slide onto a barstool across from Taylor and Max and notice Malin talking up some random at the bar. I get her attention with a wave and pantomime glugging a bottle of something. She smiles and gives me a thumbs-up.

"Did you just use my little sister as your waitress?" Max asks.

"She's young and sprightly," I answer. "It's good for her. Besides, I'm too tired to move. I spent all day yesterday on my feet watching a bunch of drunk actuaries dancing to a Neil Diamond cover band."

"Whose name is . . . ?" Taylor asks.

"Love on the Rocks," I tell them all with a grimace.

"How did that event turn out?" Taylor asks at the same time Malin slides a glass of red wine in front of me.

"What's an actuary?" she asks before sipping her own drink.

"An accountant without a sense of humor," Landon groans.

I give the group a deadpan look. "We heard that joke about a thousand times yesterday."

"But the event was awesome, Tay. Thanks for asking," Landon chimes in. "How's that big order coming along?"

I listen to Taylor describe the desks he's working on with fascination. I love anything creative, and his furniture design is incredible. It's so neat to hear about the process. How he finds the reclaimed wood or how each different kind requires a different sort of finesse to restore.

I don't know what makes me turn suddenly, except that maybe my nerve endings sense Liam before the rest of me does. He's working his way across the room, looking incredible in jeans and a sweater. His winter scarf is slightly askew, which only adds to the hotness of the fact that he's wearing a scarf in the first place. I imagine burying my face in that scarf or burrowing under it to get closer to his skin.

I'm staring at it so intently that when a well-manicured hand reaches out to touch the plaid material, my response is visceral. French-tipped fingernails tug playfully on the end of the scarf. I follow the line up her arm until I can try to take in what I'm seeing. She's tall and thin with chestnut-brown hair that falls halfway down her back. Her skirt is too short and her makeup is a little strong, but beyond that she's utterly gorgeous. She's the exact kind of woman he always brings to something like this. This isn't anything new; I've seen it fifty times at least. I have no idea why this time it feels like a betrayal. Now that we've finally acknowledged we're at least more than acquaintances, I guess I thought that somehow might change the way he acts around me. Whatever

I expected, I certainly never thought he'd be parading another woman in front of me a week later.

I look up into his determined, cold, steely blue gaze. His steps falter, and for a moment I swear he winces at whatever is on my face. He bites down hard on his molars and keeps moving towards our table. By the time he makes it to us, he has the woman by the arm. It's not at all a sweet caress; it's more like he's showing her off.

"Hey, everyone, this is Cara," he says by way of greeting.

Everyone at the table says hello. They've all met some variation of this woman plenty of times before. Liam arriving with a new woman on his arm has played out more times than I can count. They won't try to establish any kind of real relationship with her. That would be futile, since they're never going to see her again, but they also won't be rude. They engage her in conversation as she takes her seat and Liam walks off to the bar to order their drinks.

I've finished my wine by the time he comes back.

I can get through this. I can totally get through this. I've been honest with myself about how strong my feelings are towards him for a long time. In the last year I've seen him with countless women. This is just the first time I've seen him on a date since he found out how I feel. But that he would parade someone in front of me, even in some lame attempt to teach me a lesson, doesn't just hurt—it crushes me.

If he looks my way, I don't know it, because I'm too busy pretending to be engrossed in my phone. The pictures in my Instagram feed blur as I scroll through them. Oh man, I cannot cry right now! The second I acknowledge my tears, they get worse. I want to get up and walk away, but there's no chance I can do it without every single person at this table knowing that I'm upset. If they know I'm upset, there's no way they won't assume something is up, since I was fine until he walked in.

Gods, what is it about not wanting to cry that makes you feel like you have to that much more? A text from Landon pops up on my phone: *I'll create a diversion.*

I can't even look up to let her know how grateful I am, because her kindness is pushing me over the edge. A tear drops onto the screen of my phone, and I'm grateful for the hair framing my face protectively.

A glass crashes to the floor, and Landon yells dramatically, "Oh Lord, now I've ruined this dress!"

All around the table, people slide their stools back to avoid the liquid that's dripping everywhere, but I don't look up to see it. I grab my bag and jacket and mumble something about making a call, not knowing or caring if anyone even hears me. I just have to get outside before I lose it.

I hurry down the street, feeling cold everywhere except for my cheeks, hot with tears. I turn one corner and then another, dodging groups of happy people on their way to their next destination. I pass a hipster coffee shop and a hipster gastropub and a hipster barber. This part of Silver Lake all looks the same, and I'm not really heading anywhere specific; I just want to get away. Maybe if I walk long enough, it'll turn into the really shady part of Sunset, and I'll be put out of my misery by a random ax murderer or a street thug high on methamphetamines.

Even the thought of possibly getting murdered doesn't stanch the tears.

I can't believe I'm the crying woman walking the streets alone. I've read this scene a thousand times in books. I've even purposely looked for stories full of exactly this kind of angst, because I love the emotion behind it so much. But I had no idea how it would feel in real life.

I hate seeing him with someone else, but it's nothing new. It's more upsetting to know that he's done it intentionally to remind me of the distance between us. It seems unnecessarily cruel, and

I never would have imagined Liam doing anything so hurtful. If he really is this cruel, then he's not at all the person I thought he was, and that means I've been wrong about everything else too. My daydream of us telling stories to our grandkids flashes through my mind, and I cry harder.

"I didn't know it would upset you this much!" His voice reaches me long before he does.

I spin on my heel in surprise and watch as he hurries down the street to stand in front of me. Once he's there he seems at a loss for what to do next. He runs a hand through his hair in agitation.

"I don't know why you're so upset," he says finally.

I want to strangle him with that stupid designer scarf.

"Don't." I try to make it a warning, but it comes out wobbly.

"We are acquaintances." He emphasizes every word. "Work associates or family friends at most. You're fixated on this idea that there's some sort of deeper relationship between us, and it's just not there."

The mention of our fledgling business relationship is enough to make me pause. The retainer to design the restaurant for Barker-Ash is four times as much money as I've ever made on a single job. A paycheck like that means I can hire Casidee on full time. It means I can get a new Mac. It means I could propel my company further along in a way that I haven't been able to do, since I refuse to take out a loan from the bank or borrow money from Tosh. This job is important to my career for so many reasons. I just can't bring myself to care about my résumé right now. His refusal to acknowledge this feeling between us instantly dries my tears.

"Then why are you chasing me down the street, Liam?" I demand. "If I'm just some family friend with a misguided crush, why do you care? If we're just acquaintances, then why do I catch you staring every time we're in the same room? Why do you find a way to insert yourself into the conversation every time someone tries to hit on me in a bar?"

He clamps his mouth shut and looks away from me.

Coward.

I take a step closer to him. "You can lie to everyone else, but please don't lie to me. You owe me at least that much." I jab a finger into his chest. "If you're too much of a child to admit that you have feelings for me, then that's your loss. But don't you dare stand there and tell me I don't know what I feel."

He takes a step back and runs a hand through his hair. "Your feelings are based on some fantasy you've concocted in your head, Miko. They don't have anything to do with me."

The comment takes all the wind out of my sails. I take a step back like he pushed me, shaking my head in denial. "It's not—"

"It is. You're fixated on who you *think* I am, like a character in one of your damn books. All of the reasons you like me aren't based on anything real. They're based on my false charm and your imagination."

Gods, he doesn't get it at all. He thinks I like him based on what, his hair? I mean, yes, it's gorgeous, but I admire him for so many reasons, and none of those are made up. He's kind and funny and smart, and he loves his family. There are so many reasons to want him for my own, and the only reason I've never admitted them out loud is that I'd sound utterly enthralled—which I guess I am.

His sigh sounds so tired. "I'll walk you back. This neighborhood isn't safe."

When he turns around to walk back in the other direction, his head is down and he's staring at his feet, looking for some kind of answer on the dirty sidewalk. Telling him that he's funny or nice to his mother isn't going to cut it. He thinks I'm romanticizing him, that I don't know who he really is. I find my voice.

"You love dogs, but you think you travel too much to have one of your own," I call after him.

He quits walking and turns back to face me.

"I know because you stop to pet every single dog that crosses your path. And not just to pat them—you actually bend down so you can look them in the eye. I think you like big dogs the best, but you're nice to them all. Even the little yappy one that bit your finger last summer."

He looks stupefied.

I continue on nervously.

"You always have lottery scratchers in your wallet. I saw them the first time you paid for our breakfast after dodgeball, and now I notice them whenever you reach for the bill. That night you—you told me that your mom loves them, that you buy them every time you think of it and then save them up for your visits."

He takes a step towards me, but I can't read the look on his face. I flex my fingers anxiously. Now is not the time to let my nerves get the best of me.

"You hate tomatoes. You always ask the server to leave them off your dish, but you never complain even if they forget. The other night you ate Vivian's salsa, because she was so proud of it, and I could tell you wanted to gag. When you could see how happy it made her, you asked for a second helping and you ate that too."

He takes another step closer, and his eyes scan my face.

"You listen to jazz when you're anxious or sad." This one is only a guess.

His voice is whisper soft.

"How do you know that?"

"Because we've had three meetings on a Monday. And every time I've walked into your office, you shut off Miles Davis."

"And?"

"And Monday is the day you visit your mother."

His curse is loud on the quiet street.

"What's wrong?" I take a step closer. "Why are you upset?"

Dark eyes grab hold of mine.

"Because I'm about to do something really stupid."

He crashes into me like a storm, only the force doesn't push me away; it seals us together. Like we were magnets at counterpoint and someone finally flipped one of us around in the right direction. And then his lips are on mine, and through the haze of sensation and the total euphoria of being in his arms, I am aware that I am wholly out of my league. If my kiss is a question, his isn't just an answer—it's a statement of fact. I feel that kiss everywhere. I feel his hands running through my hair and the strands winding around his fingers to hold him there. My own hands itch to explore, to trace the contours of his skin, but I refuse to release the grasp I have on his shirt; I'm afraid he'll step away and I'll be grasping at nothing but air. And so I stand there, and what I cannot explore with my fingers, I try to explore with my mind. I want to remember his hands sliding down to my hips and holding me against him. I want to remember the feel of his bottom lip against my own and the sharp surprise when he nips me there. I want to remember how hard my heart is beating and that the wall of his chest is there to absorb the vibration. If I could hold on to this feeling, I could live off the single moment for the rest of my life.

When he looks down at me, I feel dizzy, elated, and a thousand other emotions I can't name. But the expression on his face isn't tender or sweet; it's flustered and challenging.

"Honesty?" he asks gruffly.

His hands are still gripping my hips, and my lip still stings from where he kissed me.

"Always," I choke out.

"I want you to come home with me tonight."

Excitement and blind panic make my heart beat erratically, and thoughts fly so fast through my mind that I can't hold on to any of them.

"For tonight," he continues. "I don't do tomorrow, but I want you for tonight. Can you handle that?"

The words are a gauntlet. Somehow I always knew it would come down to this. My experience with men is limited, and he must know that. He's daring me to make good on the lie I told him days ago, that I was fine with casual. Maybe he thinks he'll get over this feeling if we finally fully acknowledge it. Maybe it's another attempt to teach me a lesson. Either way, I'm playing with fire hot enough to match the one burning inside me. It's the ultimate means to an end. If I back out now, it proves him right on so many levels, and I don't know if I'll get another chance.

It's hard to think with him this close, with his eyes reading every thought on my face. He gave me honesty, and I answer him with the only truth I can. He wants me for tonight. Can I handle it?

"I want you . . . any way I can get you." If not an answer to his question, it's at least the truth.

The words seem to frustrate him even more but not enough to back down. He grabs my hand and leads me off down the street, and I hurry to keep up in my daze. The night is cold enough that I can see my breath in front of my face coming out in excited bursts. In the back of my mind I can hear Tosh cautioning me not to start any relationship with a beggar's mentality.

———

We ride the whole way to Santa Monica in tense silence. It feels awkward and also weirdly exciting. I've never been to his house before, but I don't even have time to admire it before he's opening my car door and tugging me inside with the same determination he pulled me down the street. He takes my jacket and hangs it on a hook by the door. That banal gesture makes me pause long enough to remember something. I cross my arms and fix him with a stare.

"What about your date? Did you just leave her there?"

I want to believe I might change my mind if he admits that he's been so callous, but I'm honestly not sure that's true.

He tucks his hair behind his ear sheepishly.

"She wasn't my date," he tells his shoes.

"What?"

"I met her out front. I thought maybe it would help you understand . . ."

Misguided, yes, but at least he wasn't intentionally being malicious. The relief I feel at this discovery is all-encompassing. I can't help my giggle, and when he looks up in surprise, I smile at him. I look down at my rumpled clothing and touch my lips, which are still on fire where he kissed them earlier.

"You sure showed me."

His grin is lopsided, and for the briefest moment he seems vulnerable, like the person I met on New Year's, not the successful businessman who's always in control. His face clears of the tender expression.

"I'll take you home right now if you want to go. We don't ever have to talk about this again."

Any hesitation I might have had goes right out the window. I know him, and whatever he thinks about this night, it is going to lead to a tomorrow. I close the distance between us by a foot. It's either the smartest or the stupidest thing I've ever done.

"Don't get cold feet on me now, big guy."

He takes a step closer to me, and when he finally speaks he sounds so sad.

"Did you know that Tinker Bell dies in the original *Peter Pan*?" He reaches out to play with the ends of my hair where blue meets black. "And when they ask him about her later, he can't even remember her name?"

I hate the melancholy in his voice and the reality creeping back alongside all of the feelings running through me. I push both of them away with an action.

My hands are steady when I slide the first button of my blouse through its hole. His eyes fly to mine, and the force of his gaze is like an earthquake; everything inside me shakes. Another button comes undone, and the one after it. His blue-gray eyes are riveted on the movement of my fingers, and my gaze is trained on the play of emotion on his face as he watches.

I can't believe I'm doing this. Somewhere in the far recesses of my mind I'm mortified. But the embarrassment that's surely staining my cheeks is nothing compared to the way it feels to be the one who put that look in his eye. My blouse falls to the floor with a whisper. Something like wonder fills his eyes. His fingertips feel hot against my skin as they slide along the pattern of shapes in every color of the rainbow that lines my rib cage and runs all the way down to my hip.

"Yet another thing I wouldn't have expected, and yet it makes total sense."

I watch then in mesmerized silence as he lowers himself to his knees in front of me. When his lips touch the first bit of artwork, I fight the urge to crumple to the floor along with him. He kisses one image after another with something close to reverence, and I give myself permission to do something I've wanted to do since the moment I met him. My shaking fingers hover over the crown of his head for a long moment like a priest offering benediction. I'm almost afraid to actually touch him, since that feels like an official invitation and the sum total of my knowledge about what to do next ended with taking off my shirt. My college boyfriend would have just sort of taken it from there, but I don't want to be the bystander here. I've dreamed about this too many times to just go along for the ride; I want to be involved in every part of it.

My fingertips slide into his hair, adding another sensation to the myriad that fight to consume me. There are so many feelings battling for attention—how do I choose? My focus flits from one nerve ending to another until I think I might be dizzy from the chase to experience it all. Suddenly he's upright again, and I'm wrapped around him like that scarf; I'm lips and teeth and tongue and fingers and a desperate need to touch every single part of him as fast as I can. We're backing down a hallway and bumping into every surface we touch. A picture frame flies off the wall and crashes to the ground as I gasp.

"Don't worry," he says between kisses. "I hated that photo."

I'm laughing into his smile when my back hits a doorknob. I can't stop my wince, and then my smile. How in the world could I explain that bruise to someone? Thank gracious it's not summertime, or my collection of backless sundresses would seriously suffer for a chance at wardrobe rotation.

"Damn!" His fingers reach around to the spot on my back. "Are you OK?"

I nod, fumbling with the doorknob behind me. The door gives way sooner than expected, and we both tumble through it in a heap. This time he's the one who gets dinged by breaking my fall on the hardwood floor. I'm laughing so hard it takes me a minute to bring him back into focus. My laughter fades but not my joy. We're both on our sides now, inspecting each other with dancing eyes. I slide my hand up to pillow my face on the hard floor. I could lie here all night and stare at him and be totally happy. His eyes are filled with laughter as he props his head up with his hand.

"I'm usually much smoother than this," he tells me.

I grin again.

"I don't doubt it."

Some of the sparkle leaves his eyes.

"You're much too sweet to be here with me."

My cheek slides against my palm as I nod at him.

"Probably."

"Do you want to leave?"

The grin hasn't left my face when I shake my head.

When he doesn't move, only continues to debate it internally, I slowly move forward to touch his mouth with my own. Because I can do that now. I can, in this moment, touch and kiss Liam however much I want to. And in this moment I want to touch him more than I want to breathe.

His lips catch mine and turn bold, then demanding. And then there are no more questions or debates, and there's no going back. I fall asleep that night with him wrapped around me, on sheets that smell like us. It's the happiest I've ever felt in my life.

I wake up in the morning alone.

Chapter SEVEN

I must read the note he left on the nightstand at least fifty times on the way home.

Wonderfully weird, was better than I might have imagined. —L

I fly through every possible reaction in the fifteen-minute ride back to my house. Elated that last night happened. Happy that, according to his note, he enjoyed it too. Anxious and unsure where this leaves us, and finally miserably sad that he'd do something as obnoxiously cliché as leaving me a note on the nightstand. How depressingly trite.

To add insult to injury, my hair is a disaster and my makeup isn't any better. I suppose I should be happy I'm not wearing a cocktail dress, but I don't think my walk of shame could be any more obvious even if I were. My Uber driver, Saul, tries to make conversation, but my gigantic sunnies and my monosyllabic answers finally put him off. Instead of talking I stare out the window and watch the bright and sunny day slip by.

Liam sent me a text as well, a confirmation of the car service he'd ordered to take me home. He mentioned that they'd wait outside until I was ready to go. I considered using it too, but in the end the whole thing made me kind of nauseous. I'm not sure how I allowed last night to happen with a man who couldn't even stick around until morning to tell me good-bye. I know he said it was casual, but I guess I wasn't totally prepared for what that meant. I flex my fingers nervously, and when that doesn't ease the tension, I give in and pop each knuckle. Saul throws me a disgusted look in the rearview mirror.

My phone vibrates with a message, and my breath catches. When I see it's only Landon, the air all comes back out in a rush.

Liam never came back to the bar last night and I haven't heard from you . . . Coincidence?

If I were more mature, I might handle this whole thing in silence. I might never talk about last night or what is quickly shaping up to be a terrible mistake and an epic heartbreak. But the truth is I'm not more mature, and all I want is my best friend—and lots and lots of sugar.

I need some chocolate.

Her response is immediate.

How much and where am I delivering?

I send her a picture meme of a little kid eating a candy bar four times as big as he is and tell her I'm about ten minutes from home.

That bad?

For the first time all morning, I feel the tears burning the back of my throat.

That bad.

Oh girl.

Her response is only two words, but I imagine it in that sweet, concerned southern voice that Landon has down to a science, and it breaks the dam on whatever has been holding my tears back. If

Saul sees them streaming silently down from behind my oversize sunglasses, he's polite enough not to mention it.

———

I left the front door unlocked, so Landon just walks right into my bedroom. She's wearing a black gingham button-down blouse under a red cardigan; she looks like she just walked out of the J. Crew fall catalogue. Me? I'm freshly showered and swimming in oversize flannel. She eyes my pj's worriedly.

"Bad enough for My Little Pony?"

I duck my head and fight another round of tears.

"Oh no," Landon whines and pulls me in for a hug. "What happened? Did your plan backfire?"

I shake my head against her shoulder and my voice comes out wobbly.

"No."

"Did you get into a fight?"

Another shake of my head.

She holds me at arm's length to study me.

"What happened last night?"

"We, uh . . . um, we . . ." My voice trails away as I sort of gesture awkwardly at the bed with my hands.

Landon's eyes widen to their full capacity. Her head may pop off of her neck at any given moment.

"*What?*"

My shoulders slump at the thought of the lecture I'm sure is coming. I grab the bag of candy she brought and start to work my way through a king-sized Kit Kat.

"You . . . you . . . you and Liam had . . ."

I don't look up from the candy bar.

"Yes."

She must open and close her mouth three times before she thinks of what to say next.

"Wow" is what she settles on.

I rush to defend myself from the look in her eyes.

"I know that's not the kind of person you are, but I—"

"That's not the kind of person *you* are either," she interrupts quietly.

My shoulders fall again.

"Please don't be judgmental, Landon." I gesture to my blotchy face and the fact that I'm wearing PMS pajamas before noon. "I'm barely keeping it together here."

She grabs for my hands.

"I am not judging," she says emphatically. "You're a grown woman, and I'm not trying to push my beliefs off on you. But Miko—a one-night stand? That's not like you."

I want to look away from her sad eyes, but I force myself to ask the question.

"Why do you think it was a one-night stand?"

She smiles kindly.

"Was it something else?"

I try so hard to keep my bottom lip from wobbling, but when I finally get the words out, I'm bawling before I even make it to the end of the sentence.

"I thought it was at the time."

"Oh girl," Landon says into my hair. I don't even remember throwing myself into her arms.

"I am such an idiot."

"You are not an idiot," she tells me vehemently.

I give her a jerky nod while I sit up. "I am. I thought I was mature enough to handle him, to handle this. I have no idea what I'm doing, and now I'm worse off than I was before."

She kindly runs her hand over the crown of my hair.

"We all make mistakes, girl. That's how we learn better for next time."

I sit back against the pillows and grab for the candy bar. I know in my head that she's right, but my heart feels like it got sucker punched. I have no one to blame but myself. I take a couple of bites of chocolate before I can find the courage to tell her what I'm thinking.

"I know everyone makes mistakes," I tell the piece of candy bar in my hand rather than my friend sitting a few feet away. "I just feel like mine are worse, or at least more plentiful. I never say the right thing. I never do the normal thing. I'm awkward and—"

"Where is all of this coming from?" Landon demands. "You are one of the most confident people I know. Who cares if you're different? Normal is boring."

I finish off the last of the candy bar. It's a pretty sad day when even chocolate-covered wafers can't make you feel better. "I think it's easier for you to say that because you're all in perfect love with Brody; you're past the need for pony pajamas."

Her smile is rueful.

"Girl, you have no idea what you're talking about. I still make mistakes all the time."

Maybe it's petty of me, but I so want to believe she's telling the truth.

"Like when?"

She settles into the pillows alongside me with a long sigh. "Like when I freaked out on Brody about that Sloan woman."

For once, I'm the one who gasps. "You didn't!"

She's already nodding. "I did."

"I thought you said you were cool with his past."

"I am. Well, I was. Something about finding out her name made it so much more real." She grabs for the bag of candy on my lap and finds herself a piece. "I mean, who has a name like Sloan?"

"Fat girls," I reply quickly.

She slaps my arm playfully. "That's so rude. Don't say that, especially when we know it isn't true. Girls named Sloan are always beautiful and tall and—"

"Prone to venereal disease."

"Not true," she says through her giggles.

"True. And she most definitely has back acne and halitosis and a tattoo of Tweety Bird on her lower back that stretched out due to all that weight gain."

Landon is full-on laughing now, which was my intention.

This Sloan creature, whoever she is, is probably lovely and kind, but as the ex-girlfriend of my best friend's man, it is my sworn duty to dislike her.

"Well, even still, I freaked out on him. I raised my voice. I was crying like an insane person and demanding to know details." She covers her face with both her hands. "It was irrational and so immature. When I calmed down later, I was mortified."

My shock makes me momentarily pause my candy consumption. I actually have a really hard time imagining Landon doing any of that. She's always so calm and cool; I can't believe she went full crazy girlfriend on him.

"How did he react?" I finally think to ask.

She smiles at the memory. "The dummy actually apologized to *me*. He said if he had been more honest with me, I wouldn't have felt so insecure about it. I told him that was dumb reasoning, because he was entitled to his privacy. I also said that I was insane and he had every right to be mad at me for at least twenty-four hours."

I feign shock.

"You gave him permission to be upset with you for an *entire day*?"

She doesn't catch my joke and plows on around it with a nod.

"Yes. He didn't take it, though. He said he loves and accepts me as I am, even if that means I get so angry and slam his front door so hard that the mirror in the entryway falls and breaks."

This time my shock is not faked.

"Not the vintage mercury glass!"

She nods gravely. "I'm sorry. I know that took you forever to find for him."

I accept the condolences and hand her a Baby Ruth.

"I was in a huff and storming out of the house after screaming at him like a fishwife." She shrugs. "The crashing sound startled me out of my anger long enough so we could have an actual conversation about it. He helped me clean up the glass. It was the dumbest I've ever felt."

She finishes the bar and starts to eat her way through a bag of candy corn for at least five minutes before I respond. I'm absolutely shocked at what she just admitted.

"Why didn't you tell me?" I finally ask.

"I was pretty embarrassed about how I'd acted. And also pretty sad about murdering the mirror. You looked for months to source that when he asked you for help decorating. I can't believe I did something so foolish." She shrugs sadly. "It wasn't one of my finer moments."

I nod in understanding. Perfect, kind, sweet Landon has had bad moments too, and she's sharing them with me now so I feel less alone in my misery. The only difference is she's having her bad moments inside a relationship, where it's OK to make a mistake. I never got anywhere close to that place with Liam. The truth brings tears to my eyes all over again.

I spend the rest of the afternoon crying and eating candy, and at some point Landon busts out the only known cure for true sadness: a Sandra Bullock movie. By the time she leaves that night, after pizza and more sugar than anyone can handle, I'm sad but much better than I was. Over the last several hours, I have come to accept that maybe I did build Liam up into someone he wasn't. The man I love couldn't have whispered those things into my ear or held me so sweetly and then been so callous the next day. I can make a lot of excuses for a lot of things but not that. Even if it wasn't his intention to hurt me by disappearing this morning, he'd made me feel cheap and honestly a little ashamed of myself. I can't fix past mistakes, but I can make better decisions going forward. I don't know how I'm going to get over him, but I know I have to make myself. I don't want to be in love with someone like that. I'd never survive it.

Decision made, I take another shower and spend an extra-long time blowing out my hair. Landon believes deeply that looking better makes you feel better. At this point I'm willing to give anything a try. I pull on some yoga pants and an oversize sweatshirt and curl up on my bed with a worn-out copy of *Me Talk Pretty One Day*. I'm too raw to read any fiction, and David Sedaris always makes me laugh. Like a million other times in my life, I do my best to escape into the pages of a book.

I like to think that in another world, that's where it all would have ended.

I would have been sad, but I would have gotten over it. It might have been awkward, but I'd find a way to carry on with my life even with that one odd night on my record. I would have missed loving Liam, but at the moment I was smart enough to know I had to get myself past it.

Would have, might have, should have: they all went up in smoke as soon as I got his text.

———

The entire way to Liam's house, I curse myself in both of the languages I know. I'd almost convinced myself that he was a douche lord, and I'd for sure convinced myself that I was going to get over him swiftly and with the strength and dignity of a young Princess Diana. Then the second he'd sent me a text saying he wished he could relive yesterday, I was so giddy with relief that I'd immediately offered to help him recreate it in detail.

I must pop my knuckles fifty times on the short trip to his house, and my face catches on fire remembering the messages we sent back and forth. Turns out, while I'm *way* awkward at it in real life, I'm kind of dangerously good at flirting via text message. All the way up PCH, I give myself a stern talking-to on all the reasons I should turn right around and go home, but I keep driving.

When I pull into his driveway, I give myself a quick glance in the mirror. I'd told myself I didn't care what he thought of me after yesterday and refused to change out of my lounge clothes. But I'm also honest enough to admit that I reapplied lip gloss three times, and my hair was already good from my earlier OCD session with a blow-dryer. I actually look kind of pretty. I scowl at my reflection. What am I doing? How have I gone through every emotion possible and still find myself wishing I had a little mascara?

I slam my fist into the steering wheel hard enough to sting. I refuse to let him get away with this. He's going to hear about every single terrible thing I've thought over the last ten hours, whether he likes it or not. My UGG boot catches on the door of the car in my attempt to flounce out of it dramatically, but I right myself and avoid eating pavement. By the time I head up his walkway, I'm composed and fully ready to tell him off.

Before I can reach out to knock, the door flies open, revealing Liam in workout clothes with hair still wet from a shower. He's clean and shiny, and even from here he smells like fresh laundry. I could handle all of that, though; it's his smile that I'm not equipped to deal with. It's the happiest I've ever seen him look, and he's looking that way because I'm in front of him.

When he pulls me through the door and into his arms, it feels so good and so right and so wonderful that I let him kiss me. Then

I'm kissing him back, demanding and angry and relieved all at once. He lifts me up and carries me down the hallway to his bedroom, and the important words, the angry words, the *right* words I meant to say fall forgotten to the floor along with my sweater.

Hours later I lie on my stomach in a tangle of sheets while Liam traces the artwork on my rib cage with his fingertips. His bedroom is a study in white. White sheets, white duvet, white walls. In fact, the only color at all comes from the hardwood floors and the view beyond the windows. It's dark outside now, but come morning the room lights up with the vibrancy of the sun reflecting off the Pacific.

The memory of the view in the early morning sunshine reminds me what it was I meant to say earlier. I prop myself up on an elbow and push wild hair out of my face.

"This morning sucked."

His hand stops its slow progression up my side, and he looks up at me in confusion.

"How so?"

"You took off before I woke up. You left a note on the nightstand." I sit up and pull the sheets along with me, though modesty is sort of ridiculous given the last twenty-four hours. "A car service, Liam, really? It's something the evil ex-boyfriend does in one of those books with cheesy covers where, like, diamonds are spilling out of a wine glass—what is that even an allegory for?" I remember my point. "Either way, it sucked."

He sits up too, and I'm momentarily distracted by his abs, because . . . seriously. He runs a hand through his hair quickly, and it falls back around his face in disarray.

"I had an early meeting today. I told you that last night."

I make sure he can see me when I roll my eyes.

"Nobody in Los Angeles has a meeting before eight a.m. And even if you did, who peaces out before saying good-bye? And leaves a driver waiting?"

"You needed a way home. I was trying to be thoughtful."

I raise my eyebrows as high as they'll go.

"You were *trying* to get rid of me."

He considers me for a long moment before looking away at the darkened windows. "Maybe."

The truth might have hurt my feelings if not for the quiet way he admits it. I clutch the sheets tighter around me.

"It made me feel like any of the rest of them."

He doesn't insult me by pretending not to know who I mean. He looks back at me both wary and annoyed. I'm positive I'm only seconds away from a lecture on how I knew the deal coming in and how he never signed up for a scenario where my feelings were a factor at all. My stomach churns, and I try to prepare myself for whatever haughty thing a man with his experience says to a woman with mine. His head drops, and he stares down at the sheets.

"What do you want me to say, Miko?"

I didn't expect that.

Of all the things I thought he'd say, that question wasn't even close. I guess that's why I answer with total honesty, even if my voice seems quiet with the admission.

"I want you to admit that I'm different . . . than the rest of them."

"That's an immature thing to ask."

I raise my chin. "I don't care."

He chews on it for a moment.

"I've never had anyone back here a second time."

What am I supposed to do with that? Does that mean I'm special? Does that mean this is the first of many sleepovers or merely that I was lucky enough to get a round two?

"What am I to you?"

I can tell the question annoys him. I doubt it's what a worldly and mature woman would ask after less than a day.

He runs another troubled hand through his hair.

"A friend?"

Wait, what?

"Is this what you do with your *friends*?" I sound utterly scandalized, which must strike him as funny, because he laughs.

He gives me the full weight of that lazy, sexy grin, and I'm powerless not to respond to it. It feels like kryptonite.

"I don't have women friends." He reaches a fingertip out and traces it along my arm. Heat licks at the trail that finger leaves behind. "Though you are making me seriously reconsider what I've been missing out on."

I tuck a piece of hair behind my ear. I need to focus. I need some clear definition of what to expect here.

"What do you want from me?"

He crawls closer across the sheets like a lazy cat and kisses my left shoulder.

"Right now?" he whispers.

All ability to speak is lost when his lips hit my skin. I nod.

"I want to make you breakfast."

It startles a giggle out of me, since it's so obviously not where my thoughts were headed. "But it's the middle of the night."

"Call it a late dinner." He leans back to look at me earnestly. "Or call it the late, late breakfast I should have made you this morning."

I bite my lip to keep from grinning like an idiot.

"You're getting better at that." Liam taps my mouth gently with his fingertip.

I'm getting better at a lot of things. Like right now I'm getting better at stopping myself from blurting out all of the things I love about him. I'm getting better at not asking more questions or demanding more answers. I'm getting better at agreeing to things like breakfast in the middle of the night and pretending I'm not worried about what all this will mean in the morning. So when all I want to do is get some reassurance from him about where this is going, I keep my mouth closed instead and let him pull me down the hallway to the kitchen.

Chapter EIGHT

The next morning when I wake up, Liam is still there, though none of his playfulness from the day before is. He kisses me good-bye in the early morning chill and tells me he'll see me later. I am too mature and worldly to ask if that means later in the biblical sense or later as in he'll just see me around. I cover up my questions with a casual response.

"Well, of course I'll see you later; we're coming over to your parents' house for dessert, remember?"

He nods quickly. "Of course, I'll see you then."

I nod, and he smiles. We both just stand there not doing anything more clever than breathing. Ugh! Why does it feel so awkward now when it didn't feel at all that way last night, even in a much more compromising position? I consider asking him if he knows the answer to that question, but I'm positive that's not the mature thing to do.

Instead I spend the whole way back to my house debating it. I consider all options and angles until I want to punch myself in the face for having turned into a woman who obsesses over a man's next move in two days flat. My parents are coming into town this afternoon from San Francisco, I haven't figured out which Thanksgiving side dish I want to attempt to make today, and Florence and the Machine released a new song last week that I still haven't memorized yet! See! There are plenty of things to focus on besides whatever it is Liam does next. I nod at this sound wisdom and turn left onto my street.

Tosh lives in Santa Monica, but his house is inland, unlike Liam's place, where you can walk outside to his back patio and directly onto the sand. My brother bought his place a couple of years ago, because it was brand new, totally luxurious, and every single part of it had the most modern amenity on the market today. It's two stories, a study in the color white, and half the walls are made of glass, which creates a gorgeous backdrop for the perfect landscaping out front. All those glass windows mean that the house reflects the sunlight like a diamond during the day and is lit up warm and inviting at night. It also means I have a clear line of sight to my mother sitting at the dining room table as she watches me pull my car into the driveway.

Damn and blast!

What are they doing here? Weren't they supposed to come in later than this? The only way she can be drinking coffee in her pajamas at this time of day is if they decided to come early and got here last night. I glance quickly at the clock, willing it to be much later than it is. But no, half past seven is way too early to be driving home from somewhere.

Well, this should be fun.

I trudge up the walkway and right into the dining room. May as well get it over with. Katherine Jin is a shorty like me, but her personality is at least six feet tall. She's still in her pajamas, a navy flannel pair I got her last Christmas, and her shoulder-length wavy auburn hair is messy from a night of sleep. I stand at the entrance to the room, pulling on the hem of my sweater and wishing at least my hair was down instead of pulled up in a bun. I could use some sort of security blanket right now.

"You're up early," I say lamely.

"I had to put the turkey in at an ungodly hour." She looks me up and down. "We usually do that together."

I have no idea how to respond, and staring regretfully at the floor isn't offering up any answers. How did I forget that she'd be here early to do that? How did I forget that I usually do it with her? Is it possible to forget such a regular part of you life just because you have someone to make out with?

I briefly remember the way Liam's hair hung down around me like a veil while he kissed his way down my neck. Yes, it is totally possible to forget getting a turkey in the oven when that's your alternative. Gods, when he's looking at me I don't even think I can *spell* turkey.

She breaks the silence by waving me over impatiently.

"Well, first of all give me a hug, Koko. I haven't seen you in two months, and I miss you."

I walk quickly to her outstretched arms and get pulled into a warm embrace. She smells like vanilla and coffee, a scent that is uniquely my mother. She runs her hand up and down my back a few times and then reaches up to smooth the crown of my hair.

"Were you volunteering at a convalescent home and agreed to work the night shift so the nurses could have the evening off?" she asks hopefully.

I smile against her shoulder.

"No."

"Did you go to a late-night yoga class and then fall asleep during child's pose, and they just left you there on the floor because they could tell you were exhausted?"

"You know I hate yoga."

"Did you go to one of those all-night raves that only just got out an hour ago?"

I pull out of her arms and give her a sad smile.

"Would you prefer that I had?"

She's already nodding before I finish the sentence.

"Yes, I think I would prefer it actually." She sighs. "Sit down. I'll get you some coffee."

I sit down at the dining room table as she disappears into the kitchen. While she's gone I trace the pattern of the wood grain with my index finger to keep my hands busy. A cup of coffee appears next to them, and she sits down across from me with her own mug.

"Did Tosh tell you?"

He might not have liked where I'd been the last two nights, but I'd told him just the same. My brother always knew where I was. He worried if he didn't know, and as long as he didn't try to lecture me, he always remained inside the circle of knowledge.

She makes a tutting sound.

"You know he'd never tell me something like that." She takes a sip of coffee. I wonder how many cups she's had already and how long she's been waiting at the table for me. "He told me you were at a slumber party."

It's a little juvenile of him, sure. But it's not a lie. It's also not outside the realm of possibilities. I've passed out at Landon and Max's place more times than I can count, and once we did convince Max to have a real-life slumber party with pajamas and party games. Well, when I say *party games*, I mean that we drank and watched *The Bachelorette*, but that's neither here nor there.

"So maybe I was at—"

"Landon and Brody left for Texas yesterday, and Max is working around the clock to fill all her Thanksgiving orders. You told me that last week, remember?"

Well, this is what you get for having a close personal relationship with your mother. Ugh! Why can't I have a properly dysfunctional family like everyone else? At least then she wouldn't know so much about my life and my friends, wouldn't see through me when I walk in the door in last night's clothes. I feel sick to my stomach.

"It's the boy you like, right? That's where you were last night."

Only a mother would refer to a grown man as *the boy you like*. I nod down at my coffee cup.

Her voice is careful.

"Does this mean that you're dating now?"

I never told her his name, but I've mentioned him enough over the last six months for her to understand that I have feelings for someone and am hoping to make him mine. Being honest is so much harder because she has that backstory. I shake my head.

Her brow furrows ominously.

"What does that mean?"

I try on worldly and mature for my mom to see if it works on her too.

"We're just hanging out." I sip my coffee as casually as possible, but it's hot and I burn my tongue. I cover it up with a pained squeal while I choke—you know, like all worldly and mature women do. "It's just a casual thing." I finish when my tongue stops throbbing.

She shakes her head slightly in disbelief.

"This isn't going to work."

I feel indignant and rush to defend myself.

"This is 2015, Mother, and I'm twenty-six years old! I know it's not a choice you would make, but if you try and lay some Catholic guilt on me, I'm going to scream. It doesn't make sense to you, but it's my life and it's working just fine."

Some of my hair has escaped the bun in an attempt to defend me as well. She reaches out to tuck a piece back behind my ear, completely ignoring my tirade. The sad look on her face tears my heart out. She reaches for my hand and grabs it tightly.

"You don't understand. What you're doing wouldn't be my choice, but I recognize that you're allowed to make your own. I mean that it's not going to work because you're not capable of this kind of relationship—"

"You don't know what I'm—"

"Yes, I do. You've got more heart than anyone I know. If you've been interested in him for so long, it means he's got a piece of yours whether he wants it or not. It's not going to work, because you won't be capable of casually"—she clears her throat—"*hanging out.* If that's all he's interested in, you're going to be hurt by this eventually. You don't know how to love halfway."

Her hazel eyes are filled with worry, but they stare me down with a bit of demand.

"Well, look who the cat dragged in," Tosh announces with far too much enthusiasm. He's already dressed for the day, and I wonder how long he's been hiding in the hallway listening to our conversation. Based on the look on his face, I'm assuming he's heard enough and totally agrees with my mother. He's going to rescue me all the same. It's a sibling code of honor.

"I thought we'd take them to breakfast, since we're going to be cooking most of the day. What do you think, Koko?"

I *think* I want to hug him for creating a distraction. I *think* I want to curl up in a ball and cry over my mother's obvious disapproval. I *think* my gut is churning with all the emotions I've experienced in the last couple of days. I *think* breakfast is a much better option than doing any of those things. When I answer it's with just as much false enthusiasm as Tosh used.

"How about doughnuts?"

———

When we roll up to the Ashtons' home later that afternoon, the holiday is already in full swing. I say *roll* because among the four of us, we polished off enough of my mom's food to warrant some embarrassment on our parts. The idea of consuming anything else should make me want to heave, but I can always find room for one of Max's desserts. I'm looking forward to it almost as much as I'm looking forward to seeing how Vivian's florist has designed the party.

I've never been to Thanksgiving at their house before, but I know from Landon that Viv always throws a huge dinner party complete with chefs and servers and centerpieces the size of a one-year-old child. For once it's fun to be the one invited to something like this instead of the one producing it for a client.

When we ring the bell, it's Charlie who opens the door in slacks and a blue sweater that matches his eyes. He greets my parents with the enthusiasm usually reserved for long-lost cousins. It's always interesting to watch someone meet your family for the first time, to wonder what they'll think now that they can fit more pieces of your puzzle together. I wonder what he sees, looking at my parents now. My mother is chic, but in the understated way of Audrey Hepburn. My dad isn't as tall as our host, but he has his own impeccable sense of style, and the salt and pepper in his hair makes him look distinguished. He shakes Charlie's hand and offers up a beautifully wrapped bottle.

"Miko tells me you're a wine connoisseur. Since we're not too far from Napa, we took the liberty of picking out something exceptional for you."

"You didn't have to do that," Charlie says, though it doesn't sound very convincing. He starts to untie the twine, eyes alight with possibilities of small boutique wineries or a vintage Meritage blend. "Though it's certainly appreciated. I love finding out what other people . . ."

His voice trails off as the paper falls away to reveal the bottle of Charles Shaw we picked up especially for this day. Anyone who's ever shopped at Trader Joe's knows that bottle costs exactly $1.99.

"We splurged and got the 2016," Mom says cheekily.

Charlie starts laughing. Not chuckles, but deep, real laughter of surprise over the bottle of Two-Buck Chuck. He smiles and looks at me.

"Well, now I know where she gets it."

Everyone laughs, and after a few more jokes about the wine, we head in the direction of the party. We don't make it more than a handful of feet before my dad stops walking completely. The entryway is muted in tones of white and beige; the only color at all comes from the large painting on the wall that's lit from at least three different directions by lights installed for just that purpose. Dad stands in the center of the room and stares at the Pollock with the rapture of a pilgrim returning to the Holy Land. I exchange a grin with Tosh. I purposely didn't tell my art-professor father about Charlie's art collection, because I thought it'd be way more fun to see him experience it with surprise. I was right.

Charlie admires it along with him. "I fell in love with his work the first time I saw the Guggenheim collection. I chased after this piece for fifteen years before I was able to snag it at auction."

"It's fantastic," Dad says with reverence.

"They have at least one of his there at Stanford, right?"

"Yes. *Lucifer* is part of the Anderson Collection, but this is—I've never seen *Number 3* in person before." As if remembering himself, he turns to Tosh and me. "Do you know why he numbered his paintings rather than name them?"

My dad is incapable of sharing information straight out. He always frames it in the form of a question. *Miko, can you tell me why those flowers are blooming, but the others are not? Kitoshi, do you know what Lichtenstein based his prints on? Koko, what can you tell me about the Bolsheviks' rise to power?* It used to drive me insane as a child, but now I understand him in a way I didn't then. A lifetime of him drilling me for math tests and high SAT scores means that I know he can't step out of his role as an educator any more than I can stop redesigning every room in my head the minute I walk into it. He believes you're much more likely to retain information if you have to work it out in your head before you grasp it, so asking a question like this is just how he operates.

"I'm not sure," I answer with a shrug.

"Because he didn't want the viewer to have any preconceived notions about the work," my mother murmurs, following the drips and splatters of paint with her eyes. "A title might tell you how to feel about it. A number forces you to draw your own conclusion—decide on your own what it's supposed to be."

My father beams at her.

"Teacher's pet," I squeeze out through a round of fake coughing.

Charlie gestures down the hall. "Come on, Miko. Let's get you a drink. I'd hate to think you might choke to death when I've got a perfectly good bottle of two-dollar wine right here."

As I follow Charlie down the hall past more priceless paintings and family pictures, my nervousness grows with every step I take. I saw Liam eight hours ago, and I should not feel this excited about seeing him again when we just hung out. But today is special. Today is a holiday. Today he'll meet my parents. Today he'll see me in this adorable red velvet vintage dress from the sixties, with its white Peter Pan collar and its short skirt. Today's outfit says *pretty, flirty, romantic*. I saved this recent flea market find for months just so he could see me wear it for the first time.

The house is packed with people, but it's easy enough to make out my group of friends lounging on various surfaces of the sectional in the far corner of the large room. After grabbing a glass of very expensive wine from Charlie, I take a moment to lust after all of Max's desserts. The little signs tell me she made bananas foster banana pudding, her famous chocolate coconut cream pie, and something that looks like homemade Oreos. Nobody has started in on them yet, so I whisper a vow to return soon and head over to my friends. Max and Taylor are sitting on the floor with Casidee around a coffee table. Malin is lying on the sofa like a fatted calf. I make my way over to them and laugh in surprise when I see what they're doing.

"A puzzle?" I ask in shock.

Max is adorable in skinny jeans and a cozy-looking bronze-colored sweater that brings out the gold in her eyes when she rolls them at me. "Apparently the Taylor family does one every Thanksgiving. I am trying to be supportive."

"You've been *trying* to put that corner together for half an hour and failing miserably." Taylor kisses her cheek without removing his hands from the pieces he's working on. "Good thing you're cute."

I plop down on the end of the sofa next to Malin's head. "And what's wrong with you, Briar Rose?"

"I went out with friends last night." Her bloodshot eyes peel open slowly to look at me. "Mistakes were made."

I scan the room again, but there's still no sign of the blond Viking god.

"Ahh, you poor lamb. Can I get you something?" I take a sip of the excellent pinot noir. "Maybe some tuna casserole or three-day-old baby food or gefilte fish that's been left out in the afternoon sun?"

Malin covers her hand with her mouth and uses the other one to sock me. "You are so rude!"

I put my wine on the table next to me before the little harridan forces me to spill it all over Vivian's designer sofa. Malin's blonde hair is spread out all over the sofa cushion, so I gather part of it in my hands to work on a French braid.

"It serves you right," I say, twisting the hair into place. "Getting drunk is so childish."

Casidee looks up from her section of the puzzle. "You were drunk twice last month!"

"Exactly." I pull the hair tie off my wrist and secure the end of the long blonde braid. "Do you really want me as your role model?"

"Too late," Tosh says, sitting down on the other side of the sofa. "When I'm finally grown up, you're exactly who I'm going to emulate. Right down to the colorful nail polish."

Malin moves slowly into a sitting position. The thirty percent of her hair that's braided flops awkwardly in her face, but she's apparently too sick to care.

"Nail polish can look really sexy on a man," she tells Tosh.

I assume she's just trying to make conversation, but it comes out as a groan. He winces along with the rest of us at how miserable she sounds.

I glance around the room again but still don't see who I'm looking for.

"Why don't you have your brother make you one of his hangover concoctions?" I ask. "As I recall it worked really well for you after last year's wine-pong tourney."

Malin falls back against the sofa with a world-weary sigh.

"I can't. He isn't here."

Disappointment crashes through me.

"Oh?" is all I can manage.

Max doesn't look up from her puzzle pieces. "He decided to go spend the day with his mom at the last minute."

I try to sound casual. "I thought he switched back and forth? I thought this year he was supposed to be here?"

My hands feel clammy, and my stomach flips over.

How many weeks did I hold on to this stupid dress in anticipation of this day? Or worse, how long did I spend convincing my family to come here for Thanksgiving? At the time I said it would be fun to try a new locale, but the truth was I'd wanted to know what it was like to spend a holiday around him, even if it was only for dessert. My heart shrivels up in desolation.

She shrugs absentmindedly. "I guess he changed his mind."

"Oh," I push out of my mouth for the second time.

Tosh is looking at me with barely concealed . . . not pity, exactly, but something really close. When I attempt to look away from him, Max is staring at me curiously. I really have to get better at not showing every single emotion on my face! I smile brightly and jump up from the sofa, not really sure of my destination, just sure that I need to move before the jig is well and truly up.

"You going to get Mom and Dad?" Tosh prompts me. "So everyone can finally meet them?"

Gods bless him for giving me a destination!

"Yes! It's about time we make this meet and greet official. Casidee!" I snap my fingers in her direction. "You brought my robe and all the ingredients for ritual sacrifice?" My voice sounds a little strained, not at all the proper delivery for one of my better jokes, but she doesn't seem to notice.

"The chicken is in a pen out back," she tells me, deadpan. "Once you've bathed in the goat's milk, we can begin."

Everyone laughs at her comment, and under normal circumstances I would have too. Instead I use it as an opportunity to escape to the bathroom.

I step inside the powder room and look at myself in the mirror. I spent way too much time choosing my look today, and now it just feels ridiculous. Would he really go to this much effort to avoid me? He might not always give me the answer I'm hoping for, but he's always been honest with me until now. Changing plans last minute seems childish and for some reason dishonest. And now I'm questioning his intentions again and second-guessing myself.

I hate that I keep swinging back and forth through emotions so quickly. This morning I was thrilled, and now I feel sick to my stomach. I'm not even sure what I'm supposed to do in this scenario. Call him on it? Pretend indifference? What I really want to do is chew him out, just like that Amazon I saw on New Year's did.

I turn the faucet on and wash my hands just to have something to do. When the cold water hits my skin, another thought occurs to me. I keep running New Year's around in my head, and with each passing second my conviction grows. I dry my hands, pull my phone out of my sweater pocket, and then bring up our latest text exchange. What if he is avoiding me and I'm going to make a fool of myself? What if he's not and he needs a friend? I stare at myself in the mirror. The woman staring back looks flushed with emotion and totally unsure of herself. I guess it comes down to what's more important. Would I rather try to keep up some pretense of detachment on behalf of my pride, or would I rather check on my friend?

When put like that, the answer is obvious. When it comes to the people I care about, pride could not be lower on my list of priorities.

I press the button to call his phone.

It rings several times, and when it eventually goes to voice mail, I hesitate before forcing myself to say what I called to say.

"Hey, I just wanted to check on you and make sure everything was OK." I push my hair out of my face. "Sorry if this message makes me sound like a stalker. I promise not to put your bunny in a pot or anything. Um, call if you need something, OK?"

As I make my way back down the hallway, my phone's empty screen mocks me. Zero new texts and no new emails. What if he doesn't write me back? What if he—

The phone buzzes in my hand, and I have to tap out my password three times before I get it right.

Hardly the most stalker-like voice mail I've ever received.

I smile with relief at his playful message, then realize he didn't actually address the reason I called in the first place.

Is everything OK?

The typing icon pops up, but it takes him several minutes to respond. The short length of his text makes me wonder if he debated the answer or just wrote and rewrote his response several times.

She's having a bad day.

My heart breaks for him. How sad that he's the only one around to pick up the pieces. How sad that he's spending yet another holiday like this.

How can I help? Do you need anything?

I stare at the screen, willing him to answer for so long that I finally start to wonder if maybe that wasn't the right thing to ask. Liam doesn't ask for help, and he doesn't strike me as the kind of man who *needs* anything or anyone. My suspicions are confirmed when I get his terse reply.

Have a nice Thanksgiving.

I have to force myself to put the phone back into my pocket without responding. Even a stalker like me knows better than to keep pushing him when he's obviously not interested in discussing it further. With another worried sigh I head back to find my parents.

Chapter NINE

I'm sure I've done stupider things.

I went bungee jumping once at a county fair strapped into a dirty harness and trusted my safety to a carney still coming off last night's bender. Last year I convinced Landon that we should start our own company, though at the time I had very little belief that we could actually succeed and no money at all in my savings account. I only knew that my friend needed *something* to go right for her, so I walked away from the security of a big salary and let my blind faith and her enthusiasm propel us forward. And just last month when that same friend said we should try aerial yoga, I went along—certain parts of my abs are still sore from that mistake. The point is I've done stupid things. None of those feel stupider than carrying this box up Liam's front walk and ringing the bell.

When I got home tonight and my parents were finally in bed, I knew I had to do something. I hated just sitting at home not knowing what was going on with him. I hated the fact that nobody was taking care of him, in particular his mother, who'd been assigned the role but was unable to fulfill it. I can't imagine how saddening that must be, particularly on a holiday when most moms—my own included—were busy fussing over everyone.

And so I snuck out of the house and found a grocery store that was still open, not even sure if he'd be here when I arrived. I figured if he wasn't, I'd just drive home and eat my purchase by myself, and if he was, well, I'd wing it.

The door opens, revealing his disheveled form in silhouette against the light behind him. His hair is pulled back in a low bun and his slacks and button-down shirt are wrinkled. I wonder if he'd been dressed to come to Charlie and Viv's or if he tried to dress up for her regardless of whether or not she'd notice. I bite back a sad little noise in my throat. I don't want him confusing sympathy with pity. Just then I catch the strains of jazz playing in the background.

I hold my box up higher with a bright smile on my face.

"I thought you could use something to eat."

I glance meaningfully at the tumbler of dark liquid in his hand.

A hundred emotions run across his face, and he seems to be struggling with what to say. How much of that alcohol has he had already?

"God, you're beautiful." It comes out gruffly, like an admission of guilt.

He reaches out for the box in my hands, and I give it over with another smile.

"I just thought that maybe you'd . . ." My words trail off and I frown when he immediately sets the box on a console table by the door along with his drink. When he turns back around, the look on his face is fierce. I know exactly what that look means.

"I don't want you to think I came over here for this again."

I jump a little when his fingertips slide under the hem of my dress to reach my skin.

"I don't," he whispers, kissing along my neck.

A tiny whimper slips out of my mouth when his fingers slide down my back along with the zipper on my dress. I need to focus.

"You're upset."

Those same confident fingers slide back and forth against the rainbow of ink that runs along my side. He always seems to go back to that spot on my skin, though he's never once asked what the tattoos mean. "And?"

I'm trying to stay on topic, but I keep getting lost in the sensation of his hands. My answer comes out breathy. "I just wanted to help."

A slow, lazy grin spreads from one side of his face to the other. "Oh, believe me—this is extremely helpful."

———

It's hours later before I remember the Trojan horse sitting on the console table and force Liam to accompany me to the kitchen. He pulls on pajama pants and a T-shirt, and his overly long hair looks almost as chaotic as mine does. I find his blue cashmere sweater lying over the chair in his room and throw it on. It's about a hundred times too big for me, but it feels like heaven and smells like him.

"You go there." I point to the line of stools sitting next to a marble-top center island and then hurry to grab the box and my bag from the entryway where I left them. When I come back into the kitchen, he laughs.

He points to the can of whipped cream in my hand. "Now we're talking."

"Exactly. We're *talking*. But first we're going to enjoy this." I remove the pumpkin pie from the container with the flourish of a magician. "What size piece would you like? Tall, grande, or venti?"

I vaguely remember the layout of the kitchen from when he made me breakfast. I pull a knife from the drawer but need some guidance from him before I can find the plates on the overhead shelf. I look to him for an answer he still hasn't given me on the size of his slice.

"I really want to make a joke right now about your use of the word *piece* and exactly what kind of piece I'd like—"

I roll my eyes.

"But you won't because that's rude."

His lips twitch.

"Right. I'd hate to be rude." He runs a hand through his hair. "I'm going to choose venti."

I slice into the pie.

"Thank goodness! I'm going to choose venti too, and this way I don't feel alone in my gluttony."

I put two gigantic pieces of pie on each of our plates and carry them around the island to take a seat next to him. After sliding a plate towards him, I shake up the can of whipped cream. I add a stream of the white topping down one side of the pie in a straight line.

"I think you can tell a lot about a person based on how they add their whipped cream," I say.

"Ahh, one of the great tenets of life."

I wish I had something heavier to throw at him than just my glare.

"Don't be a wiseacre."

He laughs.

"Wiseacre? Are you secretly a hundred-year-old man?"

The look I turn on him is solemn. "Sadly, you are not the first person to wonder that. Now back to the pie. I like to cover mine completely in this sort of uniform formation." I add one row after another, covering every square inch of my slice. "This way I can be absolutely certain of my pie to Reddi-wip ratio."

I set the can in between us and take a bite. I can't help dancing a little in my seat; it's the perfect combination of flavors, and I've waited all day to get it. I grin at the amused expression on his face.

"Come on." I nod at the can. "Let's see what you've got."

He picks up the can and shakes it for good measure. He adds a perfect dollop to his slice directly in the center. I've eaten blueberries bigger than that circle of whipped cream. My eyes fly to his.

"You can't be serious!"

His shrug is playful. "I don't really like whipped cream."

I have to take an extra-large bite of my pie to cope with this discovery. "Good gods," I despair around a bite of pumpkin filling. "I'm going to pretend you didn't say that."

He takes a bite of his own pie sans whipped topping. "Deal breaker?"

He's nearly a foot taller than me and a giant wall of solid muscle, but he's still playful enough to come to the kitchen in the middle of the night to eat a piece of pie the size of his face.

"Normally yes," I sigh dramatically. "But I've never seen anyone look so handsome while eating a midnight snack, so I'm going to let it slide."

He grins and takes another bite. He seems laid back, almost peaceful—a totally different person than the one who answered the door a couple of hours ago. I'm ridiculously happy that I played any role in that at all.

"So what happened today? Is everything OK with your mom?"

He pauses with the fork halfway between him and his plate.

"Same thing, different day," he throws out casually.

I turn to face him fully and do something I've wanted to do since the very first night I met him. I reach up and tuck a piece of golden hair behind his ear.

"It wasn't just a different day," I say carefully. "It was a holiday. That can't be easy."

The kitchen is the only room with the lights on, so when he looks away from me, it's out into the darkness.

"It was fine. How was your day?"

I try not to sigh. I want to be respectful of his privacy, but it's not like we haven't discussed this before. In fact, I'm pretty sure I'm the only one who has discussed this topic with him. I worry that he's so busy keeping up the pretense of having it all together that he doesn't have anyone to talk to. I keep thinking if I just carefully bring it up or keep throwing him underhand softballs that maybe he'll start to talk to me. Maybe that's the wrong approach, though. Maybe I need to be more direct.

"My day was fine, but I think I'd rather hear about yours."

He turns his head back in my direction, but his eyes land on the can between us. He grabs it off the counter with a mischievous smile.

"You know what I think?" He holds the can.

I'm already shaking my head. "There's no telling."

He reaches for my left hand, and since my body is his willing accomplice, I place my hand on top of his outstretched palm without any kind of coaxing on his part. He adds a dollop of whipped cream to the center of my palm and leans down close enough to warm my fingers with his breath. Then without ever once breaking eye contact with me, he slowly licks it clean.

"I think we can come up with much more interesting uses for this than pie topping."

In more than one book, the heroine describes her desire in the floweriest of descriptions. She feels like she's going to internally combust or come out of her skin or get burned up by wanton flames.

My desire isn't anywhere near as articulate.

My head fills with weird, nonsensical sayings: a flash of the jingle for a local electrician, the opening dance routine for *Kids Incorporated* circa 1991, the Mad Hatter's gibberish as described by Lewis Carroll, and He-Man yelling about the power of Grayskull. These are the crazy images that fill my head along with a million other things that are so intense and demanding I have to stop myself from attacking him like a howler monkey.

"You—you don't even like whipped cream," I stutter inelegantly.

The light in his eyes catches on fire as he shakes the can again.

"I'm thinking it all depends on what you put it on."

It isn't until much, much later that I realize he never answered my question at all.

——

Landon bounces into my office a few days later wearing way too much pink and enthusiasm for a Monday morning. She's all smiles as she deposits a coffee onto my desk.

"I'm trading caffeine for information," she says as she plops down into a chair. "Your text messages were cryptic and uninformative. I want—" She halts as if remembering something.

She jumps up and hurries to close the door, then resumes her seat and takes a big swig of her own coffee.

"OK, go!"

I eye her dubiously.

"You first." I take a sip. "How did everything go with Brody and your parents?"

"I told you this already." She rolls her eyes playfully, because she knows I'm stalling for time. "My mom would marry him herself if polygamy were legal in the state of Texas."

"And your dad?"

"They argued the entire time. They covered everything from football to workers' comp and debated each point ad nauseam."

"Crud. Really? They didn't like each other?"

She looks at me like I'm crazy.

"Are you kidding me? They *adore* each other! My father loves a good debate, and Brody thinks he knows everything. It's a match made in heaven."

This makes my heart so happy. Not that I ever worried that they wouldn't all love each other, but Landon's relationship has gotten serious really quickly, and I know how important her parents' opinions are to her.

"And he liked them too?"

She scowls at the question. "Girl, stop holding out on me. What happened?"

I glance at my computer screen, where a layout for an upcoming event is still open. I consider asking her a question about it just to throw her off, but she's like a dog with a bone. She's not going to be ignored, but I don't even know where to begin or how to explain all that's happened in the last week.

"Blessed assurance, are you *blushing*?" she screeches.

I will my face to return to whatever color it was before I started thinking about the last week. Equal parts embarrassment and annoyance make my voice come out too loud.

"I don't know, probably!"

Her blues eyes flash in amusement.

"Oh, girl, tell me everything."

I cover my face with both my hands, positive it's bright red again. She laughs and waves a hand in surrender.

"OK, don't tell me everything. Just give me the pertinent information. I left you crying and upset in a pint of Ben & Jerry's, and last I heard you hung out again, and again"—she raises her eyebrows—"and again. So where does that leave you now?"

"I don't know."

"Do you two have plans later?"

I shake my head.

"But you expect to see him?"

"If tonight is anything like the last several, then . . ."

Her perfect blonde eyebrows furrow.

"But if you haven't made plans, then . . ."

I shrug helplessly. "He just texts me, and then I go over to his place."

Gods, when I say it like that it sounds so shady.

"That sounds super shady," Landon says sternly.

I do a full face-palm. "That is exactly what I was just thinking." I take a deep breath. "But it's not like that—I swear. When we're together we hang out and laugh and . . . and . . ."

She rolls her finger in the air in a carry-on motion. "I got it."

"Yeah, well, that too. But he's—it's amazing. He's funny and charming and so sweet to me."

She's nodding along in agreement, but I can tell she wants to say something more.

"What? What are you thinking?"

"Have you gone on a date? Gone for coffee?" She winces a little. "Have you ever even gone out in daylight together?"

I make a lame attempt to lighten the mood.

"Are you suggesting he's a vampire?"

"No." She shakes her head sadly, unwilling to play along. "I'm suggesting that you're a booty call."

Ouch.

That one hurt. For a lot of reasons, not the least of which is that this is something I've been worrying about but haven't wanted to acknowledge. Liam treats me like a princess when we're together. I just can't imagine that someone who's only looking to hook up acts that way. I know there's something deeper between us. I shake the ugly words away and refuse to hear them.

"No, I think it's just new. We've only been hanging out officially for a week." I ignore the voice in the back of my head that says there's nothing official at all about us hanging out. "I think I just need to do something impactful and attention grabbing."

"You need to *talk* to him about this," she says sternly. "You need to explain to him what you want out of this relationship. You have to know if he's able to give you those things or if he's even interested in giving you those things, Miko. Otherwise this whole thing is doomed."

Sadly, the last thing Liam and I do is talk about anything serious, but I'm not about to tell her that. I paste on a bright smile.

"No, come on—it's too soon for something that heavy. I have the perfect plan. It's number eight on my list."

"Girl, I really don't think—"

"Landon. It's been six days! And even your perfect relationship isn't always perfect, so please stop trying to be my mom and just be my friend right now."

It's the harshest I've ever spoken to her, and I immediately want to take it back. The look of chagrin on her face stops me.

"You're right. You're so right. I'm sorry for getting you all worked up. I'm just worried about you."

I sigh. "I get it."

She shakes her head in disagreement. "I don't think you do get it, though. You're so fun and funny, and you embrace everyone and everything no matter how odd or broken or weird. You've never met a stranger; you literally make friends with everyone you meet." She leans towards me. "You have the biggest heart of anyone I know. I just worry that that means there's more of it to get easily broken."

I blink at her a few times. I have no idea how to respond to that. Luckily, Landon fluffs her hair and smiles happily.

"All right, I've said my piece. Tell me about number eight on the list."

I cross my arms. "Don't pretend to be interested on my account."

"Ahh, come on. Don't be a grouch. Tell me about your idea."

I could sit here and stew in my annoyance. I could brood about my current pseudorelationship. Or I could accept her worry as part and parcel of her friendship and move on. The truth is I need Landon to be my wingman on this, because I feel totally unsure of what my next move should be. Two weeks ago I didn't question anything I did; I just went with my gut. But now I've got Liam, and it's so much more wonderful than I thought was possible before. The problem is that I only have him in some small way, and I'm terrified of the idea of losing even that. This makes me question things I wouldn't have before. At least if Landon is on my side, I have someone to talk it through with.

I pull out my list, which now covers both sides of the original paper with Casidee's notes. I lay out my latest plan for her, even if I have to stop a couple of times so she can finish laughing. It is kind of ridiculous, but that's what I loved about the idea in the first place.

"The thing is," I tell her as I finish up the details of my plan, "I need to figure out a time and place to pull this off. What's the modern-day equivalent of playing poker in an antebellum jail cell?"

She taps her finger on her nose, genuinely trying to come up with an answer for me. Gods love her.

"I think they're going to the Beanery this Saturday to watch the games. We could meet them there."

I don't know anything about any kind of sport. I'm not even sure which games she's referring to. But that's neither here nor there. "Perfect!"

She grins mischievously as she stands up. "Now you've just got to figure out what to wear."

I smile along with her.

"Exactly."

She laughs on her way out the door, and Casidee comes in a moment later. Her face is bright with enthusiasm.

"Well?" she asks me expectantly.

"Well what?"

"Well, what did you think of the new Colleen Hoover book? I've been dying to talk to you about it all weekend long, but I was too afraid to text you for fear that I'd accidently reveal some kind of spoiler."

She's nearly breathless in her excitement, and I'm totally startled to realize that I completely forgot that the new book was out. I preordered it months ago. I usually stay up until midnight to watch it download onto my iPad, just for the joy of finally having it in my hands.

"Can you believe that ending?" she squeals. "When he gets the Purple Heart and he gets up out of his wheelchair to walk to the stage?"

Her eyes are filled with tears of joy, a usual reaction to reading one of our favorite authors.

"I, uh, didn't get the chance to start it yet."

She gasps. "*What?* I did spoil it for you!" She covers her face with both hands. "I'm so sorry, Miko! You look forward to a new release for weeks and weeks; it never occurred to me you might not have read it."

It truthfully never occurred to me either. Not only that I might not have read it but that I wouldn't even notice the absence. I wave her away and promise to do a full-on book-club coffee date with her about it as soon as I've finished. After she walks out of my office, I open the app on my iPad and realize that the book is there, exactly where it should be.

Maybe trying to live out your own love story means that you have less time to read about other people's.

Chapter TEN

I'm a night owl, which means I tend to do a lot of my sketching and design planning in the evening. That means that a lot of the time I've been spending with Liam is time when I should be working. To try to make up the difference, I spend the rest of the afternoon hunkered down at my desk, working on a proposal for an upcoming bridal shower. When Landon leaves for the day, I'm just starting the second one. It feels good to focus on the design instead of worry about my personal life, and I'm so absorbed in the process that I don't even know what time it is when I hear my phone vibrate.

My heart kicks into rapid staccato when I see that it's a text from Liam.

You should come over and hang out with me.

I can just imagine the sly charm he would have delivered that line with if he'd been here in front of me. I can't help but smile as I type back.

Oh really? And why should I?

Because I want to see you.

My heart lurches, thrilled that he wants to see me. I want to see him too, but even I can recognize the problem with this situation. In the last six days I've spent four nights at his place. The only reason he couldn't convince me to stay the other two were because my parents were in town. The time we spend together is wonderful, but it's always at his place, under the cover of night, and it's always at his request. As much as I'd love to see him, I really do have a mountain of work to get through. I also need to make sure he understands I'm not just going to come running every time he calls. I fire off a response before I can change my mind.

I can't tonight. I have gobs of work to do.

When I reread it and realize how terse it sounds, I add, *But I want to see you too. Maybe tomorrow?*

I have an early morning flight to NYC, won't be back until Friday. I have a ton of work too. We can both work from here. Order in dinner? Wear as few clothes as possible while doing both??

I didn't realize he had a business trip this week. Should he have told me that? Gods! I don't even know the rules of this stupid nonrelationship and whether or not I'm allowed to be annoyed by the lack of information. It also sucks that he's going to be gone all week, and it makes me feel a little panicky. What if he gets some time and space and talks himself out of whatever we've started? What if it really is exactly what Landon said it was, and I just make for a sure bet? The thought makes me feel sick to my stomach.

No, I need to look at the evidence. He asked me to come over tonight fully admitting we're going to hang out and work and order food. That's a totally couple-like thing to do. You don't order Chinese food with your booty call.

Do you?

I slam my laptop closed since no one else is here to take my frustrations out on. The trappings of design cover every flat surface of my office: linen samples and squares of tile, a box filled with tape measures, a vase filled with extra scale rulers. If Cas didn't come in here and organize me once a week, I'd probably drown under a pile of brocade fabric. I push a stack of magazines out of the way and prop my feet up on the desk. I go around and around in my head, trying to figure out the right thing to do. Another text from him pops up on my phone.

I can bribe if necessary . . .

His playfulness eases some of the worry in my head. I drop my feet back onto solid ground to properly text him back.

Oh yeah, what you got boo?

The other night we got into a long debate over which movie candy was the best. His vote was for Reese's Pieces. I made a long soliloquy on the merits of the Junior Mint, which he rebutted rather forcefully. I ended up laughing through most of his speech, because yet again, I'd gotten him to engage in a ridiculous conversation with me. I laugh even harder when he sends a picture as a response. I'm still grinning when I type out my response.

Poor Stella! Did you make her buy out the store?

His answer is immediate.

I'll have you know that I personally bought all eight of these boxes!

Really?

Well, no. But I did supervise Stella while she obtained them.

Really??

No to that too. But I did ask her to pick up Junior Mints because I know they make you happy. That counts for something, right?

Gods, he's so cute I can't even handle it.

Yes, they make me very happy.

Happy enough to come hang out with me?

I grin like an idiot. I am an idiot. This time I don't even pause to consider not going over there. I look around quickly, making sure I have everything I need for this evening. Computer? Check. Drawing pad? Yes. Total disregard for propriety and lack of restraint where this man is concerned? Absolutely. I send one more quick text and hurry out of the room.

Leaving the office now. I'll be there in a little while.

When I get to Liam's house, he greets me at the door wearing track pants and a T-shirt so old and thin I can see the indentation of his abs through the material. I can't help but notice that his eyes light up at the sight of the red leather pants I wore to the office. I'm wearing them with black Converse, a slouchy T-shirt, and a jean jacket, so they're super dressed down. But at the end of the day, they're still tight red leather pants.

"No," I tell both myself and that look in his eye. "I have so much work to do right now. I don't have time to do anything else. This is due tomorrow."

He shakes his head back and forth with mock sadness. "You shouldn't have worn those pants then."

"Liam, I'm serious." I try to sound firm, but it's lost in a squeal when he picks me up and throws me over his shoulder.

Being carried caveman-style back to someone's bedroom is not as graceful as they describe it in the books. But it *is* just as thrilling as I hoped it would be, and even if it's not the most comfortable way to travel, I'm laughing too hard to care.

———

Later on that night we're both spread out on the ridiculously comfortable sectional in his living room, working on our laptops next to the fire. The remnants of our Thai food are still in the Styrofoam containers on the countertop in the kitchen. He's busy typing out emails, and I've spent the last hour feverishly trying to make up for the time that I've lost. Landon and I have a meeting tomorrow with one of our biggest clients to go over their holiday party coming up in a couple of weeks. I'm supposed to be presenting three design options, and I haven't even started the last one yet.

I finish typing the final details of the party elements into the Google doc that we keep for every proposal and then pull out my sketchpad and pencils. If I'd had time, I would have laid this out in a CAD for them, but I can get just as much detail into a drawing and it will take me half the time. I glance at my computer to see the specs of the space we're producing the event in and then start to sketch.

I make long, fluid lines to give myself the parameters of the room. I use short curving strokes to add dimension. My fingers fly over the white page, transforming it into something else, something special. I use my black pencil for shading and red to fill in the deep drape of the linens; a dapper cobalt blue highlights the detail in the centerpieces. I get lost in the project, shading and smudging it with my fingertips as I go. I set the first page aside and start to work on a layout of the long bar with a leather front façade. The client is a purveyor of high-end liquor, so the bottles themselves are a major focal point in the design. I design the shelving behind the main bar so that pinspot backlights shine up through the gradient of glass bottles, making them glow against the dimly lit room.

At some point I become aware of his gaze on me, and I look up into blue-gray eyes. He's propped his arm up on the back of the sofa, his head leaning into his hand. I can't imagine how long he's been watching me. The room is quiet; only the sounds of the wood popping and hissing as it burns fill the space. When I raise my eyebrows in question he finally speaks.

"You're so focused." His voice is quiet. "You always put every single part of yourself into anything you do. Don't you?"

I fight the urge to frown. It doesn't feel like he's talking about just my work. I nod self-consciously. "I don't know any other way to be."

He rubs a hand through his hair, and his response is so quiet I almost miss it.

"Me neither."

Before I can figure out what that means or how to respond, he stands up.

"I better start packing."

The mention of his trip reminds me that he didn't tell me about it until today, which brings up a whole storm of questions in me. I set my notepad to the side.

"Are you—while you're gone. I mean . . ."

He cocks his head to one side, studying me again.

"Are you trying to ask a question?"

Am I? Am I really going to ask this? I shake my head in response to both of us. Even if I'm still a foot shorter than him when I stand up, I do it anyway. It feels weird to be the only one sitting down.

"No, not a question. I have a statement to make."

His lip twitches and he sits back down. "By all means." He waves a hand at me magnanimously.

I open my mouth and then feel awkward. I want to pop my knuckles, which is terrible and not even a little attractive. I'll pace instead. Pacing is a much better use of my energy, even if it's only marginally prettier than cracking my finger joints.

"I don't know what we're doing here exactly." I glance at him quickly to see if by chance he's going to enlighten me at this point. He keeps staring at me expectantly. I resume pacing. "I don't know what this is called or what we're doing, but I just want to make sure . . ." Jeez, how does one explain this tactfully? "Er, I don't . . . um, usually do this . . . whatever this is."

He swings a finger back and forth between us.

"Not *usually*? So sometimes, then? So you have done whatever this is before?"

I stop pacing, face him, and roll my eyes at his attempts to antagonize me.

"Dude. You know I've never done this kind of thing before."

He grins. Either at my admission or at the fact that he's succeeded in annoying me—I have no idea.

"And?"

"And." I put my hands on my hips. "And I don't know what the rules are or what I'm supposed to say or how any of this works."

"OK, I understand."

If he weren't so pretty, I might actually consider punching him in his stupid smirking mouth. He's purposely making this harder on me than he needs to. I take a step towards him and then another until I'm standing in between his legs, staring him down.

"OK, well, understand this." I pause for dramatic effect and try to channel someone strong and confident, like Cat from the Night Huntress books. "I don't share."

Oh snap! I've always wanted to deliver a line like that, and I'm pretty sure I totally pulled it off!

He grins. "Wow, that was actually really well delivered."

I drop any pretense of cool.

"Really?" I preen. "I thought I was pulling off the whole alpha nobody-touches-what's-mine thing, but I wasn't sure."

"No, it's totally believable. The body language, the tone." I startle when his fingertips start to slide up along my calf. "I think you should consider this new-found persona in other areas of your life."

For a second I almost cave. I almost just follow him down this road and forget the point I've been trying to make. But this conversation is important and one we have to have before he leaves on his trip. I take a single step back and force myself to be serious.

"I can't do this with you if you're still dating around."

The shadows created by a flicker of fire in the grate make his face look ominous. He opens his mouth to respond, but I cut him off.

"I'm not asking you for anything. I just want you to understand where I'm coming from." I want to tell him that my new persona, which he thinks is an act, isn't actually that far from the truth. I'm pretty sure I'd go full saber-toothed tiger on any woman who even looks at him funny. I want to tell him that just the idea of him leaving for three days makes me feel sad. I want to tell him he's made me feel more beautiful things in a week than I have in my entire adult life. But I don't, because I'm supposed to be mature and worldly and this is supposed to be casual. So instead I say, "I really like spending time with you, but I can't keep doing this if you're still seeing other people."

His brow furrows in annoyance.

"We agreed that this was casual."

I'm actually amazed that I don't flinch.

Did I agree that this was casual? I never said the words, but I guess I sort of implied it by coming to his house in the first place. Maybe I had agreed by not saying anything at all. I somehow manage to make myself sound firm.

"I can do casual. But I won't do competition; I won't play seconds, Liam." My anger grows with each word. "And frankly, if you'd even want me to, then you're not the person I thought you were at all."

"I—"

My anger feels righteous. I hold up my hand to cut him off.

"Everything else aside, if we seriously are friends, then I will tell you that that mentality is seriously screwed up. You can't sleep with more than one woman at time. It makes the entire thing cheap!" The idea breaks my heart, breaks it enough to loosen my tongue. I finally say the thing I've wanted to say to him for a year. "Actually, it makes you cheap," I whisper. "You are so special. Don't you get that? You've got to value yourself more than that."

Neither of us speaks for so long that I look down at my toes. Running headlong through every emotion I have in the last quarter hour on top of night upon night without sleep has made me exhausted. I have no idea how he's going to receive any of the things I just told him.

It shouldn't surprise me when he handles it with irreverence like always.

He reaches for my hands, pulling them off my hips and dragging me closer to him in the process.

"Has anyone ever told you that you're hot when you're angry?" he asks playfully.

My breath comes out in one big gust.

"Liam, I'm being serious."

He wraps my arms around the back of his neck and kisses my biceps. "So am I. I'm totally turned on."

He kisses my other biceps and then my shoulder and my neck. I can barely find my voice to reply.

"You're always turned on."

"Only around you, beautiful."

These words are better. So much better than all of the things I just said. I let myself focus on his words instead of my own; I let his words wash away the others. They fill up the space around us until there is no more room for questions. There's only room for us.

We fall onto the sofa in one feverish heap, the notepad all but forgotten on the floor beside us.

———

"Crap and crap and crappy crap!" I scramble around my messy desk, trying to find my notes on the presentation I'm supposed to give.

Casidee hurries into my office, carrying the coffee I begged her to get me when I ran into the building twenty minutes ago.

"They're in your filing cabinet."

I come to a full stop. "I have a filing cabinet?"

She rolls her eyes and walks across the room to the piece of white furniture in the corner. I'd brought it in because it went perfectly with the aesthetic in my office and balanced out the space against my white glass desk. It never occurred to me that Cas would actually use it for its real purpose. I've never even opened the thing up to look inside. She slides open a middle drawer and pulls out a blue-green file.

"They're color coded by client. The teal files are all Riverton."

I slam back my coffee and grab the file out of her hands. "Thanks! Do I have time to use the restroom before I go in there?"

She grabs a stack of paperwork off my desk and places it quickly into my hands.

"Landon has been making small talk with them for the last five minutes; you barely have time to walk down to the conference room."

I nod quickly and rush out of my office in a near sprint. Halfway there I realize I left the presentation packets on the printer and shout out for Casidee to grab them and bring them in once they're stapled. Then I turn back around and run-walk as fast as I can. The second I get close enough that they can see me through the glass door, I slow to a more casual pace. One of the few things I ever actually learned from my old boss in the event industry was *Never let the clients see you run.* She meant this both literally and figuratively, but in this instance I don't want Diego and his team to think I'm as frazzled as I actually am. I pull open the oversize glass doors, and the four clients at the table stand up to greet me. When I first met this group it was handshakes and formality, but we've done several events together now and they're all Latin, so we've moved up to double *besos.*

As I greet the last member of their team with a kiss on each cheek, Landon throws me a questioning look. I smile and try my best to appear casual, but I feel terrible. I've never been late for a meeting before. I've never been this unprepared either. Riverton is a huge client of ours, and it was an incredible coup to have landed their business when our firm was still so new. This is not something we can afford to lose. This is not a situation I can afford to screw up, and if I do, it won't just be my livelihood I'm messing with but Landon's too.

"We're very excited to see what you've pulled together for us, ladies," Diego tells us in his thick accent. He has to be at least fifty, but he is a caricature of the suave Latin lover. When I first met him years ago, I thought he was a super creep for trying to flirt with me. Then I realized he uses that same tone and persona with everyone he meets, both men and women. I've come to recognize it as a lure. He seems charming and laid back, but underneath all that affability is a sharp businessman with laser focus.

Casidee enters the room and smiles. "I'm so sorry I forgot to drop these off with y'all earlier," she says, putting a stapled packet of information down in front of each person. Using bubbly southern charm to ingratiate herself with the clients is something she learned from Landon. Throwing herself under the bus to save me face is a characteristic that's all her own. We really should give this girl a raise.

"We can't wait to take y'all through this," Landon tells them with her usual enthusiasm. "We have so many cool ideas."

I give Cas a grateful smile when she sets down my packet and then turn it up to ten when I look back at Diego. This is a pitch meeting, so enthusiasm is everything. I hurry to play my part.

"The party space is great too. It really lends itself to that Old World charm you're hoping to impart. Plus, downtown is so trendy right now. Your guests are going to love it."

Landon's brow furrows. Diego looks up from the paperwork in front of him.

"Downtown?" he asks me. "I thought the venue is on the Westside."

I glance quickly at Landon, expecting her to come to my rescue and explain to Diego that he's confused about which area we're producing this in. It wouldn't be the first time that's happened. Landon's smile is just as big as mine, but her brow-frown has gotten deeper. I keep the smile glued to my face while inside I'm screaming every curse word I know. She appears to be trying to read something in my face and then comes to some kind of conclusion.

"Oh, we know." She waves his question away breezily. "But everyone's using the term *downtown* now. Downtown Burbank, Downtown Hollywood—"

"So the Armory is in Downtown Santa Monica?" Diego asks.

"That's exactly right." She turns back the cover page of her packet at a precise angle. "Now if you open your proposal to page one, I'll take you through some of the installations we're considering, and then Miko will show us her design schematics."

I should be elated that she just covered for me like that. Instead I'm in full-blown panic mode. The Armory? When did we change the venue to the Armory? My palms are sweaty, and I wipe them down the front of my jeans. Last I heard we were holding the party in an old empty bank in downtown LA. I designed all three parties to fit within those specifications. Oh gods! I am so dead. This is a killing offense for sure! Diego is going to torpedo this project and the three others we're scheduled to do for him as well. I dart a look at Landon, who's happily chirping about the options available for break-dance troops to perform at their party. She's in her element. Totally polished and fully prepared. I cannot screw this up for her!

I quickly think through the parties I've designed for this presentation. The specs aren't exactly right, but I doubt Diego and his team know either space well enough to realize I planned the proposals for a different venue. Maybe if I describe it in detail, they won't pay as much attention to what's on the paper. I run through each party design in my head again, looking for ways I can expound on what they're seeing.

Landon looks at me. "Miko, you want to show them what you've been dreaming up?"

Time to put up or shut up. I pull up the first design on my computer and spin it to face them all. I don't need to look at Landon to know that she'll immediately recognize the leather-studded bar that's a signature of the original venue. I just do my best to spin it into the pitch.

"So first of all"—I grin at each client in the room—"how amazing would it be to create a custom bar like this?"

———

Despite my being wholly unprepared, Diego and his team love the designs and end up choosing the one I sketched out last night on paper. We shake their hands and promise to send over the contract and details before the end of the week. We make it all the way back to my office and close the door before Landon turns her fully incredulous face in my direction.

"What just happened?"

The sound of knuckles popping precedes my answer. "Um, our client just picked out a design for their next event?"

My voice sounds only slightly hysterical.

She wore a pretty baby-blue dress today for our client meeting, but it does nothing to soften the stink eye she gives me. "Girl."

Landon uses that one word in a thousand different ways. I never knew one word could be a question, an encouragement, or a statement of fact. In this case it's got the full implications of Tosh's favorite who-you-trying-to-kid look. She doesn't wait for me to answer.

"How could you not know the event venue? I sent you at least three emails about this right before I left for the holiday. They're putting the executive staff up at Shutters, and Diego wanted the venue to be closer by." She searches my face for some kind of recognition. "Remember the email? I mentioned that they'd added on a huge order for gift bags?"

I vaguely remember an email about Diego and gift bags. I'd gotten it the morning after that first night with Liam, and I'd been too upset to pay attention. I had meant to go back and read through those old notes, but I ended up at Liam's house again the next day and I've basically been distracted ever since.

I walk around the edge of my desk and pretend to sort out the materials on top of it. Really I'm just stacking them in nonsensical piles to have something to occupy my hands and buy me some time. I've never done anything like this before. I might be a little messy and disorganized, but I have always taken client relations seriously, even when I've worked for other companies and the clients weren't my own. We're in a consultation-based business; if we don't take care of our clients, we won't have a business anymore. This is really, really bad of me. I give up on the paper tower I'm building and fall into my chair desolately.

"I am so sorry, Landon. I don't even have a good excuse. I'm just—" Even though I told her I didn't have one, I search for one just the same. I got nothing. "I'm just sorry."

She sits down in the chair across from me and stares like she's trying to figure me out. I doubt she'll be able to. She has always been so focused on her career. In fact, if anything, Landon is the opposite of me in this situation. She struggles with not putting her career in front of everything else, and her relationships have suffered because of that. Now here I am screwing up both our careers for a relationship that's not even real. I have to fight myself to keep from crying.

"Hey," she says softly. "It's OK. You pitched the heck out of those design concepts. It all worked out."

Did it all work out? It feels like my life is just as messy as my desk. Everything is getting more jumbled by the day; nothing is becoming clearer. I nod just to appease her.

"Hey, let's call it, OK? Let's just acknowledge the elephant in the room. You screwed up. It happens to the best of us. Remember last summer when I forgot to order enough pens for the silent auction bid sheets?"

God love her for her lame attempt to make me feel better. We were down eleven pens, so we borrowed some from the hotel's front desk—it wasn't any kind of a crisis. She is one of the most organized people I know, and her troubleshooting list is typically three pages long. She doesn't screw up, not like this.

"Oh yes." I sniff miserably. "The pen crisis of 2015."

"Girl, it's *fine*. You've had a ton on your mind lately. I should have double-checked to make sure you were clear on the details."

"And now you're trying to shoulder responsibility when you are in no way to blame." I sigh. "Your being virtuous is not helping me feel any better."

"Well." She fluffs her bouncy blonde hair. "I can see that you're determined to castigate yourself regardless of what I say. Can we go get a latte at least? I'm going to need caffeine if I'm going to be forced to watch you wallow."

"Yes." I nod. "And I'll buy you a baked good too. It's the least I can do."

Her eyes light up. "How about a Milky Way cheesecake brownie with *fleur de sel*?"

I can see the plan already forming in her head. It's a ridiculous idea, given the amount of work I still need to catch up on, but I play along.

"But Landon," I say with the affected innocence of a silent-movie ingénue, "there's only one place in all of Los Angeles that makes that dessert, and it's all the way in the Valley."

"Oh come on." She bounces up from her chair. "You know we do our best work when surrounded by food, and the Flour Shop totally has Wi-Fi."

Just the idea of playing hooky and stealing espresso all day already makes me feel better. I smile in agreement. "I'll text Max and tell her to reserve our table."

———

We take seats at our usual table in the corner. All around us Max's bakery is alive with happy activity. A few customers are finishing up treats or working on laptops just like Max wanted it when we designed this space. The only thing she'd asked me at the time was that I find some way to preserve some of the raw and broken elements. Since I knew that the request had everything to do with her emotional journey at the time—that she was trying to find the beauty in the broken parts of her—I spent weeks and weeks making sure I paid homage to that. The floor, for instance, is the exact same stained concrete it was when she got the place. I had it polished and buffed until it shined. The seating area is a mix of large and small tables that Taylor made just for her. Each table is whitewashed reclaimed wood—again, an opportunity to give something new life. The white marble countertop is the anchor of the entire space, and it's topped on one side by a glass display case housing baked goods that I know from personal experience are good enough to make you cry. We found a way to marry a little rough industrial with a sort of French country kitchen, and the results turned out beautifully. The serving pieces themselves, from the vintage cake stands to the mismatched teacups, are all from a flea market. Everything in here got a second chance when the bakery opened, especially its owner.

"You look like hell," Max says.

She sets a lavender-and-honey latte down onto the table in front of me, served in one of the giant flea market coffee mugs she knows I love so much. She also slides a platter filled with glazed doughnuts towards us. They are covered in a brown-butter glaze, and I know from experience that they will be warm from the fryer. She knows from experience that Landon and I always want treats whether or not we order them.

I run a hand down one side of my mane to try to smooth it out, but there's no hiding the wildness in it today, in spite of the general calm I usually feel when I come here. The conversation with Liam, the mistakes I made with the client, the discussion with Landon—that drama is playing out in every single hair follicle to make it twice as big as it should be.

"It's not a great hair day," I grumble.

Max settles herself gracefully into the seat next to Landon. She's wearing one of the cool hipster aprons we sourced for the staff here, and her pixie cut is being held in check by the vintage scarf she wrapped around her forehead. She looks beautiful but suspicious, which for Max translates into concern. Naked concern shows too much vulnerability for her to display openly, so when she's worried about someone, she channels it into anger instead. I can guess why she's immediately hostile too.

"I hadn't even gotten around to checking out your hair. I'm more concerned about the dark circles under your eyes. What's going on?"

She actually gets super pissed off if she thinks one of us isn't taking proper care of ourselves, since health is such a driving force in her own life.

"Oh Lordy, too many things to count." Landon's accent gets more pronounced the harder she's trying to sell you on something. "Work's been crazy busy. And Thanksgiving took it out of her— isn't that right, Miko?"

I nod like a dutiful ventriloquist dummy. If she wants to try to save me from probing questions, I'm not about to stop her. I take a sip of my latte and focus on the joy of that rather than the awkwardness of this conversation. This caffeine tastes like I'm getting a hug from an angel while standing in a sunny field of lavender. They should totally put that description on the menu.

"And then there's, um . . ." Landon is still stumbling along under Max's knowing glare. "Um, that new POV book."

"POV?" Max asks.

That was the opening Landon needed. "Oh, it stands for point of view—"

"I know what it stands for, Landon. I'm not an imbecile." She stops to smile at the mother who's just walked into the bakery with a toddler in one hand and an empty stroller in the other. "Hi, guys! Back for more cookies?" Max asks this question with the joy of a first-year kindergarten teacher.

My eyes fly to Landon, and we stare at each other in shock. The little girl wiggles loose from her mother's grasp and runs headlong to our table.

"Miss Max," she greets enthusiastically. Her lisp turns the *s*'s into *th*'s, which is the flipping cutest thing I've ever heard. "I got new braids today." She leans her little head closer to Max for inspection, making her tiny waterfall of braids swing against each other. "Do you like my beads? Some of them are stars."

"So pretty," Max tells her with equal enthusiasm. "Can I touch them?"

"Of course, silly," the toddler says, shaking her head and making the colorful beads dance.

"Ooh, the stars are my favorite shape so far. Much better than the butterflies from last time." Max plays with the ends of the braids reverently. "So which colors did you choose today, Claire?"

As she starts to recite her colors, the little girl's mother wheels the stroller up to our table. Max smiles and waves her away. "Mike will help you get your order together, Sasha. She's fine."

"You sure?"

"Absolutely," Max tells her over the sound of Claire reciting *red* for the fourth time.

Max introduces us to the little girl, but that seems to make her shy, and she turns back to regale our friend with stories of something that happened at preschool yesterday. Landon and I watch in stunned silence while Max carries on an animated conversation with the toddler until her mother comes back. She wishes them well and then turns back to us without having missed a single beat.

"I know what *POV* means, Landon. I'm just not sure what that has to do with Miko looking like she's in the third stage of mono."

"There are stages of mono?" I wonder aloud.

Landon can only stare at Max; every emotion she's feeling runs across her face in quick succession. She jumps a little when my foot connects with her shin under the table, and she has to clear her throat twice before she can resume speaking. There is absolutely no way we can comment on what just happened. Later, when it's just the two of us, we will laugh and scream and rejoice over how far our friend has come. But doing that now will only embarrass Max and make her self-conscious.

Right now we have to act like nothing important happened. Like we didn't just see something incredible. And it is incredible. A year ago she wouldn't even have been able to look at a small child, let alone interact with one. For the first year I knew her, I just assumed it was because she didn't like children. It was only after learning the gut-wrenching story of how she lost her own baby that I realized how painful it was for her to see other parents with theirs.

I marvel again at the effect that Taylor has had on her life; it's been amazing to watch. They might have started out a little rocky

and unsure, but they are nearly inseparable now, and not inseparable in that creepy way that some couples are. They hang out all the
time because they are genuinely best friends. Because they were
friends first, she was able to learn to trust him in a way she hadn't
with any other man. And eventually she trusted him enough that
she could recognize the love that had been there all along. It's as
if by allowing him to love her, she was able to love herself. And
by loving herself, she's been able to grow into the best version of
herself she's ever been.

I look down into my half-empty cup and slowly let the air out
of my lungs. That's what a relationship is supposed to do. That's
what the *right* relationship is supposed to do. The right relationship certainly doesn't leave dark circles under your eyes.

I bat that unwanted thought away and focus instead on what
Landon's saying.

"—is when an author rewrites a popular book from the male
POV. It really upsets Miko." She takes a demure sip of her latte.
"Gets right up under her craw."

Max leans back in her chair and crosses her arms. "Seriously,
how can you even keep track of the amount of things that upset
Miko?"

Landon casually rests her chin in her hand. Each nail is perfectly painted in ballerina-pink polish. "Oh, I don't know. I suppose I've gotten so good at keeping track of all the things that upset
you, that keeping up with Miko's emotional dependence on literary fiction is just par for the course."

Max snorts inelegantly and Landon skillfully changes the subject. Before long we're talking about the bakery, getting brunch this
weekend, and a dozen other innocuous things that keep me from
thinking about all the stuff I don't want to focus on.

———

Since I sent the last text in our phone conversation, I make the decision not to reach out to Liam while he's in New York. I figure if he wants to talk to me, he knows how to get ahold of me.

I don't hear from him all week.

Part of me wonders if he's trying to prove something or send me a message. Part of me wonders if this is yet another move in some relationship game I haven't figured out how to play. Part of me (an admittedly pathetic part of me, in the very back of my mind) wonders if he's in Manhattan running his way through a bevy of women. All of me misses him, which super pisses me off.

I make the decision at least eight times a day to call things off. But then I talk myself around again. He did tell me he'd text me when he got back into town, so really, what do I have to be upset about? Also, maybe this is totally normal behavior. Maybe I'm being too needy. I always thought when you found someone, it would be so easy to figure out. I guess I just never anticipated having to figure it all out on my own.

Several times I consider asking Landon what she would do in my situation, but after my screwup earlier in the week, I don't think she's the biggest proponent of me and Liam. Without a better option I head in search of my original sidekick on this project.

I find Casidee in the small closet-sized room we commandeered from Tosh to use as a craft space. She's sitting at the large work table that takes up half the room, and she's surrounded by at least a dozen different vintage floral fabrics. I'd seen the idea for fabric-covered boxes ages ago and was excited to find a client who finally wanted them as favors for her bridal shower. That's how it works in event planning: you design a hundred events in your head, and eventually you find a client willing to pay to make your dreams a reality. Casidee is busy gluing the fabric around craft boxes. The box of Hello Kitty Band-Aids beside her means she's probably already hurt herself at least once. Crafting in large quantities is always hazardous. When I was an intern, I was always accidentally hurting myself, though my bandages were Ninja Turtles, which are way cooler.

"Cardstock?" I nod towards her bandaged finger.

She's in the middle of attaching a pale-pink toile fabric to the box in her hands, so she nods without stopping. "I was cutting the gift tags, and somehow my knuckle got in the way."

"Bummer."

She nods again, making no further attempt at conversation. She's been acting awkward around me for weeks.

My shoulder hits the doorframe as my sigh fills the too-small room.

"Are you going to be weird around me all of the time now?"

Her fingers still on the fabric, she finally turns around to face me. "This whole situation makes me anxious."

I straighten up in surprise. "Work makes you anxious? I know some of the clients are—"

"Your life makes me anxious," she clarifies.

"Excuse me?"

She pushes her glasses up farther on her nose, and for all her claiming to be the opposite, she seems totally confident.

"I'm acting weird because I'm *feeling* weird. I know you want my help and I know it's my job to assist you, but the whole thing makes me uncomfortable."

Dramatica extravaganza.

"Well, I'm *feeling* that you're being a little overdramatic, Cas. If you don't want to help me, don't help. But don't act like this list is some huge thing hanging over your head. I asked for your help, but it's not like I forced you to—"

Her sigh is interruption enough.

"No, you don't understand." She rubs the bridge of her nose underneath her glasses. "It's not the list. Do you think that's the weirdest thing you've asked me to do since I started working here? Or even the fifth weirdest?"

My head fills with the image of her trying to find a crown small enough to fit on a frog—a poorly conceived plan for a little girl's birthday party—and the subsequent mad scramble when our frog prince bit the big one forty minutes before the party. So no, this isn't the weirdest thing she's worked on.

"Not even close," I agree. "So what's so bad about this time? I thought you were going to be my wingman, the supportive sidekick, because that's what you've always been. What's so different now?"

Her face turns solemn, like a doctor about to deliver terrible news. "Because this time, you're the one who's going to be hurt."

She's so sure of what she's saying that I can see it in every line of her face. That assurance actually makes me pause, and my voice comes out strained. "You don't know that for sure."

"No, *you* don't know." She stands up from her seat, hands angrily fisted at her sides. "Life isn't a fairy tale, Miko. It doesn't end the way they show in books or movies. The hero isn't always kind; he doesn't always love you back, no matter how much you wish he would!"

For the first time I wonder whose life we're talking about here. We stare at each other in tense silence. I'm supposed to be older and wiser, but I have no idea what to say to her.

"I don't believe that's true" is all I can manage.

She looks like my mom did when I was little and I did something bad; disappointment is written in every feature.

"I know you don't, and that's what makes me so anxious."

The look on Casidee's face haunts me for hours that night. So does the fact that I still haven't figured out what to do about Liam.

Without anything better to help me figure it all out, I've only got my gut to go by. Regardless of whether or not we're in touch right this moment, and regardless of what anyone else thinks, Liam has only ever been lovely to me. And when I imagine how much more incredible we'd be if this were official, if I were allowed to say all the things I feel about him, that makes up my mind for me. So I don't let myself think about Landon, and I don't let myself think about Casidee. I focus instead on what I can control in this situation: myself and my ever-expanding list of love stories.

I have a really good plan for this weekend, stolen out of one of the greatest love stories ever written down. Plus, I have to try to cram in some knowledge about college football before then so I can at least keep up with their conversations. So I'm not going to worry about whether or not he misses me too; I'm just going to focus on what I do best. I'm going to design myself some romance.

Chapter ELEVEN

When I arrive at Barney's Beanery midmorning on Saturday, I briefly reconsider my plan. Initially, I had no greater goal in mind than to do a little attention grabbing. I wanted to remind Liam that I'm different and special and not someone you can forget—even just while you're away on business. This scene was the obvious choice because it is the quintessential *I'm totally confident in myself and I don't need you* moment in literature or film—even if the opposite is true for both that heroine and myself. The problem is that since I've never been to a sports bar before, I didn't really think about how casual and sloppy it is. Oh sure, I'm wearing an old T-shirt just like everyone else here. It's just that I paired it with a voluminous skirt large enough for a princess or a mad game of parachute at the nearest preschool.

I look out into the sea of jeans and T-shirts until I find the table full of my friends on the other side of the room. They're all staring at the flat-panel TVs that line the walls, engrossed in things that make them yell at the screens.

Hmm, I didn't count on how truly laid back this bar really is. That makes a bold wardrobe choice all the more daring. Is it too bold? When Landon looks up from the table, wearing a vintage T-shirt and her UT cap, and spies me from across the room, she answers my question by managing to do a spit-take *and* choke on her beer simultaneously. Brody pounds her on the back while hurriedly asking her a question, but she's clearly asphyxiating too hard on her drink to answer him.

Oh well, it's not the first time I've been the only one in costume. And besides, I look super hot in this baby tee. I pick up the front of my skirt and make my way around tables surrounded by groups of guys yelling at various TVs. Almost every table I pass has a person or two who looks down long enough to eyeball my ensemble, but at the end of the day, this is Los Angeles and a full ball gown–style skirt isn't the oddest thing they've seen this week by half.

As I get closer to my destination, Liam looks up from his phone and actually does a double take. He's staring at me with the same confusion that Brody and Taylor have on their faces. Max, unsurprisingly, is the one who calls me out. "Did you get that skirt at Ikea?" she yells over the noise of the bar.

I smile down at my creation.

For good luck I actually made the skirt out of my old bedroom curtains, but in their original iteration, they did grace a rack at the Swedish big-box store.

Scarlett had Mammy's help when she created a dress out of the living room drapes in order to make a bold statement for Captain Butler. I didn't have help, but it's amazing the things you can learn to construct with a sewing machine and a YouTube tutorial. Cas isn't the only one who's crafty with fabric.

"I'm actually totally impressed that you recognize this print," I tell her happily.

"I'm pretty sure they can recognize that print from deep space," she quips. "It's louder than the TVs in here."

The woman wearing a T-shirt that says *Bakers do it for the dough* is going to question my outfit?

I beam at her. "Do you like it?" I do a full spin to show off my skirt, and when a group of frat guys at the table next to us turn to watch, I wink at them.

"Can I buy you a drink?" the tallest one of the group asks me.

I feel like Glinda smiling benevolently at the munchkins. He's barely old enough to legally be drinking in here, but his offer is flattering just the same.

"That's so sweet—"

Liam's voice cuts me off. "We just ordered a round of Bloody Marys. We're all set, champ."

Even though I'm annoyed with his high-handedness, his ignoring me all week, and his assumption that I even like Bloody Marys, I still fight a grin. That little interruption was downright possessive—just like an antebellum war hero! Never doubt the power of a large skirt.

Before I can retaliate, he stands up and pulls out the chair next to me. I stare at him for a moment, and he stares right back. It's not like we're going to have any kind of real discussion with everyone we know sitting three feet away. My skirt puffs out around me like a tuffet when I sit down.

"The skirt turned out just darling," Landon tells me with a smile.

Brody looks from her to me in confusion and then startles.

"Oh—yes." He appears to be rubbing his shin. "Excellent craftsmanship."

"Thanks. The hemline isn't exactly straight, and the hidden zipper is actually not even a little bit hidden, but I still feel pretty happy about how it turned out."

Liam resumes his own seat across from me.

"You *made* that skirt?" he asks.

OK, so maybe I did a shot before the Uber driver picked me up. I was trying to calm myself down for our first interaction since he left town, but now that I have to look at him in his stupid vintage concert T-shirt and his stupid well-worn jeans, it just feels like a reminder of all the things I can't have. So rather than calm, I actually feel sort of combative.

My voice comes out a little demanding. "Are you surprised?"

He crosses his arms. "I suppose I should be."

"Hmm." I pretend to consider it. "I suppose you *should* be a lot of things—"

"Oh look," Landon chirps in an attempt to save me from myself. "The cocktails are here!"

I accept a Bloody Mary from the waiter and drink a huge spicy gulp while Landon slides the paper menu across the table to me.

"We were all just deciding what to order." She delivers this pronouncement in an overly loud tone usually reserved for deaf senior citizens.

It's like she's trying to coerce her wily grandmother into taking her meds. I am only able to ignore her attempt to manage me because I see how many different kinds of breakfast skillets they have on this menu. Home fries are enough to distract any red-blooded woman. Besides, it's probably not a bad idea to get a carb base going if I'm going to keep drinking today. I'm debating the merits of sausage crumbles over chorizo when my phone buzzes with a text message.

I've always wanted to watch football in formalwear. Good on you for starting the trend.

It shouldn't surprise me that he'd lead with a joke. It also shouldn't surprise me that even such a casual comment is playing out over text rather than in direct conversation. Heaven forbid anyone here knows we have even the friendliest of relationships. I keep my head down while I type my response.

So you haven't lost the use of your opposable thumbs? Or the data plan on your cell phone? One would wonder.

I slide the phone back onto the table and surreptitiously watch him pick up his own to read my text. When my phone buzzes again, I take a sip of my cocktail before reaching for it. Wouldn't want to appear too eager.

"One would wonder"? Are we having an argument from the 1940s and nobody told me?

He's such a brat. I absolutely refuse to grin at him. Instead I stare down at my menu like it holds all the mysteries of the universe.

When the waiter comes to take everyone's order, I make a spur-of-the-moment decision and splurge on a breakfast that easily includes two days' worth of calories. A woman should be entitled to dairy-based comfort food in times of crisis.

I reach for another sip of my drink just as Liam places an order for Belgian waffles. When he adds in a request for extra whipped cream, I almost swallow my tongue instead of my beverage. He grins at me like a lecher, and I have to look away to keep from laughing. OK, so ordering whipped cream was hilarious, and I can't help but love the inside joke. It's funny that no one called him on it either; he doesn't even like whipped cream, and he just ordered a sidecar of it. Those were his exact words.

Then it hits me. Nobody called him on it because nobody here actually knows him well, not even his siblings. Not that knowing how he eats his waffles is vital one way or another, but it's symptomatic of a much bigger problem. I know that Landon hates dill pickles and wants to be embalmed in a vat of sweet tea when she dies. I know that Max doesn't like oatmeal cookies but does like oatmeal cookies with raisins. Landon is genuinely afraid of Bigfoot, and Max is genuinely afraid of ever being trapped in a room with Landon while she explains that fear to us for the fiftieth time. I know that Taylor found his cat in a Dumpster the first week he moved to LA and that Brody won't drive his car down La Cienega because he once saw a really bad car accident on that street and the memory still freaks him out. I look at the table of them laughing and talking and showing each other things on their phones. I know a million different little things about all of my friends, so how is it possible that nobody knows even the smallest detail about Liam?

Because in order to know him, they'd have to have a deeper relationship, and Liam only does surface level. I suppose it should make me feel better that it's not just the way he is with me but the way he is with everybody, but the truth of it makes me sad. My anger deflates like the makeshift petticoat under my skirt. Once again my grand scheme turns obsolete. Once again I find myself wanting to hug him when I should want to punch him for ignoring me all week long.

A foot taps the top of mine under the table. When I glance up at him, he seems genuinely confused. His blue-gray eyes look lost, and that golden hair nearly shields his face when he bends his head forward. He mouths the words at me before anyone else can see him do it.

Why am I mad?

I sigh. I'm not mad at him. I'm frustrated and worried; I might even go so far as to say I'm obsessed. I want to make his life better. I want to make him happy. I want to make him realize that he wants those things too. I've lost all my anger, and in its place is a need to comfort him so fierce that I feel desperate with it. I walked in today righteous in my indignation. Twenty minutes in his presence and I'm right back where I started.

Malin asked me to meet her for coffee to discuss web design—apparently she has some idea for starting a blog—which is how I find myself trudging into Culver City and the most hipster coffee shop the world has ever known. Seriously, I love me some organic cold brew as much as the next caffeine addict, but this place is out of control.

Every single person behind the counter has a beard, gauge earrings, and a look of disgusted ennui generally reserved for titled royalty or spoiled socialites. The specialty iced teas are stored on the countertop, ladled out of small wooden buckets that might have been used with a mop in another life. And the featured house-made snack is a full menu of various kinds of toast. As in, an entire blackboard full of options for eating pieces of warm bread with various toppings. On second thought, goat cheese and honey sounds kind of delicious; maybe I do need to try one of those.

"Miko!" I turn and see Malin sitting in the corner and head over to join her.

A drink is already waiting for me, and I take a sip as soon as I'm seated.

"That is an Americano with organic cocoa, coconut milk from a local farm, and a hint of crushed almond," she tells me.

"So it's an Almond Joy?"

She nods her pretty blonde head. "I knew you'd understand."

I settle myself in. "You had some questions for me?"

She grabs a notebook out of her purse with a beaming smile. "I do," she says, flipping through the pages. "I have an idea, and I know you've designed websites before."

"I've designed them, but you'd still need a developer to code everything."

Her face falls a little. "Oh? Cripes. Is that difficult to find? Is it expensive?" She bites her lip nervously.

"Mali, this is Los Angeles. Half the nerds in this room could probably code for you. Don't worry."

Her face clears. "Oh, great then. OK, so I have this idea, and I think it could be a really cool website and—I don't know—maybe even a business, but you should totally tell me if it's the dumbest thing you've ever heard of, OK?" She looks down at the notes on her page. "I'm actually kind of an expert at that."

Malin is always so alive and full of energy. I've never actually seen her unsure of herself before. I lean closer across the table. "Hey, I'm sure it's a great idea. Tell me about it."

She grins happily. "So, I was thinking about becoming a fashion blogger."

I don't hide my wince very well.

She holds her hands up in surrender. "I know, OK? I get that there are a hundred thousand people trying to be fashion bloggers and that the vast majority of them live within a twenty-mile radius."

I open my mouth, but she cuts me off. "And before you mention it, yes, I also know that I got my degree in education—but that was really just a last resort, because my parents were freaking out about me not picking a major." She shudders. "Can you imagine me trying to mold America's youth?"

I grimace. "Good gods, no."

"Exactly." She takes a sip of iced tea that presumably came from one of the wooden buckets on the countertop. "So I know the competition is fierce, but I think I have a pretty unique idea."

"Which is?"

"Terrible fashion!" she announces joyfully.

"Pardon?"

"Terrible fashion, as in, an entire blog and Instagram that's devoted to styling really terrible clothes in a beautiful way."

My forehead knots.

"Max is actually where I got the idea from. You know how she's always wearing those horrible T-shirts with ridiculous and/ or totally inappropriate sayings on them?"

When I saw her last, Max's T-shirt had a picture of a piñata on it under the words *I'd hit that!* I grin at the memory.

"Yes, I'm familiar."

"Well, I saw her wearing one of those terrible shirts, and I thought, well, actually, if she styled it with a cute skirt and the right pair of heels, that could totally trend. You know?"

"Sure."

"It could totally be a thing—like, a sort of make-the-nerdy-girls-cool thing."

I give her the stink eye.

"Careful, Blondie."

"Please, you aren't anywhere close to nerdy now, if you ever were."

I love her for thinking that's true.

"And that's not the point anyway. The point is that it's a different angle, one that hasn't been done." She takes a breath. "And I'd like to try it. Do you think it could work?"

The truth is, the idea isn't bad, but it's nearly impossible to break out of the saturation of the blogging market nowadays, particularly in fashion. But she's looking at me like a hopeful little bunny, and I'll be damned if I'm going to dream-crush her, even if I don't think this is the best I've ever heard.

"I think that if you want to do this thing, you should do it. Everyone should be allowed to pursue their dreams."

To my surprise she slumps down in her chair again. "That's the problem, though. All I do is follow my dreams, one after another, and none of them lead me anywhere. Sometimes I realize it was a bad idea, or sometimes it doesn't work no matter how much I try. Either way, I've got a long list of careers I've attempted, and since I'm currently working in a boutique selling clothes on commission, I'm sure you can guess how well any of my other ideas have turned out."

She looks so lost all of a sudden, and I want to reach out and hug her. The thing is, though, Malin doesn't need a hug, and she doesn't need to be coddled. That's what her family has been doing her entire life.

"So give up."

Her head flies up in shock. "What?"

"Give up," I say it clearly. "You've got a rich daddy; you can live off your trust fund forever."

Hurt settles over her face, followed quickly by anger. Attagirl.

"I don't want to be that kind of person. I want to make my way."

I fling a dismissive hand out at her spiral notebook. "Doing this?"

Her eyes narrow. "Why not this? It's a cool idea and it's entertaining. It's a way to elevate a style that lots of people look down on. It might help other women feel better about themselves." Her words become hurried in her excitement to explain it all. "I could have guest posts where people submit their own pictures, or we could take the worst thing from someone's wardrobe and show you five different ways to wear it. There could be a weekly segment where I show off something I got at the Goodwill for less than five dollars." I didn't even know Malin knew what Goodwill was. I'm wildly impressed. She stabs her notebook with an angry finger. "This is a good idea!"

I smile at her sincerely. "Of course it is. Now don't let anybody talk you out of it. Not me, not your family, and definitely not yourself."

She sits back in shock at my abrupt change in direction. So I lean closer across the table and look her right in the eye. "Mali, everybody has dreams and ideas. The difference between the people who succeed and the people who don't isn't about whose dreams were better. The difference is that the people who succeed refused to give up."

She sits up eagerly and grabs my hand. "So you'll help me?"

I roll my eyes and feign a long-suffering sigh. "I mean, you did buy me a coffee, so I guess."

The sound of her squeal startles the guy at the table next to us. He's unironically wearing beaded moccasins, though, so he totally deserved it.

———

"So where does this start exactly?" Charlie looks down at the blue-prints in his hand and then back up at me.

I walk across the dusty and cracked floor to stand next to him. After everything that went on at work with Landon, I feel even more pressure to make sure I don't screw up this meeting. I prepped for hours and tried to think of every question they might throw at me. I pull the tape measure off the waistband of my jeans and measure out the appropriate distance from the wall.

"The bar would begin just about there." I point out the area to the left of us. "And it'll run down the wall until just before the entrance to the kitchen."

I came to the restaurant today to do a walk-through with all of the Ashton men. Liam and I have discussed the schematics for the space several times already. Since it's his project, he's the one tasked with making the majority of the decisions. At the end of the day, though, this place is a Barker-Ash property, and I am on con-tract with Barker-Ash. That means taking the other two members of their executive staff through the plans as well. Since the space was a former restaurant, they're going to get off easy with several codes and permits, but before they break ground on the design, they all need to have a clear understanding of how it'll be laid out.

Charlie is looking dapper in his slacks and a bespoke blazer that probably costs more than every piece of clothing I own com-bined. His blond hair has the slightest bit of gray in it; he's well on his way to becoming a silver fox.

"It's an awfully long bar," he tells me with a worried frown.

I smile back confidently. "Ahh, but some allowances must be made in the pursuit of great design."

"The design is beautiful, Miko," Brody tells me sincerely. "But something that large cuts into our capacity for the restaurant by an additional ten percent. That's a significant loss of profit on what could be more patrons. Especially when we really only need a bar half this size."

Behind both of their backs, Liam fights off a grin. This is the same argument we've been having about the plans for weeks. Sticking my tongue out at him would be childish, so I don't do it, even though I really, really want to. I turn my attention back to Brody and Charlie and look at the room with them. The image is in my head, as clear as it is on the plans they hold. It's exactly what the space should look like, and that bar is central to the whole idea. Each design needs one grounding element, one thing that makes it stand out. In this case it's the bar, and I'm prepared to battle for it. They brought me in on this project because I know what I'm doing when it comes to design. They brought me here because they needed a fresh perspective to set the stage for the high-end clientele who care almost as much about the ambiance as they do the food. I know what I'm talking about; I have years of design credit to back up my belief—now I just need to convince them that I'm right.

"It wants for a major focal point, you guys. Can't you see that?"

Their smiles are kind, but I can tell design is going to be a hard sell with them when the profit is being affected. I set out to explain it the same way I would with event clients: by selling them on the experience, not the way it looks.

"People are going to pull up out front and find this place glowing like a firefly." I point out the front door. "Imagine that you're them and you're stepping inside this restaurant, with its hideous vegan food"—Liam rolls his eyes—"for the very first time. You stop first at the front door. You can't help but admire its ironwork and the scrolling inspired by the spires of Sagrada Família in Barcelona. And then you walk inside." I hurry over to the spot where the receptionist will stand. "And you find an antique Cuban desk that serves as our reception stand."

"Given that the embargo has only recently been lifted, thus driving up the price of goods, would another country's antiques be more cost effective?" Brody asks, bemused.

I snap my fingers for him to be quiet. I suppose I should be a little more deferent to his position here, but we're just too good of friends now for me to pretend otherwise.

"Cuba will be fine. Don't worry about it. And it'll be gorgeous and so is the receptionist; his name is Paolo—"

"Here we go," Liam interrupts, only to be silenced by his father's chuckle and my refusal to be stopped right when I'm getting to the good stuff.

"His name is Paolo," I continue, louder now. "And he's tall for a Dominican."

"Dear Lord!" Liam is laughing now too.

"And he's not one of those regular receptionists who's really rude and actually wants to be a backup dancer. He's the consummate professional and so happy to greet you when you walk through the door. In another situation, in another restaurant, perhaps, you might stop to chat with him for a moment. But not here. No, there's something even sexier than Paolo in this restaurant, and it's just beyond where you're standing. Your eyes quickly slide past him to the room, drawn there by the play of pattern and texture so beautifully harmonized you can't not look at it. It's not what you expected. So much bigger and brighter than you thought it would be. And then you see it; the bar beckons to you, an oasis of bold color in the large airy space. You and your date make your way over to sit at the stools, amazed by the detail and ironwork in their base."

All three of them are smiling at my story as I knew they would, but they're also looking out over the empty space along with me, which is what matters most. I hope they can see it too.

"The façade on the bar is a statement in and of itself. Black-and-white tile shipped here from a tiny artisan outside Mexico City."

"Did they figure out how to ship it properly?" Liam asks.

The tile was another item we argued over, since I'm insistent we use a pattern I remembered from a small hotel I visited years ago in Baja. One of many issues with this merchant, besides the fact that I needed Landon to translate for me since they can't speak English, is that they had no idea how to ship it to the States without it breaking.

"We're figuring it out, Liam," I say to him for what must be the fiftieth time in reference to that tile. "My point is, the bar is part of the story of this space. More than that, it's the heart of your restaurant." I shake my head defiantly. "You can't cut it in half."

They all look a little sorry, likely because they're dead set on disappointing me, but Liam is the one who speaks. "Miko, I appreciate your passion for this—we all do. But ten percent is too great a percentage to miss out on in the name of style. We have to find some way to make it work in a smaller size."

It's impossible. The entire design is based around the bar standing just as it is. And not only that, but this will be my most significant design ever. This is the kind of thing that will put me on the map after years of scraping by with freebie work and low-paying design jobs. I remember my conversation with Malin about the people who don't give up on their dreams.

I cross my arms and look around the room, trying to come up with some way to make this bar work. And then I remember the design I worked on for Riverton and the highlight of the party they're throwing. I spin around and nearly trip in my excitement.

"Have you considered only serving organic liquor?"

They all glance at each other.

"Providing a top shelf and widely stocked bar is imperative to the success of any restaurant," Brody tells me. "Getting a full menu of items to offer that are entirely organic would be difficult."

"But not impossible," I hurry to add on.

They still looked confounded by the direction I'm headed.

"I believe it would be extremely difficult to educate people on exactly what they're drinking and why their favorites aren't on the menu," Charlie says kindly.

"But the exclusivity would also mean you could charge a lot more than you could for regular liquor." I grin at them. "A lot more than a ten percent markup, I'm sure."

Brody frowns. "But how could you convince them to order the more expensive option?"

"You don't give them the option," Liam says. The understanding on his face makes me feel like a superhero. "You only put high-end organic alcohol on the menu, and they don't have a choice."

I nod at him. "You make the bar the focal point of the whole restaurant, both within the design and within the menu. You have Max come up with some incredible cocktails. She'll use unique flavors and specialty ingredients. Give them long names and have the servers regale your guests with some histrionic backstory of how each drink came to be and how it earned its name. They won't question the upcharge; they'll accept it all as an exclusivity of eating at a place like this."

Liam smiles.

Brody smiles.

I smile.

Charlie breaks into loud laughter. "Come on, girl. We're going to take you to lunch. I want to hear what other crazy ideas you've got tucked up there with Paolo and organic tequila."

On the way out of the building, Liam calls after me. When I turn around to speak with him, he tells them we'll meet them there. As soon as the door closes behind them, Liam pulls me to him and kisses me so well I feel light headed.

I can't help my grin. "What was that for?"

"You are always a surprise."

"And you like surprises?"

His eyes are sparkling with mischief, and I think he might answer with another joke, but then his smile grows soft. "I like *you*."

———

After that pronouncement I decide not to push him too hard on things like text messages or labels or what the normal progression of a relationship should be.

When Liam and I are together, it's incredible—the happiest I've ever been in my life. I stay at his house almost every night when he's in town. The next time he goes out on business, he keeps in contact with me through funny photos and the occasional borderline-inappropriate text message. We never actually get around to arguing about why his radio silence during the last trip bothered me so much.

He goes away for a couple of days on a business trip again not long after, and the next time we see each other is at Sunday Supper. We end up making out in a closet, surrounded by winter coats and scarves like teenagers afraid of getting caught.

Whatever else our relationship is, it is exciting and fun. I decide to just focus on enjoying myself rather than trying to figure everything out. We do sneak around a lot, but that becomes a game in and of itself. I tell myself our relationship is more special somehow because it is something nobody knows about but the two of us. Whatever this is, it has turned into some kind of relationship. That is more than many other women could boast. I count myself lucky.

At some point our clandestine meetups are going to turn into the real thing. At some point we'll walk out of his parents' house hand in hand instead of leaving in separate cars and meeting up later that night. At some point he and I are going to spend enough time together that he'll realize he is in love with me, just like Marianne Dashwood and Colonel Brandon. The way he feels about me is evident in his touch, the sweet things he says, and the little gifts he gets me for no reason. If it isn't a normal kind of relationship, that's OK—I'm not a normal kind of girl. Not that he needed to be reminded of that; it's always popping up in conversation.

"I'm sorry—it's called what?"

I just took a huge bite of my Corn Flakes, so I have to chew quickly to answer him.

"Cosplay."

He looks at me incredulously. "And it's like . . . a costume party?"

I start to shake my head and then reconsider. I guess you could call it that.

"Well, I guess sort of. But it's not really a party; it's just people who like to dress up in costume as their favorite character."

"And they go through life like this?"

I'm clearly startling his delicate sensibilities, but this is nothing knew. Plenty of people are thrown off by the idea of groups of people dressing up in costume en masse. Liam, who was born and raised in Beverly Hills, who has always been popular and pretty, wouldn't understand the desire to become someone or something other than himself.

"Not through *life*, Liam. It's not an affliction. It's really more like performance art. They just dress up for conventions or conferences or fan events."

He shakes his head and looks at me like I've just told him the world is flat. "Dress up as what?"

Why do I find his dismay so endearing? "Oh gosh, everything." I take another sip of coffee. "Harry Potter, *Game of Thrones*, manga, anime, *Lord of the Rings*, Marvel—"

"I think I have a great uncle who's into Civil War reenactments," he tries to add helpfully.

I bite my lip to keep from laughing. "Um, yes, I guess that's sort of the same thing."

"But this group of people you're talking about is mostly teenagers, right?"

"Sure."

He's still totally baffled by what I'm talking about, and it's throwing off his whole view of the world. I don't have the heart to tell him that the year I went to Yukicon, I was one of the youngest people there. Or that there's a whole society of grown men called Bronies who love My Little Pony more than any toddler girl ever could. Or that the greatest Sailor Moon costume I've ever seen was worn by a woman old enough to be my mom—who also happened to be a super high-powered corporate lawyer. I think I've disturbed him enough just by mentioning that it's something I'm into.

"You should try it with me sometime." I grin mischievously. "I'm sure you'd love it."

"I'm good, thanks." He grabs my now empty bowl and his own and walks around to the island to rinse them both in the sink.

"Well, if we're going to try and do something together, I think it would be fun to do the other person's favorite thing."

This is how this whole conversation started in the first place. After a month of sleepovers, I suggested we try to do some kind of activity not based in his bedroom.

He puts the bowls into the dishwasher and reaches out to tap my nose across the island.

"Beautiful, we do my favorite thing almost every day of the week."

I hide my blush by taking a sip of coffee. When I glance up and see his grin, I do my best to look stern. "I'm serious. Let's each plan a joint activity based on what we like to do. I'll even let you go first."

He considers me. "I guess we could go to dinner or something."

I should *not* get this excited over him suggesting something so simple. I should actually be embarrassed about my reaction. It's just that it's the closest he's ever come to mentioning anything even sort of like a date, and that makes my heart want to sing. Sadly, though, that isn't the point of this exercise, and there's also nothing unique about dinner. I imagine he's taken a hundred women to dinner, and I have no desire to be like any one of them.

"I'm not looking for dinner, Ashton. I'm looking for an activity that you like to do."

He nods.

"OK, let me think on this."

"Think all you want, pal, but I've got three holiday parties to produce this week, so you need to come up with something good. OK?"

"You're so bossy," he says playfully.

"Not even!" I take one more sip of coffee and then stretch up on tiptoes on the edge of the barstool to hand him my mug. "I am running late, though. I've got to jet."

He takes the mug with one hand but quickly grabs my wrist with his other. I've put the sweatshirt and yoga pants I wore over here last night back on, so he has to push up one sleeve to get to my skin. He rubs his lips back and forth across my pulsing wrist, which started to hammer as soon as he reached for me.

He's got that look in his eye.

"Liam, I really have to go. Didn't you hear the part about my three events this week?" It would be so much more convincing if I didn't sound so out of breath.

His grin is almost dangerous. "This will only take a second."

"You always say that, and then it's three hours later and I can't . . ." I stutter when he kisses the center of my palm. I try to remember what I was about to say. He bites the flesh just below my thumb.

Talking is overrated anyway.

He tugs on my wrist, and without even stopping to consider how odd it might be, I crawl up to sit on top of the marble island. I'm sure the look on my face isn't far from the one on his. His hands trace slowly up my calves and hook under my knees, and before I realize what he means to do, he slides me all the way across the counter until I collide with him.

I'm going to be late for work again today.

Chapter TWELVE

On the way to the office, I run by our favorite coffee place and grab gingerbread lattes for myself, Casidee, and Landon. They'll serve as penance for my showing up late again for work when we're already so busy. I carry the tray of coffees in one hand while teetering a little on my new DVF pumps. They're not that tall actually, but I'm more of a wedge kind of girl. Liam loves pumps, though. I know this because he basically attacked me the first time he saw me wear some, and so I've been finding ways to incorporate them into my wardrobe ever since.

I find Landon and Cas set up in one of the conference rooms. There is tissue paper everywhere and huge stacks of beauty products, couture sugar cookies, and the custom water bottles I designed for our next party. I wince when I see how many gift bags they've already stuffed on their own. I totally forgot we were going to do that this morning. I hurry into the chaos.

"I come bearing gifts!" I call brightly.

"Thanks," Cas calls from the long end of the table.

Landon doesn't manage more than a tight smile. Oh cripes! I wonder if she and Brody had a fight or something.

"Where do you want me?"

Landon shoves the tissue paper she's holding down into the open paper bag in front of her but doesn't look up. "Wherever."

I drop my purse on the console table by the door and set down the tray of coffees nobody seems to want. When Landon still doesn't look up or make conversation, I decide something really bad must be going on.

"Hey, Casidee," I say before I've come up with a good way to finish that sentence. "Can you, uh, grab some of these empty boxes and take them down to recycling?"

It's a lame excuse to get rid of her for a bit, but she doesn't seem to mind. She makes a huge stack and then carries it from the room in one awkward heap. As soon as the door closes, I give up all pretense of work and turn to face Landon.

"Hey, what's up? Did something happen?"

She puts down the product she's holding and turns to me. She searches for words for at least a minute. I get the impression that whatever has upset her is going to be bad. Gods, what did Brody do?

"Did something happen?" she asks the room at large.

I'm surprised by the anger in her voice.

"Yes, Miko, something happened." She takes a deep breath. "The florist never got the final centerpiece options for the shower this weekend."

My stomach drops.

"And because she never got them—even after you assured me they'd been sent—she couldn't place the order for amaryllis in time."

I stumble over my apology, hopping quickly to ways to fix this mistake. "We can sub out for stargazer lilies or maybe—"

"Amaryllis was her grandmother's favorite flower. It was Michelle's way of remembering her nana as part of the bridal shower. It was the only thing she truly cared about in the design."

Crap.

I do remember the request for amaryllis now that she mentions it; in fact, I designed the whole party around it. The sketches were beautiful, and we even found linens with a print that looked like it was made to hold the ornate cut-crystal vases Michelle's grandmother had collected all her life. I had everything ready to go over to our florist; I just needed to run through it once more to make sure quantities were right. I took it home with me, fully planning to send it in that evening. But then Liam called.

"I'm sorry," I tell her quietly.

Landon's look is pitying; her voice is just as quiet as my own. "You're sorry a lot lately."

I rear back like she pushed me. "That's not fair. Why would you say that?"

Her smile is sad. "The truly cruddy part is you're so far gone right now you really don't know why. What's *not fair* is that I've taken the last four client meetings by myself. What's not fair is that the reputation of *our* firm is based on the fact that we *both* do our jobs well. What's *not fair* is that all I do is make excuses for you these days!"

I can't help but feel defensive. Feeling defensive makes me angry.

"What are you talking about? What excuses?"

She ticks them off on her fingers. "The design for the Klein Bat Mitzvah was pink when they specifically told you that Talia hates that color. You mixed up the rental orders for last week's cocktail hour. We had to pay a restocking fee and the cost of the labor. That is money we don't have! You were forty-five minutes late to that walk-through with the lighting company, and you're never disrespectful like that. You didn't even show up to the bakery last Thursday, and it took you two hours to even notice enough to text us some lame excuse about being caught in traffic."

My ire deflates like a balloon. I don't have any good response, because I haven't really thought about any of those things. I've only been focused on the reason I keep getting pulled away or distracted. When I hear all of my failures laid out in a row like that, I can totally understand why she's pissed off. We're supposed to be in business together, and she's been carrying way more than her share of the load. Event planning is really stressful, and one of the reasons we've been able to manage it so well is that we lean on each other.

"You're right. It hadn't really occurred to me how many things I've slipped up on lately, but you're totally right. It won't happen again. I promise."

She clasps her hands in front of her, looking unsure of how much she should say.

"I'm worried about you, girl."

I nod. "I get that, but I'm going to get the work stuff together. I promise."

She nods sadly and turns for the door. "This isn't about the company, Miko. Your work ethic sucks right now, but I trust that it's just a season of life for you. What I'm worried about is that you're letting so many people down and you don't even notice."

I watch in shock as she turns and walks out of the room.

———

"And then she said something about me letting everyone down," I tell Tosh around a bite of orecchiette.

Our favorite overpriced Italian place is dimly lit, but even from here I can see him wince. He doesn't say anything, though; he just continues to listen. All he's been doing since the second course is listen to me lay out my problems on the stark white linen between us. I suspect he knew that's why I called him for dinner in the first place. But of course he came anyway. He's been asking me to meet him for dinner or coffee or anything for several weeks, and I've had more than enough excuses to keep putting him off. It isn't like us to go so long without hanging out, and I worried he might be upset with me. But the second I called him, he moved his schedule around so he could meet me here tonight. He came because listening to my problems is what he's been doing all of my life. He also came because he's far too nosy to miss out on an opportunity to learn all of my business.

I stab the last meatball on the plate between us desolately. Right before I pop it into my mouth, I realize how rude I'm being.

"I'm sorry, did you want this one?"

He waves me away. "That's all you."

"Thanks," I grumble before shoving it into my mouth.

"Remember that time we made spaghetti and meatballs for Christmas Eve dinner, but we thought the salt measurement was in cups, not in tablespoons?" he asks out of the blue.

I can see that he's trying to cheer me up, so I do my best to let him. "And Mom and Dad didn't want us to know we'd screwed up, so they tried to eat them and pretend it was good. But then he gagged—"

He's chuckling now.

"Just once, but that was all it took. She gagged too, and then you realized something was wrong and took a bite, and you started crying."

"I was eleven." I smile at the memory. "I was very emotional then."

He sips on his Peroni and looks out at the restaurant buzzing around us, I think in an attempt to make his next statement seem more casual than it is.

"She says she's been trying to get ahold of you."

I twist the napkin around in my lap. "I know. I keep meaning to call her; I just keep forgetting."

He frowns. "Christmas is this weekend, Miko. They just want to figure out plans. They need to know when you're coming home if they're going to do that."

I know I need to make up my mind about when I'm flying home for the holidays. I was just trying to wait until I had a better idea of Liam's plans before I booked my travel.

"I know. I'm totally going to call her tonight. I promise."

He nods but doesn't look convinced.

I stare out at the room rather than at that disappointment on his face. The tables are placed closely together, forcing patrons to overhear each other's conversations. It's a hodgepodge of LA. Aging celebrities feign an attempt at privacy while catching the eye of everyone who passes them, hoping to be recognized. A table of junior agents in the corner is way too loud and sharing the tab on the chef's menu they ordered to seem cultured. Next to us are two people who are dressed so sloppy they look like they could be homeless. But they ordered their two-hundred-dollar bottle of wine with the discretion of a seasoned sommelier, which just shows you that in Los Angeles you can never judge a book by its cover.

"So what do you think?" I ask just to break up his brooding silence.

"I think you should fly home with me, and we can share a cab to the house."

"You know that's not what I'm asking about."

"I know." He sighs and then looks me right in the eye. "I think that Landon is right to be worried." He takes another sip of his beer. "I think if you were being honest with yourself, you'd be a little worried too."

Wow. Where did all this seriousness come from? I try to think of something I can say, but nothing great pops to mind.

"I'm just having some fun," I offer up lamely.

His eyes narrow at my words. "And you're *just* losing yourself in the process."

I scowl. "What are you even talking about?"

"What are you even wearing?" he counters.

I look down at my outfit in confusion. I bought this designer sheath dress at a huge discount, and it looks great with my pumps. So what if it's more conservative than I normally wear? It feels grown up and mature.

"What's wrong with my dress?"

For some reason my question seems to make him angrier. "Nothing. There is nothing wrong with your dress—it's just not you. Since when do you wear high heels? Since when do you do your hair that way? It's not you. Nothing about this is you. Not ditching your friends, not ignoring Mom and Dad's phone calls, not neglecting your career—"

"I missed a few meetings. That's not neglecting my career!"

"Really?" He leans across the table towards me. "Jess from VidiFilm told me he's left two voice mails for you about designing their executive suites. He was sure he must have the wrong number since you hadn't returned his calls. So imagine his surprise when I gave him your cell phone, and he said that's the one he's been calling. That's potentially a huge commission, Koko. Have you even called him back yet?"

I open my mouth to speak and then close it abruptly. I did get the voice mails, but I still haven't decided whether or not I'm interested. VidiFilm's offices are based in Emeryville, which would mean a lot of travel back and forth for the next several months. I'm already struggling enough with my workload. Liam has to travel so much already, and I don't know how that would affect the time we're able to spend together.

"I haven't had the chance."

He looks at me like he doesn't even know who I am.

"This is your *life*, Miko. You have worked so hard to get here, and you have become such an incredible person. That person loves her friends and her family fiercely. She does weird things like dressing up as a Harajuku zombie for Halloween or taking synchronized swimming lessons. She's a talented designer and a business owner, and she always speaks her mind and shares her heart." He leans in closer to look me right in the eye. "And you are throwing away all the best parts of yourself for a guy who won't even acknowledge you in public."

———

Screw him!

I slam my hands down on the steering wheel of my car and shout the words for added effect. I barely made it out of the restaurant without cursing Tosh to the ends of the earth. I only just made it into my car before I started crying. I can't understand why everyone is so down on me right now.

OK, I can understand on some level, since I've been a little bit of a slacker lately. But not enough to warrant this kind of freak-out. Not enough for everyone to be so upset with me. When I think of the way my brother was looking at me, it makes me cry harder. And then I think of Landon and how sick it makes me feel to have her upset with me. Her more than anyone, because even when we have disagreements, Landon isn't the kind of person who walks away. She's the kind of person who makes you talk about your feelings and work through your issues. But she never came back into the conference room after she left, and she didn't seek me out before she went home. It makes me feel sick and so sad, and I can't believe I'm fighting with my best friend, especially when I know in my heart this is entirely my fault.

I need to talk to someone about this. I need to discuss it with someone with a clear head so that I can find a way to make Landon forgive me. And there's only one person I can think of to discuss Landon with. I check my mirror before flipping an illegal U-turn and driving back in the other direction.

I knock hesitantly on the front door, not really sure how this is going to go. I see the peephole go dark and then hear the sound of several different locks sliding back. I can tell she's upset when she opens the door, because she's in the biggest pajamas she owns. We both turn to flannel in times of extreme stress.

"I got in a fight with my best friend," I tell her sadly. "I wasn't sure who else to talk to about it."

"Girl," she says with a smile.

We reach to hug each other at the same time. I'm sure if any of her neighbors walk by right now, they'll think we're ending a lovers' quarrel. Landon opens the door wider, and I follow her into the living room of the apartment she shares with Max.

"Where's your roomie?"

She sits down on the sofa and tucks her feet up underneath her. "Out with Taylor."

I slide out of my shoes and do the same. The TV is paused on a chaotic frame. "What are you watching?"

"*Hoarders*," she tells me with way too much enthusiasm. "I only meant to watch a single episode, but I don't think I've moved in three hours."

"I'm sorry," I blurt out.

She looks at me kindly. "I know you are. I really do know that, Miko. You would never in a million years intentionally try to hurt someone or do a bad job at something. It's not in your nature."

The TV screen goes blurry as my eyes fill with tears. I really needed to hear her say that.

"I'm just so worried about you."

"I know," I tell her. "But I'm not really sure how to make you feel better about what's going on. I know what you think I should do. I know what Tosh and my mom think I should do. I just . . . I can't make decisions based on what you guys would prefer."

She stares at the frozen TV screen for a long moment, in thought.

"Girl, I don't want to tell you how to live your life. If you want to take up extreme sports or run around in hot pants whistling Dixie, I'm still gonna love you. I just think you have to be a little more conscious of the people around you. I know you care about him—but you care about a lot of other people too. Just don't get so wrapped up that you forget that."

"OK."

"OK." She smiles happily. "Now hand me that remote. This woman has seventeen years' worth of the Sunday paper stacked in her guest room, and they're about to start bagging it up."

Chapter THIRTEEN

I end up flying home on Christmas Eve.

Landon is right. I have other relationships besides the one with Liam, and I can't forget about them. Besides, Christmas is a really big deal in my family, and my parents would be devastated if I missed it.

As worried as I was about things being weird with my family, it isn't that way at all. The second I walk through the front door, I am attacked with love and kisses from my parents and both of their small breed-ambiguous shelter dogs. Tosh doesn't even wait for them to clear out all of the way before he grabs me and hugs me too.

"I'm sorry I upset you," he whispers into my hair.

I nod. He's not sorry for the things he said; he's only sorry that he made me sad. It's such a Tosh thing to say.

"You're such an idiot," I whisper back and then hug him harder.

Every year we celebrate Christmas Eve the same way. We go to mass with my grandparents and then come home to have "Fancy Dinner." Fancy Dinner is something my mom started when we were little. We all get into our fancy clothes (when we were children, that meant things like feather boas or cardboard top hats) and eat dinner with her best china. Each person is responsible for one course of the meal. This year Granddad is doing the amuse-bouche. Gran is making a soup. Tosh is creating a salad. And Mom and Dad are covering the main course and side dishes.

It's always so fun, because there are no rules or regulations about what you can choose for your section. This means there were years when my peanut butter on graham crackers would serve as the appetizer for my grandmother's vichyssoise. Or my mother's roast turkey would be served alongside Tosh's Top Ramen. This year, despite everything that has been going on, or maybe because of it, I've brought my A-game. I packed my favorite vintage dress, and I volunteered for dessert. I spent all morning prepping and baking one of Max's best recipes. It was the banana pudding from Thanksgiving, the one everyone loved so much but I barely ate, because I was anxious about Liam. I made every part of it from scratch. That meant I spent the time to make pudding—and I don't just mean the add-milk kind either. It also meant that I nearly burned down my mother's kitchen when I tried to flambé the fruit with a chef's torch. The results of my brush with culinary greatness are perfectly formed in the trifle dish and waiting only for us to devour them after dinner; while the results of my last-minute online shopping spree (since I've been too preoccupied to do real Christmas shopping) are already wrapped and lying in wait under the tree, courtesy of rush shipping.

Today has been a great day, and I hadn't realized how much I'd needed it. I was able to lounge around with my mom and watch movies. I was able to visit with my grandparents while eating too many cookies. And as much as it's a holiday and I shouldn't be working, I was able to sneak up to my room for an hour and catch up on a lot of work.

Getting a little distance makes me realize that I can't keep ditching my family and then wonder why they get upset about it.

It's unsurprising that I got a talking-to from Tosh. I'm actually surprised only that it took him as long as it did. I'm going to do better. I'm going to be present. This Christmas is going to mend some of the hurt I've caused. I head upstairs to get ready for church, feeling much better about everything.

I don't see Liam's text message until I'm curling my hair.

Headed to Santa Barbara now. Hope the pudding turned out OK.

I feel a pang of sadness for him that he's going to spend yet another holiday alone. At the same time I feel happy that he's at least talking to me about it again, even if only in small bits and pieces. I know that he'll be staying at his parents' vacation home like he always does when he goes to visit her. He's supposed to go to her facility to meet her for dinner tomorrow night, and then he'll drive back home. The rest of his family was sad that he'd be missing another holiday, but he's the only one who understands that without his presence, his mother would spend it completely alone. I keep my response light since I know he'll likely listen to jazz and brood all the way up the 101.

Don't you doubt my culinary skills! That pudding is going to be epic. Will you text me when you get there so I know you survived?

Yes, dear.

I smile at his cheeky response and then switch my phone back over to Pandora while I finish doing my hair. We leave for church and make it all the way through Mass before I realize he never texted me to say he'd arrived.

By the time we're gathered around the table eating my granddad's caprese skewer, I'm nervous because he hasn't responded to either of my follow-up texts. I excuse myself and go into the other room to call him. Relief floods my system when he answers his phone.

"Hey, you forgot to tell me you survived the drive. It's been hours. I was worried."

"I'm sorry." He sounds exhausted. I can hear the jazz music in the background.

"What happened?"

The ice tinkles in his glass as he takes a drink. "Same old, same old."

The problem is I don't know what to do with that. I don't know what the same old thing is, because he never tells me. Pushing him now won't make anything better, though.

"Is there anything I can do to help?" I ask quietly.

He takes another drink, and when he speaks again he's pulled on his charm, as if I could forget the desolation in his voice from just a moment ago. "Oh, there are all kinds of things that you could do," he says suggestively. "But you're so very far away." He sighs. "I'll be fine. I have big plans. I'm all signed up for a whiskey-drinking contest with myself. I plan on winning."

"Liam—"

His voice changes again, becomes sincere. "Hey, I'll be all right. It's just been a crappy day. You go back to your family. I'm sure you've already missed the next course."

He's right, of course. I can hear them in the other room, proclaiming the wonders of Gran's butternut-squash puree. I do need to go back in there and be with my family. I've barely repaired the damage of my absence over the last month, and they won't realize why I'm here talking on the phone. They'll just see it as another sign that I'm too focused on him.

Saying good-bye feels gut-wrenching, though, like I'm just another person who's failing to take care of him.

"I'll call you tomorrow, OK?"

"OK," he whispers. "Sweet dreams, beautiful."

I head back to the dining room just as Dad is opening another bottle of wine. Tosh and Granddad are arguing over politics while everyone else ignores them. My soup is the only one still untouched, and I hurry to eat it so that I'm not slowing down the progression of courses. I don't taste anything, though.

All throughout the rest of the meal, I take bites and answer questions and do my best to stay in the conversation, but my thoughts are miles away. Literally, three hundred miles away in a big gorgeous mansion on the side of a hill overlooking the water. Everything about that home is a celebration of the Ashton family. Having spent time there, I know that the game room and the pool out back are made for parties and cookouts. The kitchen is massive, made to welcome big groups of people for family get-togethers and holidays. It's eight thousand square feet dedicated to spending time together with your family, and yet again Liam is sitting there alone without his. I can't stand it.

I volunteer to help Tosh clean up the dinner so I can talk to him alone in the kitchen. Our parents and grandparents settle down in the living room, and the second I hear the sounds of *A Christmas Story* blaring from the TV, I launch into my plan.

"I have to go."

Tosh turns to me with a look of total disbelief.

"No. No way. They're going to freak out, Miko. It's Christmas Eve."

I shush him quickly before everyone in the front room clues into what I'm talking about. I pull him to the far side of the kitchen.

"I have to go, Tosh. He's all by himself and it's Christmas."

His anger is growing more palpable by the second. "If he's alone on Christmas, isn't that his choice? He has a family, so why isn't he with them?"

I know if I could explain it all to Tosh, he'd totally understand. He knows as much as I do what it's like to worry about your mother's health. He'd totally sympathize with Liam. But I can't betray Liam's trust. He's protecting his promise to his mother by not saying anything, and I won't be the one who makes him break it.

"Please don't be mad at me," I whisper sadly.

The shake of his head tells me it's too late for that.

"OK, be mad at me then. But help cover for me with them." I jerk my head in the direction of the living room. "Tell Mom I promise to explain to them later, but I have to go now. I'll call you tomorrow."

I can tell by the look on his face that he's losing respect for me; it's breaking both of our hearts. But everyone in this scenario has someone. My family will be sad without me, but they'll still have each other, just like the Ashtons are celebrating with a big group of people. Liam, once again, is the only one on his own. Whether or not he admits it, I'm his person, and I'm not going to sit here playing board games while he drinks his way through another holiday. I turn my back on my brother and the look in his eye before running up the back stairs and grabbing my overnight suitcase and my purse. I'm waiting at the gate to board my flight when the first call comes in from my mother. I send her to voice mail before typing a quick text apologizing and promising to call the next day. She doesn't write me back.

Getting a flight back to LA wasn't actually hard, since more than one airline has one running every hour on Christmas Eve. The only crappy part is that I have to take an Uber to my house from the airport to get my car. It does give me time to run inside and grab the present I got for Liam before I drive the hour to Santa Barbara. When I arrive in the city, I stop by a gas station to change before putting my coat back on and hurrying back to my car. It's nearly eleven thirty by the time I creep up his parents' long driveway and pull up in front of a house that's straight out of a Nancy Meyers movie.

Most of the lights are off, save the ones in the front room. I hope that means he's still awake. It would be sort of awkward if he's passed out somewhere and unable to appreciate my plan. I don't even make it halfway up the walk before the front door swings open. The sheepish smile on his face makes the last few hours totally worth it. I know I've upset my family, but I would probably do much more than that to keep that look in his eyes.

I want to rush at him headlong. I want to jump into his arms and say things he doesn't want to hear. I have to keep it light, though. When I get a few feet away from him, I slide the jacket off my shoulders and let it fall to the ground at my feet. At first he laughs, a sound of pure joy that makes my heart dance around along with it. I knew it was totally worth the rush shipping to have this sexy Santa costume sent priority overnight when I thought of the idea the other day. His smile starts to die away, replaced by that look.

"This is easily the best idea you've ever had."

I take a step closer and walk right into his arms. "Better than the organic tequila?"

I slide my hands up under his sweatshirt.

"Way better."

"Good." I giggle self-consciously. "I was going to do a whole bit here about my list and whether you'd been naughty or nice, but—"

He pulls the Santa hat off my head, sliding a hand into my hair. "But?"

"But it feels weird now. I'm hoping the costume is enough."

He's nodding, pressing kisses across my forehead and down my jaw to my neck. "You are more than enough." He stops kissing me long enough to look into my eyes. Something desperate swims around in his, all the things he feels, all the words he won't say. For an instant—a single instant—I think it will all come tumbling out. Either I'll say things or he'll say things, but one way or another the barrier is going to crumble and fall, and we'll come out of the rubble stronger than before. But he doesn't say anything, so neither do I. I watch that lazy grin slide into place, and it's like seeing a door slam shut. I fight the urge to wince.

"Now then, Santa," he says between kisses. "I think you need to sit on my lap and tell me all the things you want for Christmas."

I laugh at his absurdity. "I think you've got this backwards."

He nods gravely. "I'm sure I do. Why don't we head on back to my workshop and you can explain exactly how this all works."

I let him lead me down the hallway and force myself to enjoy this moment with him. I won't wish for something more; we're together on Christmas—it's more than enough.

The next morning the smell of coffee hits me before I completely open my eyes. When I do, Liam is grinning at me like a maniac, holding a mug in one hand and a little blue box in the other. I fully awake and sit up in bed with a shocked smile.

"Merry Christmas," he says happily.

I take the coffee from him and stare at the little blue box like it might come alive at any moment. Nobody has ever bought me jewelry before, and I never anticipated that we'd get each other any kind of real gift. That's why I went with the gag gift of sorts; it didn't feel too heavy or real. But Tiffany's? That seems super legit. That seems like the kind of thing you get your girlfriend for Christmas. Or I don't know—do wealthy men buy Tiffany's the way the rest of us buy extra ChapStick when we see it at the checkout line at Target? I always see those packs and think, *Well, it's so cheap it'd almost be silly not to get it, right?*

He places it on the sheets in front of me, and I must be grinning like a crazy person when I stare back into his eyes.

"I just want to—" I stop myself abruptly and hold up a finger to pause the conversation. I jump out of his bed and hurry across the room to the restroom, because I refuse to open luxury jewelry without brushing my teeth first. In the bathroom mirror I look mussed and happy. My skin is flushed and my eyes are bright.

"I woke up on Christmas morning in bed with Liam Ashton," I whisper to the girl in the mirror.

Neither one of us can believe it.

I've never spent a holiday away from my family, and now here I am. My smile falters. At home in San Francisco, Mom is already blaring Christmas music to rouse everyone from bed. She's probably adding the glaze to Aunt Sarah's cinnamon rolls before popping them in the oven. Dad will probably be—

No. I won't do this. I shake off the sadness. I've had a lifetime of holidays with my family; this is the only one I've ever had with Liam. I refuse to spend it feeling melancholy in any way.

When I come back a few minutes later, the jewelry box is exactly where I left it, and Liam is lounging against the pillows, drinking his coffee. He laughs when I run across the room and leap onto the bed with the enthusiasm of a flying squirrel. I sit on my knees in front of the box and look at him expectantly.

"Are you going to open it?"

I nod quickly. "I'm just memorizing this moment." I look around us at the bedroom with framed movie posters and monogrammed bedding that must have been designed for his teenage self. The bed is as rumpled as the man lying in it. The winter sun is streaming in through the French doors. The room smells like coffee.

"Come on now—don't romanticize this." His voice is playful, but there's a tension in his posture that wasn't there a moment ago. "It's just a little something."

I pick up the box and keep the smile on my face, though inside I feel like I just got reprimanded like a child. Can't I even have a small moment for me? Does everything—even my own reaction to the situation—have to be mandated by what makes him feel most comfortable?

He sits up and taps the box, playful once again. "Come on. Open it."

I slowly pull the end of the white ribbon and untie it. I've never had anything from Tiffany's before, and I wouldn't ever really think of them as having something that would suit my style; they're pretty conservative. But I'm dying to know what he picked out for me. I lift the lid carefully and find a small pouch the exact same color as the box. Liam watches me, and I can feel how excited he is to gauge my reaction, even if he says this isn't a big deal.

"There were so many things to choose from." He launches in as I untie the strings of the bag. "Tons of hearts and charm bracelets, and none of that really felt like you." I pull open the cinch of the bag but still can't see inside of it. "And then I saw this, and I thought that it was weird." My breath catches as a gold chain slides out of the bag into my palm. "So wonderfully weird," he whispers as we both stare down into my hand.

It's a gold pendant—actually, it's a rose-gold pendant, which is so much prettier. At the center of a dainty chain is a perfect golden bean. Like, an actual bean—as in lima, as in kidney, as in coffee—a bean, made of gold. He's right; it is weird. And so pretty, and so me, and so very, very expensive.

"It's perfect, thank you," I tell him sincerely through a dozen kisses. "I feel badly I only got you a scantily clad Santa costume."

He brushes my hair back from my face. "Hey now, don't hate on the Santa costume. That's my new favorite Christmas memory."

I giggle while fighting to open the tiny clasp on the necklace. When I have it on, I look to him for some reaction. I'm wearing an oversize T-shirt, a necklace, and a smile—all of which he gave me.

"You are beautiful." He's said it to me too many times to count over the last month, but I never get used to it. It makes my heart stutter and my stomach flip over every time.

"So are you," I whisper back.

He runs a hand down my hair, to my arm, and then down to my fingertips.

"All right, nymph, I don't know what we have here for breakfast, but I think we better go figure it out. I have all sorts of plans for you today, and all of them require that you keep your energy up."

He doesn't have to ask me twice. I let him pull me from the bed and downstairs to the kitchen. Once we're there I make him stop removing things from the cabinets long enough to show me how to work the sound system. It isn't long before the sound of Christmas music fills the whole house.

"Really?" he asks when I come back into the kitchen accompanied by Dean Martin singing "Rudolph, the Red-Nosed Reindeer."

"Yes, really." I ignore his imperious tone. "If you can't listen to members of the Rat Pack sing about cartoon reindeer, then it doesn't feel like Christmas."

He smirks. "All right then, any other traditions I should know about?"

I consider making up something along the lines of *If you can't watch a hot blond guy make your breakfast without wearing his shirt, it doesn't feel like Christmas either.* But then, Liam doesn't need any extra excuses to try to get either one of us out of our clothes.

"I'll keep you posted," I tell him with a wink.

I jump up on the counter to watch him work. Yes, sitting on a granite countertop wearing only his T-shirt is a tad chilly. But the way his eyes keep darting to my legs and my shoulder, which is bare where the T-shirt is hanging off it, makes the chance of catching a cold totally worth it. I watch between sips of coffee as he pulls out the ingredients for pancakes.

He turns on the griddle on the massive Viking stove. "Luckily for us both, the just-add-water mix doesn't require any fresh ingredients. I didn't get a chance to go to the grocery store."

The Ashton family uses this house pretty regularly but not enough to keep perishable food on hand. Each time I've spent the weekend with them here, a trip to the grocery store has always been one of the first things on the agenda. Every single one of them is obsessed with food, so each meal ends up being a production. Me, on the other hand? I'm always just happy to eat. I hope whatever someone puts in front of me will be delicious, but I also think a breakfast sandwich or a Twinkie can be just as tasty as a five-course meal.

"I actually won't know the difference," I tell him. "Just-add-water pancakes are the only kind of homemade pancake I've ever known."

He glances down at my legs dangling off the edge of the counter and stares at my toes swinging back and forth. "How upsetting for you," he says absentmindedly.

I throw a kitchen towel in his direction, effectively drawing his attention away from whatever dirty thought is flitting through his head. I'm starving, and I need some kind of snack if he expects to lock me in a room all day.

"Food first, pal!"

"What?" He looks back at the heated griddle and the bowl of pancake batter all but forgotten in his hands. "Oh, yes, of course."

He pours the batter out into large pancakes and then sets the rest of it on the counter. He turns back around and leans against the counter opposite me; his eyes are back on my legs again.

"I put them on the griddle." He jerks his head towards the stove. "What in the world are we going to do to occupy ourselves while they cook?"

I know that look in his eyes; this is going to go downhill in a hurry. The song switches over to Bing Crosby, and the sounds of a ukulele fill the house as Liam closes the distance between us.

"I always thought this was such a random song." Maybe if I keep him talking I can at least eat, like, half a pancake or something before he attacks me. "I mean, Bing Crosby isn't even—" I gasp when his lips touch my collarbone. "He isn't even Hawaiian," I finish breathlessly.

Liam makes some sort of noise in his throat, an attempt to pretend to be listening to whatever I'm saying. But based on the direction his hands are headed and the kisses he's raining down on the expanse of exposed shoulder, I think we both know Bing's allegiance to the Islands isn't even registering right now.

I let my head fall to the side to give him better access to my neck. My fingers slide through his wavy hair, holding him closer to me.

"Well"—the sardonic voice breaks through the fog of lust with the tenderness of an ice pick—"I'm pretty sure your pancakes are burned."

Liam rips his hands out from underneath my T-shirt, and we both turn to stare in horror at Max standing in the entryway.

Craaaaaaaaaaaaaaaap.

But worse—so much worse than my best friend, who is clearly super pissed—is the entire Ashton family standing in the entryway behind her.

Charlie and Viv are staring in openmouthed shock. Landon is holding a casserole dish, and her face is almost as red as her sweater. Beside her Brody has his arms filled with grocery bags and his head down. Even from here I can tell he's trying to cover up laughter. Cas and Malin look like they're fighting laughter too.

"Mele Kalikimaka" continues to trumpet through the house while I want to shrivel up and die. Liam's parents just caught us going at it on their kitchen counter, and his hands were up my shirt. Liam's eyes dart quickly to mine, and I can't make out a single emotion in them. Everything is locked behind a totally unflappable façade.

Just then Taylor bustles down the hallway, bogged down with presents, and nearly slams into everyone gathered there.

"Wait, what did I miss?" he asks everyone's back. Then he looks beyond them to me half naked on the countertop next to Liam in his pajamas, and he draws his own conclusion. He sets his packages down slowly, his eyes darting repeatedly to Max, who looks like she's about thirty seconds from going full-on Chernobyl and taking me and her brother down with her.

"Well, Jennings," he drawls. "I'd say I told you so, but that doesn't seem very charitable on Christmas morning."

Max's head turns sharply in his direction like a shark smelling blood in the water. If I had the advantage of clothing right now, I'd actually walk across the room and hug him. I'm not sure if he's doing it to try to dispel the tension around us or to draw her anger on himself, but either way it's more than I expected or deserved. Maybe it was Taylor's joke or Max's change of focus, but it's like someone pressed "Play" on the scene again, and everyone hops into motion once more. Vivian steps forward a bit awkwardly.

"We're sorry to uh . . . disturb you both. We just all felt so badly about spending another holiday without Liam. We thought if we came here, then you could more easily split up the day between us and your mother. Bring the mountain to Muhammad and all that."

I can tell by the way she stumbles over the words that even if Taylor had a clue that something was going on, Vivian definitely did not. And now she not only knows but has *seen* what we've been up to. How perfectly mortifying. I feel like such an absolute trollop. I slide myself slowly down off the countertop, hoping that Liam will say something. He could explain everything or even make a joke, but some explanation from him would go a long way towards easing the tension in the room. When he only stands there biting down on his molars, I try to think of something appropriate. What do you say when your family friends discover you half naked on the countertop?

"I'll just . . . go get dressed."

As far as epic responses go, this has got to be one of my best. I cross my arms in front of my chest and hightail it out of the kitchen as fast as I can without breaking into a full sprint.

When I get back upstairs, I consider going to the guest room I've used every other time I've stayed here. But if someone caught me switching rooms, that would seem more awkward than just staying in Liam's. I close the door behind me and lean up against it while willing my heart rate to slow down.

Good gods! That has got to be one of the most mortifying things that has ever happened to me in my life. The look of shock on Vivian's face, the embarrassment on Landon's, even Brody fighting the urge to laugh. I'll never forget it as long as I live. It's horrible, and . . . and . . . the funniest thing I've ever seen.

Laughter bubbles up out of my throat, and I have to cover my mouth with my hand to keep from making loud guffaws that would lower their opinion of me even more. I laugh and snort until my eyes water, and when the giggling subsides, I take a deep breath. OK, that was embarrassing. But if the worst thing that happens in your life is that you walk in on your son getting to second base, you're pretty flipping lucky. I'll apologize to Charlie and Viv. I'll apologize to everyone, but someday we'll all look back on this and laugh. I'm just starting that party early. I nod at this sound wisdom and hurry to take a quick shower. I don't bother washing my hair, because I've got no time to style it and I don't want to face them downstairs looking like a drowned rat. I pull on a pair of skinny jeans with some boots and a cozy sweater that's almost exactly the color of Liam's eyes. I swipe on a little mascara and some lip balm before cleaning up the mess I made in the bathroom. Suddenly it occurs to me. They know.

His family knows.

All of our friends know.

After all of this time sneaking around, we just became official. We're together on a holiday and buying each other gifts, and now we can just be together out in the real world. I grin at my reflection happily. I never really go about things the normal way, but I do get there eventually.

There's a light knock at the door, and I take a deep breath before turning to go answer it. Time to face the music.

Landon is standing in the hallway holding a doughnut in one hand and a cup of coffee in the other. She starts to smile demurely, but her lips barely curl halfway before she breaks into full cackling laughter. I take the doughnut and coffee before she spills them all over the carpet. She runs her fingers under her watering eyes to make sure no mascara has run.

"Lord, girl, I haven't had such a shock on Christmas since Mama's cousin Jimmy Paul announced that he was leaving his wife, Carol, because he was actually in love with a teller named Michael down at the First National Bank."

I lean against the doorjamb and take a bite of the doughnut. "I'm so glad my mortification amuses you. Jerk."

She shrugs, still giggling a little.

"How is everyone reacting to this . . . uh, Christmas surprise?"

"They may have busted into the eggnog a bit earlier than usual, but I think that's more for embarrassment than from any real anger."

I nod, finishing up the last bite of doughnut. "Good to know."

"I did come to get you, though," she says, straightening herself upright.

"I'm invited to the eggnog party?" I ask cheekily.

Her smile drops a little. "You are, but I actually came to get you so you can talk to Max."

I wince. "How mad is she?"

Landon winces too. "She's sitting out on the back patio staring at the water. Even Taylor has stopped trying to get her to talk. I think you need to go out there."

It was only a matter of time before I was going to have to have this conversation with Max. I just sort of hoped one or both of us would be drunk when it happened to make it a little easier. I grab a scarf out of my bag and wrap it around my neck as I follow Landon downstairs. Luckily I don't see anyone on the way there.

When we get to the French doors that look out over the patio, I can see Max sitting on a chair, staring silently out over the Pacific. I swear the tension in her spine is visible even from here.

"You want me to come with?" Landon asks.

"Yes." My sigh is resigned. "But I should probably do it by myself."

She nods sagely. "May the odds be ever in your favor."

"Oh man, I'm not even sure a *Hunger Games* reference can give me courage in a time like this."

She grins. "Hey, I lived through this with her, and you will too."

With that, I head in the direction of the angry girl at the other end of the yard. When I reach her she doesn't look up at me; she just continues to stare out at the ocean. The day is gray and cold, and also foggy enough that I know she can't be out here admiring the view. I wonder if she's playing with her medical bracelet to keep her fingers from reaching out to strangle me. I sit down on a chair next to hers and hug the sweater around me to ward off the chill.

When she still doesn't say anything, I decide it may as well be me who does.

"Are you super pissed?"

Max from a year ago would have let me have it. In fact, she wouldn't have come out here to calm down at all. She would have chased me up the stairs hurling accusations and making sure I knew exactly how angry she was. I can tell that this Max is battling with herself, trying hard to calm down enough to speak, and she still won't look at me.

"Of course I'm pissed," she says finally.

I shrug my hands up inside the sleeves of my sweater and hold on to the fabric, bracing myself for wherever this is going. I knew she wouldn't be OK with Liam and me dating. I knew it would be the thing that pushed her over the edge.

"I know it's weird for you," I start carefully. "Because I'm dating your brother."

She turns her head to look at me finally. Incredulity and something else I can't name are written all over her face. I try to speak faster.

"But I, um . . . I promise I wouldn't have done it if it wasn't serious. I—" Probably better not to announce the whole love thing when she's already so pissed. "I really, really like him, Max. I have for a long time. And he's wonderful." I reach up under the scarf to touch the necklace at my throat with a small smile. "But I don't need to tell you that, you—"

"Stop." The word is wrenched from her throat, like it's actually painful for her to say it. The look on her face morphs again, and my stomach drops when I recognize what it is. Pity. "Miko, I am pissed at you. So mad I want to shake you or punch you or anything that might knock some sense into you."

My voice is barely a whisper.

"What?"

She shakes her head slowly. "How could you put yourself in this situation?"

"I don't understand."

"You're sleeping with him," she says emphatically.

I nod. "Yes."

"You're sleeping with him when I know that's not normal for you. You've been sleeping with each other long enough that you're slipping away on vacation together."

"That's not how it—"

She stands up in one angry burst.

"How many times since you got together have we all hung out? How many times have we all met up for drinks? How many dinners? How many movie nights?"

"I know it maybe feels like we were dishonest by not mentioning—"

"Miko." She cuts me off again. "Wake up! He's not *dating* you. Dating would imply that he acknowledged you to us even once.

He's hooking up with you. He's keeping you a secret. It's not about him being dishonest; it's about him being disrespectful. And why in the world would you let him get away with it?"

Blood is pounding in my ears. I take in a gulp of air to try to clear my head. I need to try to think of what I can say. I need to explain how it's not like that at all, but she's still ranting.

"I am pissed. I am super freaking pissed that you've let yourself be put in this situation! You've been ditching us and messing up at work. You have dark circles under your eyes and—" She stops walking and looks right at me. "And you're here on *Christmas.* How many times have you told me how special Christmas is for your family? How many times have you told us about the Mexican Bus tournament—"

"It's Mexican Train."

"Whatever! How many times have you talked about the gifts and the food and the board games and the champagne tasting you guys do on Christmas Day?"

The guilt I've been fighting since last night—since last month, really—comes bubbling to the surface and makes me feel like I'm drowning. Her angry words slam into me, making my heart pound harder with every sentence.

"Because December was when your mom found out she was cancer-free. I know this because we've done three walks for breast cancer awareness in the last year alone. I've heard the story so many times I could tell it myself. December was the month she went into remission, and that year you celebrated Christmas for days because you were so grateful to know you'd have so many more as a family. It's a really big deal in your family. What in the hell are you doing here?"

I open my mouth to respond, but I'm afraid a sob will come out. It takes me a few tries to answer.

"I'm allowed to change my plans," I tell her lamely.

The look that comes over her face then is so angry I flinch. She turns away to stare at the ocean, and when she finds her voice to speak again, the sadness in it devastates me. "But not your life." She turns around to stare at me. "You can change your plans. But you don't change your life around for a man who won't commit to anything more than a sleepover."

I have to look down at my lap rather than see the disappointment on her face. I need time to process all the things she's said. I thought I was coming out here to apologize for sneaking around her back. But she's actually mad because she feels like I'm letting myself be taken advantage of. The words take root in my stomach, making me feel sick. The things she's saying are exactly like Landon said . . . and my brother said . . . and my mom said too. For the first time in months—no, more than that, for the first time in almost a year I wonder if maybe I don't see this relationship with Liam for what it really is. I reach up to touch the necklace again.

No. I shake the ugly thought away. I know what we have. I know who he is. I trust the feelings that are between us. I have to clear my throat to speak, but I'm proud of how strong my voice sounds when I do.

"You don't understand." I look right at her. "I know it's not conventional and we didn't go about it the normal way, but we are in a relationship."

Another sad shake of her head. "You're too far inside the forest to see the trees, and I know that you're not going to listen to me. But I also know my brother and how hard he's fought to keep himself unattached all these years. He's awesome and I love him. He's also incredibly selfish. What he wants takes precedence over what anyone else does."

"That's not true—"

Her eyes narrow.

"Really? Then let me ask you this: the holiday with your family, the games and the presents and the special meaning behind them. Does Liam know that story?"

I stare at her in confusion, unsure of how to answer or why she's asking. Liam doesn't know about that; we've never discussed it before.

"You're allergic to walnuts, you speak Japanese, you volunteer once a week teaching charcoal drawing to elementary school students. How about those things? Does he know any of that?"

I am mute. I shake my head.

"You're giving him everything, and he doesn't even know the most basic information about you. You left your family to be with him today. Did he even ask you about them? Did he even wonder what you might have been doing instead?"

Now I'm the one looking blindly at the ocean—at anything at all besides the pity in her eyes.

"Last summer when things were really bad, you told me to stop being an idiot. I'm going to say the same thing to you now: stop being an idiot. Open your eyes and look at the facts in front of you. Please do not be this cliché."

———

The problem with not being able to see the forest for the trees is that it's easy to lose your way the second you're on your own. I know in my heart that I should at least think through some of the things Max said. But then we go back inside, and it is still Christmas and everyone is doing their damndest to pretend it isn't awkward now that they know about me and Liam. It is easier for me to pretend too.

So we fall back into a familiar routine that day. He and I act just like we always do when we're in a group, which is to say, we barely acknowledge each other at all. I don't blame Liam when he has to leave that afternoon to go spend time with his mother, though I am the only one who knows how hard it is for him to do it.

Later that night he texts to tell me that he is going to drive back to LA rather than go back to his parents' vacation place, and even that I can't blame him for. I wish I could leave too, but that would have added more drama to the situation. The next day the guys go golfing, down a fourth member due to Liam's absence, and the ladies basically lounge around watching movies on the giant TV in the den. I suspect movies were the easy choice, because watching a screen is better than interacting awkwardly; Max and I don't really know what to say to each other.

I drive back to LA the day after, feeling utterly exhausted emotionally. Tosh is still at my parents' house, and I haven't spoken to any of them yet to apologize. I recognize that I have been hiding out, but it is so much easier than the alternative. I take a shower when I get home and am just changing into pajamas when my phone buzzes.

A text, just like every other time. On the one hand, I am kind of shocked that he would so casually fall right back into our regular routine. On the other hand, part of me is relieved. No matter what Max thinks, nobody really knows what goes on between me and Liam other than the two of us. I have managed to upset almost everyone I care about in some way or another over the last month. When I am with Liam, I only ever seem to make him happy. And he makes me happy too. It isn't even a question. I text him back that I am on my way.

"You're going to Twenty-Five on Thursday, right?" I ask him later.

We are lying in his bed playing cards when I remember to mention everyone's plans for New Year's Eve. He slides a card out of the draw pile and puts it into the stack in his hand.

"I am. Though I'm curious why everyone doesn't want to go to a different place this time. We have several other options."

I frown at my cards and draw two from the pile. "Because it's tradition, and we all had so much fun last year. And it has special meaning for Brody and Landon."

He'd told her later it was the first time he'd seen her and known he wanted to make her his. I want to tell Liam that it has special meaning for the two of us as well, but I'm not sure how he'd take that. The idea makes me sad, and I reach up to touch the necklace I still haven't taken off.

"How come you've never asked me about my tattoos?" I ask suddenly.

He looks confused. "I love your tattoos."

"I know, but they're pretty unique. I'm just surprised you're not curious about what they mean."

He considers me for a moment. "I didn't want to pry."

I wish I thought that were the truth, but since he hasn't asked about anything else either, I'm worried that's just a nice way of saying he didn't want to know.

"My mom"—when I realize I've never even said her name to him before, my throat nearly closes—"Katherine—was diagnosed with breast cancer six years ago." His eyes widen in surprise, but he doesn't say anything. "My family is really close, and we were devastated by the news. There was chemo and surgeries, and she was so freaking strong throughout the whole thing." My eyes water at the memory. "We wanted to come up with something we could do as a family in solidarity. There's a Japanese legend about paper cranes—have you heard it?"

He shakes his head.

"It's an old legend that says if you fold a thousand paper cranes, you would be granted one wish. All of us had only one wish in the world, and that was for her to get better. It sounded like the perfect choice for us. Me, Tosh, and my dad went to get the tattoos at night while Gran stayed with my mom. We each got two hundred and fifty—which took forever and hurt *so* bad." I run my fingers down my side, where two hundred and fifty teeny-tiny colorful paper cranes swirl across my skin. "Tosh got his on his back, and Dad got his across his chest—over his heart, he said. Theirs aren't colorful like mine. Not sure they were manly enough to handle the pain." I wink at him, and I'm surprised to see how uncomfortable he looks. "When we showed her what we'd done, she must have cried for days."

"I'm sure she was touched," he says stiffly.

"No, she was livid. She hated tattoos, said we'd all marred our perfect skin and we'd regret it later." I can't help but smile. "When she went into remission, she got the last of the cranes tattooed along her side."

It's a good story. One of my favorites to tell, and I expect him to be charmed. I expect him to ask me more questions or tell me something about himself that I don't already know. But that's not what happens. What happens is that he says something charming about needing to inspect my tattoos in further detail. He rains down kisses on my skin and praise for how beautiful I am, and for the first time since we've been together, all of it feels wrong.

Chapter FOURTEEN

I walk down the hallway towards Max and Landon's apartment just like I did last year on this night. This time around I've got on a tight black minidress, which I know Liam will love. Even if I've been feeling weird about us this week, that didn't mean my feelings for him are less intense or that I don't want him to think I look crazy hot on New Year's Eve. So I'm rocking big hair and great makeup, and I even put on the black pumps he loves so much. On the way out the door, though, I imagined the suck factor of wobbling along all night in those too-tall shoes, and I swapped them for my high-heel wedge sneakers. When I get to their door, I knock on it with the bottom of the champagne in my hand.

Max is the one who answers the door, and we end up standing there staring at each other. I hate feeling this way. We might be a lot of things, but awkward around each other isn't one of them.

"Are we still fighting?" I ask with fake petulance.

She smirks. "I don't know. Are you still acting like a jackass?"

"Probably."

"So long as you're aware of it." She moves aside. "Come on in."

I follow her into their kitchen with a smile on my face. That is the Mackenzie Jennings version of kissing and making up, and that's likely as good as it's going to get with her.

We head into the kitchen, and I watch while she opens the bubbly and pours it into juice glasses for us.

"I like your dress," I tell her.

She looks down at the bright-blue dress she has on. It's made of layers of shredded silk. One might go so far as to suggest the skirt almost, *almost* looks ballerina inspired. It's her style but with a softer effect than she ever would have worn before.

"Thanks." She turns towards the back of the apartment. "Landon, if you put any more mascara on your lashes, you're actually going to weigh them down rather than boost them up. Get out here!"

Landon yells something neither of us can make out and then hurries down the hallway in a tiny gold dress. I'm actually kind of startled to see her in it.

"Not that I'm judging, but didn't you wear that dress last New Year's?" I ask as she makes a beeline for the glass of champagne waiting for her on the countertop.

She runs a hand down the sequins with a soft smile. "I know. I hate to repeat myself, but Brody asked me to wear it again."

"Here we go," Max grumbles.

Landon's eyebrows shoot up. "Oh really? And who bought the dress you're wearing tonight, *Mackenzie?*"

Both Max and I give her odd looks.

"Dude, why are you using her full name?"

Landon smiles and then laughs. "I don't know. I was trying to be funny . . . and also, I started drinking an hour ago, so my humor barometer might be a little off."

Gods, I love these weirdos!

I hold up my juice glass in salute. "To Sandra?"

They smile in unison, and we clink glasses to the oddball toast we made up when our friendship was still new. "To Sandra!"

I can already tell this night is going to be epic.

Brody meets us at the door to Twenty-Five, and the crowd of people there part for him like Moses and the Red Sea. Probably because he owns this club and has made an incredible reputation for himself as an arbiter of cool, sophisticated venues—also because he has a security guy with him who looks bigger than the magical prisoner in *The Green Mile*.

"You're looking dapper this evening, pal," I tell Brody as I lean up to give him a hug. He smiles down at his dark suit; it's a perfect compliment to Landon's dress.

"Thanks, so do you."

As we head through the club en masse, Taylor comes down the stairs from the VIP section. His suit is a charcoal gray cut slim, sort of *Mad Men* style, and he's rocking a skinny tie. I've never seen him dressed up before. It's totally adorable. He gives Landon and me a hug and then leans in close to whisper something in Max's ear before kissing her there. She grins and beams at him with total unrestrained joy. I know for a fact she never imagined this for herself. I am so happy for them.

We walk up the stairs to the VIP area and the lounge we're commandeering for the evening. I couldn't care less what my friends do for a living. If Brody were a manager at Chick-fil-A, I'd still love him simply because he made my best friend so happy. But on a night like this? It's pretty flipping cool to know the guy who can hook you up with a lounge that typically requires A-list celebrity status or an Amex black card.

The club is pulsating with music and people, and the energy is electric. I'm sure my hair is growing bigger by the second. A server hurries over to Brody and starts taking everyone's drink order, but Landon is already bouncing to the music. One more drink and she'll be bringing out her sprinkler or a really bad rendition of the Dougie.

We slide onto the sofa just as Malin shimmies her way over with Casidee. They both look gorgeous tonight, and I tell them so, though Malin's outfit is a surprising change of pace.

"You do look so pretty, Mali," Landon tells her uncertainly. "But is that . . . Are you wearing your sister's shirt?"

Malin smiles proudly and stands up to show off her outfit.

"Do you like it?" she asks us happily.

A worn-out Jesse and the Rippers T-shirt with a hole in the sleeve is half tucked into silk ankle-length skinny slacks and designer heels that are a mile high. She looks gorgeous, even if it's not the short designer dress we're used to seeing her in on a night like this.

"It's my new style."

"It's fabulous," I tell her sincerely.

Everyone else agrees, just as the server arrives with our drinks in record time—which I suppose makes sense, since Brody is the one signing paychecks. We settle in to hang out. I sent a text to Liam letting him know we were a few minutes away. I wonder why he's not here yet. I really can't wait to see what he's wearing. Is it a suit? Is it classically cut like Brody's or more stylish like the one Taylor has on? I take a quick swig of my cocktail just as the opening beats of a Lady Gaga song come on. It's New Year's, the drinks are strong, and Gaga is bringing her A-game. There's only one option here.

I jump up and grab Landon's hand to pull her with me to the dance floor.

We dance forever. At some point every member of our group comes to join us. Even Max lets Taylor drag her up for a song, which is a miracle in and of itself. They all come in for a while here or there, but nobody can hang on a dance floor like my girl Landon and I can. We laugh and dance and make up routines. We do shots with a group of girls celebrating a bachelorette party and pretend we know how to break-dance until a guy who actually knows how to break-dance comes out and shuts us down. When we finally head back to the lounge area, we each grab bottles of water and collapse in a heap with our friends.

"Fifteen minutes, everyone! We've got fifteen minutes until the countdown!" the DJ calls out over the music.

Fifteen minutes? How did it get to be so late? Where is Liam? He was supposed to meet us here, but I haven't heard from him. I start to panic a little. Did something happen with his mom again? I grab my clutch and pull out my phone. I must stare at his text message for a full minute before I can process what I'm reading.

Not going to be able to make it tonight, I'm meeting up with some friends. Have fun, I'll text you later.

My joy, which was so encompassing a moment ago, deflates like an old balloon. He's not going to make it? But it's New Year's Eve and everyone is here and . . . wouldn't he want to spend this night with me? I know we're not *together* together, but I was looking forward to finally having a date—sort of—on New Year's. And friends? What friends does he have besides the ones assembled here? I'm sure there are other people he hangs out with, but none of them are better friends than the ones at this table.

The DJ announces that we have ten more minutes, and the anticipation in the room builds. Beside me Malin finds sobriety long enough to ask the question that's pounding in my head along with the bass.

"Hey, where is Liam?"

Brody looks up from laughing over something with Landon. "He was meeting up with some buddies from college, I think. He said he'd try to catch up with us later."

Malin is too self-involved to understand how the words might affect me, but I get varying degrees of pitiful looks from Max, Landon, and even Casidee. How flipping terrible. When your twenty-two-year-old assistant feels sorry for you, something has probably gone really wrong in your life.

It feels hard to breathe and hard to sit there without crying. But I absolutely refuse to draw more attention and force myself to stay seated. But unfortunately I can't force myself to stop remembering Max's words. They echo over and over in my head, telling me how Liam is selfish and how what he wants takes precedence over anyone else's feelings.

I shake it off—literally shake my head to make the thoughts leave my brain. I plaster a bright smile on my face and bounce up from the sofa.

"We better get on the dance floor. It's only five minutes until midnight!"

Everyone smiles and comes to join me. Landon is the only one who grabs my hand to stop me.

"Hey, girl, are you OK?"

I give her a watery smile. "I don't want to cry on New Year's, OK? It's got to be terrible luck. Let's go dance it off and have fun. I'll figure it all out later, OK?"

She smiles and throws an arm around my shoulders to lead me to the dance floor. Once we push our way into the mass of bodies, Brody snags her arm and pulls her in for a dance. Beside me Malin is dancing in a way that suggests she drank her body weight in hard liquor this evening. That sounds like a really good idea right about now. I grab two glasses of champagne off a tray that the servers are passing around and then make quick work of both of them. The bubbles make my head swim, dulling some of the questions.

"All right, you sexy beasts," the DJ calls out. "Get ready!"

Everyone is all smiles and giggles and laughs, exactly how you should feel in this moment. It shouldn't feel like your heart's been stomped on; that is not what this is about.

"Ten! Nine!" Everyone starts to chant along with the DJ. "Eight! Seven!"

A hand grabs my forearm in a viselike grip. I look up at Max in shock, but she's not looking at me, only holding on to me. I follow her incredulous line of sight to see Brody on one knee in front of Landon, holding a small red box.

"Five! Four!"

Landon's face is filled with total awe, even as she leans closer to hear the words he's whispering into her ear, since it's too loud in here. I put my hand on Max's and squeeze her fingers tight.

"Two! One! Happy New Year!"

Landon nods and throws herself into Brody's arms, nearly knocking him backwards onto the floor. But he's laughing and she's laughing, and she can't stop kissing him. Their joy is palpable, and all around the room even the jaded LA socialites in the VIP section are cheering for them.

I watch as Brody stands up and presents the ring again to Landon, who hasn't even put it on yet. She looks at it like it's magic, and I guess it is. Even from back here I can see it sparkle. I don't realize I'm crying until Max hands me a cocktail napkin. Her eyes are suspiciously bright too. Landon lets him slide the ring onto her finger and then leaps into his arms again. The kissing and laughing repeats itself until she finally turns away to look back at us. Max and I are still holding hands and watching her with watery eyes. Apparently witnessing our best friend get engaged turned us into old women. When they walk the few feet back over to where we're standing, we envelop her in a group hug, and though she'll never admit to it later, Max giggles and squeals along with us. I look at Landon's gorgeous ring and feel like my heart might burst for her.

"I just knew this night was going to be epic!" I yell over the music.

Landon nods happily, apparently too overwhelmed to speak.

"We need more champagne!" Malin declares.

Brody points back at our lounge area, which has been stocked with obnoxiously expensive bottles of champagne on ice. We hurry back over—high on everything that's happened—and take our seats just as several servers walk up with tray after tray of food. When they start to unload the plates onto our table, Landon's smile threatens to break her face in half.

Pancakes. Every kind, every shape, every size you can imagine are piled high on the plates. When the last plate gets put down before us, Landon gives up on any pretense of calm and just goes ahead and starts crying. She looks at Brody with so much love and joy that it's hard not to get emotional along with her. It's too loud in here to make out what she says to him, but I read the words on her lips.

His smile is tender, and though the room is packed with energy and people and a chaotic mess of color and sound, he doesn't seem to notice any of it. He only has eyes for her.

"You're my favorite thing too," he says back.

I reach out for a plate of pancakes and give them their privacy.

———

It's past two o'clock in the morning when we leave, and I feel heartsick by the time the car service drops me off at home. Tosh's car is in the driveway, but he's asleep when I wander in, and all the lights in the house are off except for the hallway to my room. I wonder if he ever even left here at all. When I invited him to go out with us tonight, he declined. He blamed it on having too much work to do, but I know he's still upset with me for Christmas. The reminder makes my heart hurt more.

When I get to my room, I head straight for the shower. I just want to wash this night off of me, put on my favorite pajamas, and sleep until noon tomorrow, when we're all supposed to meet for brunch to celebrate. As I stand under the hot spray, I can't help but smile when I remember Landon on the way home. She couldn't stop looking down at her ring, she couldn't stop telling him that she loved him, she couldn't stop smiling every time he said it back. They describe it sometimes in books—the giddiness, the stars in their eyes, the electric current that runs back and forth between two people in love—but the words don't do it justice. In this instance, the book isn't better than real life. No book could ever clearly describe the palpable joy that my friends are wrapped up in. Max made jokes about gagging over their PDA, but it was a halfhearted attempt at best. Everyone was swept up in their love. It was like stepping near a fireplace: it was impossible to be around it and not be warmed by it.

I am so happy for my friends; nobody is more deserving of that kind of joy. But I can't help but think how their situation compares with my own.

I keep telling myself that we're still new and that I have to give Liam time, but is that the case? Is enough time ever going to pass for him to stop holding me out at a distance? I reach up to finger the chain at my neck. I haven't taken the necklace off since he gave it to me, and all of a sudden that feels embarrassing. It feels like Gollum and the ring, and coveting things that were never supposed to be yours to begin with. Even with that knowledge, I still can't make myself remove it now.

Ugh! Is this what relationships are like? Never knowing what's going on? Always being confused? Always wishing, hoping, praying that you'll do the right thing or say the right thing? Feeling desolate when you know you've missed the mark?

I shake my head sadly as I dry off in answer to my own question. No, my friends are in relationships, and theirs aren't like this at all. They might argue sometimes, and they might have to work through their problems, but they're supportive and respectful of each other. Both Landon and Max are totally confident that they are loved unconditionally. They never try to change themselves into someone new or worry that they're doing the wrong thing, because being loved makes them utterly confident in just being themselves.

I rub at my gritty eyes. It is *so* time for sleep. I absolutely cannot think about this for one more second today.

I slip into pajamas and pad across the floor to my bed. My phone on the nightstand is showing a text message.

You should totally come over and hang out with me.

How many times has he sent me the exact same text? How many times have I immediately dropped whatever I was doing and gone to his house? I'm frozen, stock-still, unable to move for the anger bubbling up inside me. Tonight, of all nights, he's going to try that? After he couldn't be bothered to show up when he said he would? After he missed his own brother's engagement because—what, he knew there would be too much commitment in the air? Now he wants to text me at three o'clock in the morning so I'll drive over? It's New Year's and he must know that I've been drinking; how does he propose I get there? Does it even matter as long as I show up? Anger gives way to rage and with it comes clarity.

What am I to you? I asked him once.

A friend? he answered.

And I believed him too, because we have fun and we laugh and I thought it could be enough. My parents are best friends. Charlie and Viv, Max and Taylor, Brody and Landon: I've watched these couples all around me who are definitely close friends with each other, and so I convinced myself that this was a solid place to start a relationship. I shake my head.

But we're not friends. Friends don't treat each other this way.

It's like a switch is flipped and I can see clearly for the first time in months. Friends don't waver back and forth on whether or not they like you. Friends don't constantly make plans and then break them. Friends talk. Friends ask each other questions. Friends care enough to try to keep you from being hurt. Friendship was the minimum I was hoping for from him—but we're not even friends, are we?

I look over the last eight weeks and the ten months before that with a new kind of clarity. I chased after him like a puppy, but whatever I did, it was never enough to interest him. So I gave him everything I had to give and didn't ask for anything in return.

Tosh always told me, *In business you're worth whatever someone is willing to pay for you.* The idea being that you should charge a prospective client more because the value you have in yourself increases your value in the world. I've placed no value on myself at all, and worse than that, I've allowed Liam to treat me as if he agreed with the price.

The realization makes my knees feel weak, and I have to sit down on my bed.

How have I become this person?

If someone had told me a story about a friend who found herself in this situation, I would have felt pity. I probably would have said something snarky about self-esteem and higher standards. It would never have occurred to me that I would, or even *could*, become this person. It would never have occurred to me that Liam, who I've loved since the very first time I met him, was the one who would help me get here.

I lie back on the pillows, resigning myself to the truth. I have to have a conversation with Liam—and not the kind that happens over text.

———

I get up midmorning and go about getting ready with slow, methodical steps. My hair is big and wild; my T-shirt is the size of a regulation flag and just as many colors. My boyfriend jeans have almost as many holes as they have denim, and my red low-top

Converse make me smile. I feel like myself—for the first time in a long time, I feel just like myself.

I drive to Liam's house, feeling totally confident in what I'm about to do. I ring his doorbell with hands that don't shake. When he opens the door, looking sleep mussed and sexy and so, so happy to see me, my heart kicks into a higher rhythm, but I ignore it.

"I'm so happy to see you." He reaches for me.

I dart around his outstretched arm and into the entryway. I don't want to let him touch me; I don't want anything to cloud my thinking right now.

"I need to talk to you." I look him right in the eye.

A little furrow appears in between his eyebrows. He's never seen me so serious.

"Is everything OK?"

Too many answers pop into my mind, but I ignore them all. I reach into my front pocket and pull out the tiny blue pouch.

"I came to give you this," I say, handing it to him.

He looks down at the Tiffany's pouch that holds the necklace he gave me.

"I don't understand."

"I don't want to see you anymore." I say it with total calm sincerity. "I know we'll have to see each other, but I don't want to do this"—the old words taste bitter on my tongue—"whatever this is with you anymore."

He scowls. "You're this upset because I didn't show on New Year's."

He just doesn't get it. Maybe he never will.

"I'm this upset because you didn't show up ever. Not once in the last two months."

"What is that supposed to mean?"

"It means I can't be with someone who thinks it's OK to treat me this way."

Pain and confusion race across his face. He takes a step closer to me, and I step closer to the door.

"You're with me, but we're not really together. You like me but just not enough to acknowledge me in public. You called me your friend, but friends don't treat each other this way. I can't keep going on like we have been."

The last part comes out with a bit of a sob, and I have to take a couple of deep breaths to regain my composure. I refuse to break down right now. I've cried over him enough already. I can tell that my emotions make him uncomfortable.

"I don't do relationships. I told you this months ago." He crosses his arms and anger seeps into his tone. "I also don't do ultimatums."

How sad. How totally, utterly sad that this man has been so affected by his past that his first instinct is to think I'm trying to manipulate him into change. The understanding strengthens my spine again. It's sad and I want to comfort him and make it better, but it's not my job to do that anymore. Actually, it never was my job in the first place. I swallow and force myself to look him right in the eye.

"I love you." I ignore the shock on his face. Saying these words isn't about him or his reaction to them—this is for me. "I've loved you almost as long as I've known you. I just wanted to be able to say that to you at least once. I truly hope you'll find happiness." I reach for the car keys in my back pocket. "Please don't text me anymore."

I make it to the door before his voice halts my progress.

"You—you feel that way about me and you're still ending it."

For once I'm not the one someone is looking at with pity. How upsetting that he can't even say the words, even just to repeat them back. It makes me sad, as does the bittersweet truth in what I'm about to say.

"I love you, Liam." I take another calming breath. "I've just realized that I love myself more."

I walk out of his house into the bright sunshine and never once look back.

———

He doesn't listen to what I asked. He texts anyway. He tries playful, he tries sexy, he even writes some that clearly show his frustration. When I don't respond to a single one, he starts calling. I send him to voice mail each time. I know I can't answer, or we'll be right back where we started.

When you break something yourself, you feel the force of the explosion; you can see every part of the destruction and watch the pieces fall. But at least then you can find them again when it's over; at least that way you have a chance of putting the pieces back together. I find it ironic; this whole time I've lived in fear of Liam breaking my heart. But I did it all on my own.

So I cry.

I cry so long and so loud and so hard that Tosh finally stops politely asking me questions through my closed bedroom door and eventually uses some unknown key to unlock it. When he sees me wrapped up in blankets in the same pajamas I put on three days before, with a face that is splotchy and puffy with tears, he lets out a long string of curses I didn't even know he knew.

First he turns off the iPod dock, which is probably a good thing. It can't be healthy for anyone to listen to Beyoncé sing "Best Thing I Never Had" on repeat for three hours straight. He comes over to my bed and sits back against the headboard with his feet stretched out in front of him.

"Don't put your dirty sneakers on my bed," I chastise him weakly.

He raises one brow sardonically.

"Koko, you're lying on a pillow covered in mascara and chocolate sauce. My shoes aren't going to hurt anything."

I sniff. "I made myself a hot-fudge sundae for dinner last night," I say by way of explanation.

"Did it help?"

I force myself to sit up against the headboard with him.

"It did, actually."

My bedroom looks like a bomb went off in it. I wonder how long it'll be until all this chaos makes his OCD start to itch.

"What are you crying over?" he asks carefully.

Liam is the obvious answer, but there's so much more to it than that. I'm crying for every crappy choice I've made over the last several months. When I tell him as much, he nods in understanding.

"I sincerely want to hurt that guy. Not kill him or anything, but beating the hell out of him or maybe leaving a few noticeable scars would go a long way for me right now."

I never knew someone wanting to maim another person on my behalf could warm my heart.

"Can you fight?"

He stares at me in total affront. "Of course I can fight. All guys can fight."

The image that comes to mind is of my friend Lonny from last summer. A bee buzzed too close to his face, and he went fully spastic trying to shoo it away. All this while wearing a thirteenth-century troubadour costume.

"That is patently untrue."

My brother shrugs. "Well, I'd figure out how, Koko. I'm sure my rage could carry me pretty far, if you're willing to let me have at him."

My head falls against his shoulder, something I haven't done since we were kids.

"Thanks for the offer, but this was as much my doing as it was his. You get that, right?"

Something like relief fills his voice. "I totally get that. I'm so proud of you for getting that too. Most people would only blame the other person, or worse, they'd refuse to see the reality of the situation."

"Which was that he didn't love me back."

"Which was that he was a damn idiot!"

I can't help but laugh at this quick retort.

"Did you tell Mom what was going on?"

He looks away from me, suddenly finding the framed print on the wall infinitely interesting. "Of course not. You know I wouldn't do that."

And they say I'm a bad actor?

"Because she called on repeat until I finally answered the phone. And then when I apologized for Christmas, she told me she would only forgive me if I explained to her why I'd been crying for two days straight."

"Is that right?"

I bump him with my shoulder. "You're a rat and you know it."

He sighs. "I didn't know what else to do, Koko. You won't call Landon—"

"She just got engaged. I don't want this to bum her out—"

"And you won't call Max—"

"Because she'd probably punch me in the face for sobbing all over the place. I just wanted to wallow in peace."

"I was worried about you."

"I know, and I love you for that, but I'm going to be OK. It might take me a minute, but I'm going to be OK."

And even though my heart is broken and my emotions are shredded and I hate the part of me that wants to rush back over to Liam's house, I know the words are true. I am going to be OK. Whatever issues have been going on between my family and me are mending themselves. I'm heading back to work on Monday with a full docket of projects to throw myself into. So I didn't get the ending I thought I would; who cares? Badass, confident, strong leading heroines are one of my favorite literary tropes.

He leans over and kisses the crown of my head.

"You know I support you in all things, yes?"

"Yes, I know."

He turns to look right in my eyes, gravely serious.

"Then please understand that the love I feel for you compels me to say . . . that you smell. Like, actually smell like a dirty person who hasn't showered in days."

He laughs when I throw a pillow at him and dodges another one on his way out of the room. When he's gone, I take a breath and then another.

For the first time in days, I drag my carcass out of bed and take a shower. I don't try to style an outfit, and my hair is only in a bun. I don't even consider opening my makeup bag; that's way more than I can handle right now. I need to face the music, but I'm going to do it as comfortably as possible.

I shoot a text to Max and Landon, and an hour later I'm driving to meet them for coffee. I'm the first person to arrive, and I order enough pastries to feed a family of four. I'm halfway through the cheese Danish by the time they arrive. Landon is in workout clothes, her favorite weekend-wear regardless of whether or not she actually plans to work out. And Max is still wearing her vintage scarf, and there's flour on her clothes, which means she came right from work.

And that's friendship, isn't it? Friendship is no matter what happens, if you need me, I'm going to drop everything and come running. I'm going to be there for you.

"You look terrible," Max says by way of greeting.

I do the mature thing and stick my tongue out at her while they both take their seats. We make small talk while the server takes their order, but the second he walks away, Landon starts in.

"What's happened?"

My eyes dart quickly to Max, still not totally sure how to have this conversation with her about her brother.

"Out with it," she states imperiously.

"I told him I was done."

Landon winces.

I don't need to tell them the details; I only need to tell them the conclusion they helped me come to. "I realized that he and I want very different things. He's entitled to his choices. I'm entitled to mine."

"And what do you choose?" Landon asks carefully.

I take a quick sip of coffee. "I choose not to chase after love. If it was right, it would come find me, not the other way around."

They're both quiet. Maybe they don't know what to say.

"That's very mature of you," Max tells me sincerely.

Huh.

It is, isn't it? For months I've been trying to be mature in order to catch Liam. It's only by letting him go that I actually got there. Maturity isn't something you wrap around you like a coat. Maturity is like the T-shirt you get for walking in a 5K: you can only put it on if you go through the experience first. The irony, of course, is that had I been more mature, or worldlier, I never would have put myself in this situation to begin with.

"I hope so," I tell them both. "Now. Landon. It's been roughly sixtyish hours since you got engaged. Have you planned the entire wedding yet?"

Max doesn't even try to cover up her snort.

Landon's eyes begin to sparkle with excitement, and she clutches the edge of the table like she's trying to hold herself in place. "Girls, wait until I show you the bridesmaids' dresses I found on Pinterest. Y'all are gonna love them!"

Chapter FIFTEEN

I was sort of hoping it would be months and months before I had to run into Liam again. I got exactly seventeen days.

As I park and walk up to the restaurant for our meeting, all sorts of gross euphemisms about dating someone you work with run through my mind. I totally get them now. It's incredibly awkward trying to do business with someone you are no longer intimate with but have intimate knowledge of. Beyond that, I'm worried my heart might not be ready for me to act casually with him again. I pause long enough to catch my breath on the sidewalk. Today my outfit says *Hi, I'm Miko*. My blouse isn't an adjective, my skirt isn't a design element, the shoes I picked out to wear can't make me into something I'm not. I'm just me.

Through the new glass façade I can see Liam deep inside the shadow of the space, pacing, on a phone call. I wonder if I'll ever be able to look at him and not see the most handsome man I know. Will his face someday lose its effect on me? Will there be a day my heart doesn't skid out of control whenever he's close by? Gods, I hope so.

"Today is not that day," I mutter.

With one last deep breath, I open the door and walk inside.

"No, Brody," he barks into his phone. "I don't care if she's upset, she—" When he sees me standing there, he stops abruptly. "I have to go."

He hangs up without waiting for a response.

As he stalks across the room, I steel myself mentally. One quick glance around the space shows a great deal of progress since I was last here. The electrical is almost finished, and everything looks fine with the drywall installation. I'm unsure what might have happened to require my presence, but he asked for this meeting to discuss the design, and since I'm on retainer until the end of this project, I couldn't deny him. *Never let them see you run.* In business and in life. I won't let him see me get flustered either.

As he draws closer, I can see the tension coming off of him. Maybe I should ask him why he's fighting with Brody and—*No! Bad dog!*

Not my problem.

"What can I help you with?" I ask him.

He comes to a stop in front of me, a foot inside my personal space. His voice is gruff.

"Why won't you return my calls?"

Oh gods! This is what he called me here for?

I turn and look at the space.

"Is there something work related you need to discuss with me?"

"Don't pretend we're just business associates, Miko." He's so frustrated that he nearly spits the words at me.

An anger I didn't even know existed bubbles to the surface, and I scream the words before I can stop myself.

"Yeah, that feeling just sucks, doesn't it?"

He's shocked by my vehemence, and so am I. I deflate considerably at the hurt on his face. I knew I wasn't ready to see him yet.

I rub my forehead with my fingertips. "I don't want to fight with you, please. Is there something you needed me for work-wise?"

"I want to talk about what happened."

I'm already shaking my head. "There's nothing left to say, Liam. Don't you understand?"

He looks away from me, out over the empty building, and bites down hard with his jaw. "I miss you."

I clench my fists so hard that there will be marks from my nails. There is so much real sadness in his voice; it takes everything I have not to go comfort him. My voice comes out just as sad as I turn and head for the door.

"Missing me was never the problem."

I almost get there. I almost make it out to the street and away from him before he calls after me.

"Who are Bella and Edward?"

I shrug off the question and don't turn around as I ask, "What?"

"Or Mac and Jericho? How about Jamie and Claire?"

I whirl around in confusion. My heart stops when I see the piece of paper in his hand. He walks across the dusty floor until he's right in front of me. Even from far away, I can tell it's my list. Now that he's standing closer to me, I just feel more mortified to see all my various notes and additions written on it.

"How did you . . . ?"

He holds the paper up between us. "This is crazy."

Embarrassment floods my body, and I'm sure my face is red. I have no idea what to say, though I try several times to start a sentence. He takes another step closer.

"You would go to these lengths—you would do something this crazy to get my attention—but you won't return my phone calls?"

My head flies up in surprise.

"I miss you." He emphasizes every word like the knowledge makes him angry.

My traitor heart starts to pound wildly in my chest, and I do my best to squash the hope that follows after it.

"You won't even let me explain myself. You won't answer my calls, you don't show up to Sunday Supper—"

"I, uh—"

He takes another step until there's only an inch between me and another bad decision. His fingers trailing up my arm feel like heaven, like coming home.

"Come over to my place, please. Let's talk about this."

My eyes fly open in shock.

"We're right back where we started!"

His face goes from coaxing to panicked. "That's not what I meant at all. I just thought it would be private, but we can go anywhere—"

I put both hands up to ward him off.

"No. I'm sorry. I can't do this with you again."

I turn around to leave.

"You made a list! You cared enough once to make a list to try and get me. That's the truth. Don't ignore it. I'm right here. Don't walk away now."

I stop in the act of opening the door to the restaurant.

"The truth is, I made that list because I thought you were Colonel Brandon." My voice is barely above a whisper. "You were Willoughby all along."

He looks baffled. "I don't understand."

"I know you don't, and that's why I have to leave."

———

When I storm into Landon's office, she and Casidee are already waiting for me. I point an accusing finger at them both.

"Judas!"

"Girl, calm down so we can—"

I drop my bag into the nearest chair. "No, I will *not* calm down! How could you do that to me, Landon?" To my mortification, tears start to color my words. "You know how hard this has been—"

"I did it."

I stare at Casidee in shock. Landon takes a protective step closer to her.

"Liam is friends with my boss—I mean, my other boss, at the restaurant. And he's been in there a lot lately, and he just looked so lonely and sad. And you look so lonely and sad—"

I swipe stupid tears off my face. "My life is none of your business!"

"Girl, calm down, OK?"

I glare at Landon. "I will not calm down. She is a child and it's immature, not to mention beyond unprofessional, to take matters into her own hands!"

"Wrong." Casidee startles me with the strength in her voice and the steel in her spine. "You made it my business when you involved me in all this. I asked you not to. I even tried to warn you, and you wouldn't listen. You wanted an accomplice? You wanted a sidekick? Well, guess what, this is what the zany friend does in the rom com: she involves herself; she tries to make it right. Don't be pissed because you got hoisted by your own petard!"

I fall into the nearest chair and stare at her, totally dumbfounded.

"My gods." I can hear the wonder in my own voice. "I have *always* wanted to use that term successfully in a sentence. I'm so jealous that you found a way to incorporate it into modern speech."

She raises her eyebrows in silent demand. "And?"

My smile is begrudging, but a smile all the same. "And I guess you're right. I got myself into this. I brought you in against your will." I roll my eyes. "It really sucked, though, Cas."

She frowns. "I'm sorry. I really was just trying to help. If this had been a romance novel or movie, it would have worked."

Who can argue with that logic? I've made life-changing decisions based on that very principle.

"But you still love him?" Landon asks sadly.

I remember the way my heart leapt just from being in the same room with him.

"Of course I still love him, and I used to think that was enough." I cross my arms over my chest in some sad attempt to hold myself together. "I used to read those bits about finding your other half, and I totally bought into it. But that's not the way it works. Two half people don't make a whole. You've got to be completely whole on your own before you can be one half of anything. Does that make sense?"

"No," Casidee says.

At the same time Landon says, "Absolutely."

I smile at them both, though my eyes won't stop watering.

"This is depressing. Does anyone have any candy?"

Landon jumps up and hands me a bag of M&M's from her desk drawer.

"So you're not going to give him another chance?" Casidee asks.

She and Landon share a quick look that I don't even try to decipher. I pop a handful of chocolate into my mouth and chew it up before responding.

"He didn't ask for another chance, Cas. He asked me to come back to his place."

"I'm sure that's not what he—"

"You know, in all the books I've ever read—and there are gobs of them—I never once saw a happily ever after that started with *Hey, baby, let's head on back to my place first.* That's how I got myself into this mess."

"But maybe if you—"

I stand up with the bag of chocolate cradled protectively in my arms like a newborn. "I'm done. Let's move on."

I turn to leave, picking my purse up off the ground before I go.

"Oh, girl, I forgot to tell you." Landon's voice sounds a little manic. Maybe the strain of not being able to solve all of my problems is finally getting to her. "The engagement party start time got pushed up an hour. It's begins at six now."

Vivian, Max, and I have been planning their engagement party for a couple of weeks now. It's odd that Viv wouldn't just call me herself.

I frown in confusion. "Six o'clock is a little early, isn't it?"

"Something about guests from out of town or something like that."

The bag of candy shudders with my shrug.

"OK, I'll be there with bells on."

———

Tosh and I arrive at the Ashtons' house a few minutes after six.

"Where is everyone?" He asks the same question I'm wondering.

Landon and Taylor are both here, because their cars are parked out front, and so are the Ashtons themselves, but you'd think we wouldn't be the first guests to arrive, especially since Vivian was trying to be accommodating to the out-of-towners.

"LA is the worst at start times." I open my door and step out into the chilly evening air. "Every wedding we do has two start times. The one on the invitation, and the one that we actually expect people to be present for."

Tosh comes around the front of his SUV and wings an elbow at me gallantly. Since I'm in the highest pumps I own and the driveway is paved cobblestone, I totally appreciate the assistance.

When we make our way to the front door, there's a beautiful handcrafted sign covered in blooms instructing us to head on back. Our florist did a gorgeous job on this, and I don't doubt the rest of the party will be just as pretty. As soon as we're inside, we can hear the sound of violin music coming from the patio, and we make our way out there. There isn't a soul around.

"I wonder where everyone is?" Tosh asks.

"Dunno," I mumble, too caught up in the transformation of the backyard to care much where anyone is.

They had to tent the backyard for the event, because late January made it too cold to do otherwise. But any kind of tent is nearly unrecognizable beyond the incredible garden they built within it. Trees of every shape and size have been brought in so that it looks like an enchanted forest, and every single one of them is covered with white twinkly lights and lanterns of cut glass. Flowers and bushes glow in hues of amber and blush, and Regency-style furniture is scattered throughout to make small, inviting salons. It's feminine and so romantic, beautiful for sure—but not at all what I helped Vivian plan out. We'd planned out shabby chic with a base color of chocolate brown and every shade of pink we could find. It was supposed to be in homage to Landon, but while this look is so pretty, it's also far more whimsical than I would ever choose for her. A server appears holding glasses of champagne, and Tosh and I take them, still confused. The bubbles hit my tongue along with the crisp bite of perfectly chilled champagne. Seriously, where is everybody?

The music drops lower just as Charlie's voice rings out into the yard, startling us both.

"But soft! What light through yonder window breaks? It is the east, and Juliet is the sun."

He's walking across the yard grinning at us—in full Elizabethan period dress. I can't help but chuckle. "This is awesome, Charlie. Is this part of your speech or something?"

He winks and walks right past us to stand near an orange tree and then just waits patiently. OK, now I'm confused.

"Uh . . . Charlie, did you—"

"I come here with no expectations," Casidee's voice calls out into the yard. She looks beautiful dressed in a Regency-era style, the flowing gown suited perfectly to the line she quotes as she walks towards me. "Only to profess now that I am at liberty to do so, that my heart is, and has always been, yours."

She grins at me and takes a place next to Charlie. What in the world? Why is my assistant quoting *Sense and Sensibility*? I look at Tosh, who shrugs, clearly as thrown off as I am.

"I have for the first time found what I can truly love—I have found you." My heart starts to race when I recognize the quotation. I've read that page in *Jane Eyre* so many times that the paper is worn thin. Taylor looks so handsome in his Georgian costume of a brocade waistcoat and britches as he continues as Rochester. "You are my sympathy—my better self—my good angel."

He takes a place next to Casidee, and the whole lot of them grin like crazy people.

I take a step closer. "Guys, I don't get it—"

"Something magical has happened to me," Malin says as she steps out onto the patio. Her red velvet dress looks like it was plucked out of nineteenth-century Russia, just like her lines. "Like a dream when one feels frightened and creepy, and suddenly wakes up to the knowledge that no such terrors exist. I have wakened up."

She goes to stand with the group.

Next comes Brody, and I let out a loud laugh when I see him in costume as well. "I cannot make speeches, Emma . . . If I loved you less, I might be able to talk about it more. But you know what I am. You hear nothing but truth from me. I have blamed you, and lectured you, and you have borne it as no other woman in England would have borne it." Knightley's declaration from Jane Austen's *Emma* is made sweeter by his bad delivery and the fact that he keeps glancing down at the crib sheet in his hand. Brody is clearly uncomfortable acting, especially in high-waisted button-front trousers. I wonder how much whiskey Landon had to ply him with to get him to agree to do this for her.

Landon is right behind him, and when I see her dressed in a gorgeous pink Regency dress with an empire waist, I grin. When I see the tears shining in her eyes, it startles me, and then when I notice the bonnet on her head, my heart starts to pound frantically. I thought she'd set this up as part of her party, but surely she wouldn't be in costume too—she'd never willingly flatten her hair right before an event. I don't know what's happening around me, but for the first time it occurs to me that this isn't about them.

"Emma has been meaning to read more ever since she was twelve years old," she says. "I have seen a great many lists of her drawing up at various times of books that she meant to read regularly through—and very good lists they were—very well chosen, and very neatly arranged—sometimes alphabetically, and sometimes by some other rule. I remember thinking it did her judgment so much credit, that I preserved it some time; and I dare say she may have made out a very good list now." Landon walks towards me, and I can see that her tears have started to fall. At the mention of lists, my own start as well. "But I have done with expecting any course of steady reading from Emma. She will never submit to anything requiring industry and patience, and a subjection of the fancy to the understanding."

As she finishes her lines, my voice comes out on a wobble. "What's going on?"

She looks so happy, but her tears keep coming. "You'll see."

She squeezes my fingers and goes to stand next to Brody.

My heart starts to pound so loudly in my ears that I can barely hear Vivian reciting Juliet's speech as she walks over to take her place next to Charlie. I look around wildly. Max comes out of the house in full Georgian costume to match Taylor.

"I am not an angel." I'm so shocked to hear her reciting the lines from *Jane Eyre* that it actually makes my pulse slow down.

"And I will not be one till I die: I will be myself. Mr. Rochester, you must neither expect nor exact anything celestial of me—for you will not get it, any more than I shall get it of you: which I do not at all anticipate." She stops in front of me for a moment, smiling so big I don't buy the bite of her words for a minute. "Only for you would I degrade myself like this." She walks over and takes Taylor's hand.

"For me? What do you mean for me?"

No one in the lineup will do anything but smile at me. I turn in confusion to my brother, who's just unzipping his jacket to reveal a linen shirt and a perfectly tied cravat hidden underneath it. When I recognize him as the other half of Malin's *Anna Karenina* duo, I start to cry like a baby. When did he get in on this?

"I always loved you, and if one loves anyone, one loves the whole person, just as they are and not as one would like them to be."

Unlike Malin, he doesn't attempt an accent, but that doesn't mean his involvement affects me any less. The words feel like an apology, but more than that, they feel like an acceptance. He takes his spot in the line, and I wipe my face with my hands. Surely every bit of makeup I had on has dripped right off. A hand appears next to me, holding a tissue. My eyes travel up the familiar contours of his forearms, and I rear back in surprise. Liam—Viking god, male model, two hundred pounds of corded muscle—is dressed as Peter Pan.

"Wha . . . what's going on?" I sort of sob.

I swear he blushes. "Can't you tell?"

He looks around the yard at our family and friends, who are laughing and smiling and sniffling along with me. He looks down at his bright-green tights.

"It's a grand gesture." He takes hold of my hand. "I've never made one before. How am I doing?"

I laugh and sniffle. "Oh, not bad."

I look back at everyone watching us, hanging on each word. "You brought in all kinds of help."

He nods and his expression grows serious. "I wanted everyone to see. I wanted you to know that everyone knows that I'm in love with you."

I suck in a breath. "Don't say that. You don't even really know—"

"You put grape jelly in your scrambled eggs."

"What?"

"And when you fall asleep at night, you rub your feet together back and forth eight times each."

Well, now I'm just going to go ahead and bawl.

"And when you draw, you wrinkle your nose in concentration—it's the cutest damn thing I've ever seen. You're kind to everyone you meet, and you have a freakishly fast metabolism, because I've never seen anyone eat so much sugar and not gain a pound. You make me happy. You make me laugh. Even if I didn't want to let myself get to know you, it still happened. I know you." He emphasizes the words. "There isn't one thing about you that I don't like. And I'm sorry that it took losing you for me to understand that. But I do love you, and you have to give me another chance."

Back behind me I can hear sniffles from every female member of the peanut gallery. My heart wants to pop out of my chest, wants to expand to swallow everyone in the room. Liam Ashton loves me. He loves me back.

I wipe my cheeks again and smile up at his face.

"What's your line?" I ask playfully.

His smile is unsure. "What?"

"Everyone else had a line, Peter. What's yours?"

That slow, lazy grin slides across his face, and he takes a step closer until we're almost touching. I tilt my head back farther when he cups my cheek in his hand. Blue-gray eyes flash with emotion.

"In the beginning, when the first toddler giggled—the first baby to laugh," he begins haltingly. It takes me a moment to realize what he's trying to say. That very famous line from Peter Pan, the one about how fairies were made—and he's messing it up abominably. I know the words by heart, and I open my mouth to correct him before slamming it shut again. There is something so much more precious about his version. "The laughter went shooting out all over the place." I shake my head in bemusement even as the tears run down my face. J. M. Barrie would roll over in his grave. He leans in close enough to kiss, so proud of himself. "And *that* was how fairies were born."

My eyes fill up and so does my heart. This man—this beautiful, imperfect, terrible-at-memorizing-literature, hardworking, charming man that I love—loves me back. I grin at him and touch the tip of his hat with a shaky finger.

"You believe in fairies?" I squeak the same line I asked him the first time we met.

He closes the distance between us to whisper against my lips, "I do now."

Epilogue

*Three years later—because if ever there
was a character who'd love for her book to
have an epilogue, it would be Miko.*

"You cannot be serious!" Landon calls to me across the table while handing a platter of grilled corn off to Charlie.

The July evening is warm even in the shade, and the breeze that rolls across the Ashtons' back patio is a welcome break. At least, I think it is. The wind keeps blowing the tablecloth up, and Vivian keeps smoothing it back down in frustration.

"Of course I'm serious." I roll my eyes. "I don't understand the attraction. I never have."

Landon looks genuinely distressed. "But it's . . . it's Brad Pitt. He's classic."

I shrug and pile a heap of coleslaw onto my plate. "Doesn't do it for me."

"What about in *Legends of the Fall*?" Landon tries coercion. "Remember that scene—"

"When he touches the brim of his hat and the water flies off it?" Vivian apparently does know the scene, because she interrupts with a near swoon.

Landon points at her mother-in-law in agreement.

Charlie looks up from his wine glass to his wife. "I didn't know you liked cowboys."

"Who doesn't like cowboys?" Landon asks in confusion.

I shake my head and reach for the platter of veggies.

"What about *Meet Joe Black*?" Malin jumps into the conversation.

"Or *Fight Club*?" Max asks. "I mean, those abs are"—Taylor gives her the side eye—"nothing compared to yours." She winks at him.

"Good grief," Landon says when I still shake my head. "He's gorgeous and fit and he looks good no matter what is happening with his hair. Several of the most beautiful women on this earth have either married him or tried to. What more do you need?"

I flutter my lashes at Liam, who's sitting next to me. "Oh, nothing at all."

Someone throws a bread roll at my head. I shrug happily and add it to my plate.

Liam kisses my cheek as his fingers find the back of my neck. I shiver and keep filling my plate with food. It's usually better not to pounce on him until we're away from others. They've threatened more than once to put us on probation from Sunday Supper if we didn't agree to stop "accidentally" going at it in public. I've learned to restrain myself.

"Since you're all here, I just wanted to remind you about your father's birthday party next weekend. We're heading up to Santa Barbara on Thursday, but the actual dinner is Saturday night. Now remind me: Who's coming?"

"We'll be there with bells on," Landon announces.

"Which days?" Vivian asks.

"All of them, if you can believe it." Brody reaches out to play with Landon's fingers. "This workaholic is actually delegating their event that weekend to another staff member. It's like some kind of miracle."

Landon sticks her tongue out at his playful ribbing.

For the first couple of years we were in business, we worked ourselves sick doing events. It's kind of what you have to do to make a name for yourself. In the last year, since we've really started to see a bigger profit, we've been able to hire more staff. That means that we don't have to work so many parties on the day of, which means we actually get to have some kind of social life.

"And since I am the staff member that's been delegated to," Casidee calls from her end of the table, "I won't be there. But thank you so much for inviting us." She grins at her boyfriend, and he smiles right back.

He's almost completely unrecognizable as the gruff, brooding man she brought to meet us two years ago. It's amazing how love has changed them both.

"We're coming," Malin says. "What day are we going up?" She leans into the handsome man next to her like a cat looking for affection. He slides his fingers down along her arm before reaching to hold her hand. I never would have known how badly Malin needed that kindness, the almost constant reassurance of his touch, but he's understood it from the very beginning.

"Whenever you want, babe."

She looks back at her parents with eyes still shining with love. "We'll be there on Friday then. I have some client work to finish up with."

Max is busy piling second helpings onto her plate. "We'll be there," she throws out quickly.

Taylor rolls his eyes. "We don't know that for sure—we should check with the doctor."

Max is already shaking her head as she reaches a hand down to rub her belly. "We'll be there, Mom. Put us on the list."

"Jennings, why do you have to be so obstinate?" Taylor picks up her left hand and toys absently with her rings. "You know the doctor said—"

"Hey, Liam, how about you guys?" Max asks her brother. "Which day are you coming up?"

I can't even blame her for trying to change the subject. We've all had to listen to a million arguments between the two of them about her health lately. Two months ago she fainted, and even though the doctor said she was totally fine and there was nothing to worry about, Taylor hasn't been able to settle down since. Everyone at the table is aware of how quickly this topic can turn heated.

Liam has been sliding his fingers gently across the back of my neck, but he stops to answer his sister.

"That depends," he says casually.

I frown even as I take another bite of potato salad. I thought we'd already agreed that we'd go up on Friday too.

"On what?" Charlie asks.

Liam slides his hand alongside my plate. When he pulls it back, there's a small black box in its place.

"On whether or not she says yes."

More than one person at the table squeals, and I hear Landon gasp in shock. I stop chewing; the piece of bread in my mouth is wedged in my cheek like a squirrel. My eyes are as wide as they'll go, and I can't stop staring at the box in awe. I finally come out of the trance long enough to swallow and turn to look at Liam. His eyes are as watery as my own.

"Are you going to open it?" he chokes out.

It's the same question he asked me years ago, on that first Christmas when he gave me the necklace I've never taken off since the day he gave it back to me.

I nod quickly, and the tears in my eyes run down my cheeks. And just like the first time he asked me the question, I answer in the same way. "I'm just memorizing this moment." He smiles and the blue-gray eyes I used to think were so troubled are filled with happiness. The table is surrounded by so many people I love. Casidee is crying almost as hard as Landon is, as both of their men try to console them. Taylor has stopped worrying over Max long enough to grin at us, and she's using the reprieve to fight some tears of her own. Charlie is smiling broadly with one arm thrown around Vivian, who's sobbing happy tears into her dinner napkin. It's my little sisters and brothers, my second parents, my best friends, my new friends. I smile at Liam in understanding; Sunday Supper was the perfect place to do this.

"Miko," Liam says quietly. "Will you be my wife?"

I used to wonder if there would ever be a time that I would look at his face and not see the most beautiful man I've ever known. Now I know that seeing anything but his beauty is an impossibility. Over the last few years, Liam has become so much more beautiful because I haven't just seen his face—I've seen his heart. I've watched him learn to love without reservation, and that love is the greatest gift I've ever been given. Even when we fight, even when things are difficult at work and one or both of us are stressed out, I have never doubted his love for me and his commitment to our relationship. As his mother's health continued to deteriorate and it became too much to deal with on his own, I watched him allow himself to be vulnerable—even when he was afraid. Even when that meant leaning on his family and breaking a promise he should have never been asked to keep.

He has come so far. We both have. I like to believe that we've both grown to become beautiful, even if it's a radiance that only we see in each other.

I grin into his beautiful face now. "Of course I'll be your wife."

He laughs and pulls me into arms, and the whole group breaks into cheers. At some point we stop kissing long enough for him to open the box and slide the ring onto my finger. It's a gorgeous cushion-cut diamond in a setting that's obviously antique. It's not the normal engagement ring, but then again, I'm not a normal kind of girl. I kiss him again, so thrilled to have found this man who understands me so well.

We get hugs and pats on the back and kisses on the cheek, and I think my face might split in half because I'm smiling so much. And finally, after hugging my way around the room, I make it to Landon. She pulls me in for a hug, and we're still holding each other and laughing when Max waddles over to us.

Even though it's almost the end of her pregnancy, I still fight the urge to cry every time I see her beautiful belly. I place my hands on it now and lean down to speak to her stomach just like I always do. At first it drove Max crazy, but she's learned to ignore me.

"Baby, did you hear? I got engaged! That means you get to be a flower girl."

"He can't be a flower girl when he's a boy," Landon counters.

This is a debate we've been having for about eight months now. Taylor and Max refuse to find out the sex of the baby, so they can't really blame everyone for arguing about it endlessly.

"Of course it's a girl." I straighten myself back up. "That's why she and I are already so close."

I turn back to Max for confirmation, and I'm shocked by the tears rolling down her cheeks. She rolls her eyes and scowls but keeps right on crying. "Stupid pregnancy hormones." She pulls me in quickly for a hug. "I'm so happy for you guys."

"Me too," Landon adds, grabbing for my hand.

Landon's blonde curls are practically vibrating with energy, and Max is glowing with joy. I look at them, my two very best friends, and add this moment to the memory of *The Night I Got Engaged*.

Almost five years ago, this little blonde moved to Los Angeles. Who could have ever known that one little girl with an accent as big as her hair, who just wanted to throw parties, could have been the catalyst for all of this?

Back then we started this journey as girls. I can't believe the women we've become. I can't believe the adventures we've already had and the ones still out there waiting for us. Babies, weddings, businesses, family, hard times, sickness, laughter, and tears. The good and the bad, we'll take it all. The baby kicks in the exact spot my hand is resting on Max's tummy—one more girl to add to the mix, I'm absolutely sure of it—and we all laugh.

As long as I've got these girls, I can handle anything.

Acknowledgments

Oh readers, I can't even believe we've made it to the end of another book! It still boggles my mind that I wrote one of these girl's stories down, let alone three! But here we are, and once again I have some gigantic thank-yous to make, so bear with me.

My sincerest thanks to Jodi Warshaw and the team at Lake Union. I am so grateful for your belief in Landon, Max, Miko, and me.

To my agent, Kevan Lyon—who I am positive will figure out any day now that I'm a total poser and drop me like a hot rock—I can't believe I get to work with you and ask you advice. This blows my mind and tickles me pink. Thanks for all your help!

Mad love to Eryn Kalavsky for being the first reader, the eighth reader, and the hundredth reader of everything I write. Thanks for letting me whine about how I can't figure out this plot or these characters or these words. You've heard it so many times, and it has to be annoying. Thanks for taking it like a champ just the same!

Thank you to Wendy Haworth, the incredibly talented designer of Los Angeles's Gracias Madre, which was the inspiration for Liam and Miko's restaurant project. Wendy's aesthetic is incredible, and she's an absolute peach for answering a million questions about design for me. Also, upscale vegan Latin cuisine is actually totally delicious—nobody is more surprised than I am.

Thank you to the amazing staff at Chic Media, who are my work family. It can't be easy to work for a woman who spends half her time freaking out about a looming deadline for her next book, but you guys just take my crazy in stride. A big shout-out to Cortnee Brown for another beautifully designed cover. Thank you for always illustrating my dreams.

So much love to the members of my street team—affectionately known as the FORs. You guys are the coolest, and I can't believe you like me enough to want to hang out on a private Facebook page and talk books, but I really appreciate it!

Last, but never least, thank you to my Brody, my Taylor, my Liam, my inspiration for every dream man I write. David, were it not for our first year together, I wouldn't know how to write angst. And were it not for the thirteen years that came afterwards, I wouldn't know how to write a happily ever after. Thank you for filling my life with so much love that it spills over onto the pages of my books.

About the Author

Rachel Hollis founded the LA-based event planning firm Chic Events at only twenty-one. Six years later *Inc.* magazine named her one of the top thirty entrepreneurs under thirty. She went on to turn Chic into the extremely popular lifestyle website TheChicSite.com, where readers log on daily for the tips and tricks she's acquired after years of planning fancy parties for celebrities. She has designed and produced fabulous events for many of Hollywood's elite, including Bradley Cooper, Al Gore, Jennifer Love Hewitt, Ivanka Trump, Rashida Jones, Jaime King, Sara Rue, and Cuba Gooding, Jr., just to name a few.

Rachel moved to Los Angeles to go to college and promptly met a boy named David, who was as handsome as he was funny. First she made that boy her best friend, and then she made him her husband. Eleven years later they have three equally handsome and hilarious little boys named Jackson, Sawyer, and Ford. They live in LA, where they spend their time doing super cool and sexy things, such as going to soccer practice and hitting up any restaurant where kids eat free with the purchase of an adult entrée.

Take this friendship to the next level by hitting up Rachel on any of the websites below. She's so excited to be an author that she'd probably pee her pants if you actually brought it up on social media!

Twitter: @msrachelhollis
Facebook: /msrachelhollis
Instagram: @msrachelhollis
Pinterest: @msrachelhollis